M000215857

Breathless

Also by this Author

Feast of the Antlion

Breathless

A novel

Caro Ayre

Greenham Hall
TA21 0JJ

Breathless

Copyright © Caro Ayre 2013

All rights reserved.

This is a work of fiction. Names, characters and incidents are the product of the author's imagination or are used fictitiously. Any resemblance to actual persons, living or dead is entirely coincidental.

The author asserts the moral right under the Copyright, designs and Patents Act 1988 to be identified as the author of this work.

All rights reserved. No part of this material may be reproduced or transmitted in any form or stored in a retrieval system without the prior written consent of the author.

ISBN 978-0-9572224-1-0

Greenham Hall
Greenham
Wellington
Somerset TA21 0JJ

This book is dedicated to all who have been touched by Cystic Fibrosis.

A donation from the sale of this book will go to raise awareness of the disease and towards finding a cure.

Chapter 1

"Sometimes I think you'd like Hannah to die, so you can gloat."

Clare spun round.

"How dare you say that?" Her voice came out an octave higher than intended.

"Say what?" He huffed on the silver christening mug in his hand. He kept on huffing and buffing as if nothing was wrong.

"That I want Hannah dead?"

He still didn't bother to look at her.

This was their fifteen-year-old daughter he was talking about. Had he gone mad?

"Stop. I'm sick of you telling me she's ill and that my genes are to blame." He picked up a cotton bud, dipped it into the ammonia-based cleaning liquid he used to get rid of dried out deposits in decorative details on new purchases. The task had his full concentration.

"That's not true. I've waited fifteen years for you to admit she has a problem and tried to get you involved, instead you just sit there polishing silver, pretending nothing

1

is wrong."

"Rubbish. I visited her in hospital. What more do you expect?" His tone was flat. He could just as well have been discussing the weather instead of their child's welfare.

She couldn't stop herself. "Two five minute visits in the last two weeks hardly count."

She blinked back tears. Today should have been a double celebration, Hannah coming home from hospital, her latest crisis over, and their eighteenth wedding anniversary.

"I never satisfy you." Mike put the polished mug down and picked up a silver button-hook which he used to point in her direction. "Do something about that before you stain the floor."

Clare looked down. Blood dripped off the half-peeled potato she still clutched. Splatters of blood were pooling on the dazzling white marble floor tiles. She remembered the knife slipping at the shock of his accusation. She hadn't registered the cut, his words hurt more than the knife.

Now he was adding to the pain, his concern for the imported marble, a special marketing feature of the house, ranking above her injury.

How had they reached such a low? She pushed the temptation to respond aside. The sight of blood made her queasy. She dropped the paring knife into the sink, tugged a length of kitchen paper off the roll to wrap round the cut. Then, for the sake of peace, tore off a couple more sheets and dropped them onto the floor and tapped them down with her foot, half-hoping an indelible memento of his insensitivity would remain.

Wood screeched on marble as Mike pushed his chair back and stood up.

"Don't wait dinner for me." He carefully packed his silver treasures and his cleaning materials into his briefcase. "Oh, I suppose I ought to give you this." He tossed an envelope on the table, snapped the case shut, snatched up his keys and without giving her time to respond, headed towards the door.

Their two children, Edward and Hannah stood in the doorway. Edward looked as if he was about to say something, but when he realized she was looking at him, he clamped his jaw shut and tightened his grip on his sister's shoulder.

"Goodnight," Mike muttered as he brushed past them. The roar of the Porsche and the crunch of gravel confirmed his departure.

Hannah started to cough. Clare stepped forward but an outstretched hand halted her. Adjusting to Hannah's new-found desire to deal with her problems herself was more difficult than Clare had ever expected.

"Sorry, this wasn't the welcome home I planned." Not much else she could say under the circumstances.

Hannah shook her head and gasped. "I'm going to my room."

Edward released his grip, allowing Hannah to back away.

Her maternal care spurned, Clare wished there were rules for dealing with teenagers and awkward husbands.

Hannah was getting more like her father about keeping things to herself. Clare prayed it would not lead to her becoming removed from reality in the way Mike had. His latest bout of disconnectedness had started weeks before Hannah became ill again. The first tell-tale parcel of silver arrived soon after the new school year started. More followed building up to a steady trickle. Mike never actually asked her to stay at home to sign for his parcels, but somehow he expected her to be there. Clare had other plans, so arranged for the postman to deliver any parcels to Dovedales Nursery where she worked, which saved her having to go to the post office in Taunton to collect them.

The internet made his bouts of obsessive collecting much easier. When he first started buying silver he'd had to go searching in antique shops. In the early days of their marriage, Clare had enjoyed going with him, but after

Edward arrived, easing a buggy round crammed shops and market stalls took the fun away. Fatherhood led to an interest in christening mugs. He bought a few, but she had a feeling he was searching for a specific silver christening mug, though he would never let on whether it was the period, the shape or the maker that mattered most. She remembered asking and getting brushed off with an unsatisfactory response, in the same way that he never told her why his interest in mugs became almost secretive after Hannah was born. He began collecting buckles and button hooks instead and his passion for collecting dipped and soared in turn, as did his desire to spend time with the family.

Edward crossed the room and towered over her. He had the same dark hair and eyes as his father, though Edward's eyes shone with honest warmth that had long since vanished from Mike's.

He pulled out a chair. "Show me your hand."

She sat and rested her arm on the table and turned away as he peeked under the sodden dressing.

"Wow, that's deep."

She risked a quick look, but was happy when he applied a fresh wad of kitchen roll to the wound and placed her good hand on top.

"Hold that, I'll get the first aid kit."

To be alone was a relief. Her head reeled. Muffled voices came from upstairs. Guilt sat on her shoulder. Seventeen was too young to have this sort of burden thrust on him. But she couldn't stop Hannah's illness having an impact on Edward, any more than she could hide her pride in his cheerful, caring approach to life.

She picked up the envelope Mike had thrown on the table, touched that he'd remembered. She hadn't found time to buy a card, but had planned an anniversary dinner with all his favourite dishes. Now he had stormed off, thinking she'd forgotten. Eighteen years of marriage and she wondered if she understood him less now than she did at the start. She put his card on the table and saw the unopened letter from the records office. It must be the certificates she'd ordered to help Edward with his family history project. She didn't have the energy to check if they had sent what she requested so shoved it in the drawer so Edward wouldn't see it before she had a chance to look.

Edward reappeared and deposited the first aid box on the worktop. "Tea?" He filled the kettle without waiting for a response.

"Is Hannah okay?"

"Yeah," he mumbled, as he fiddled with mugs.

His tone worried her more than the teenage monosyllabic answer. She wanted her cheerful, confident son back. In a couple of months, he'd be driving a car and heading off to college. The last thing he needed was the pressure of parental warfare.

Clare steeled herself and asked, "How much did you hear?"

Edward glanced back at her. "The bit about you wanting her to die… yeah, all that… Are you going to get divorced?"

His question sounded so casual. She'd never considered the possibility. If he'd asked, "Are you happy?" the answer would have been easy, a simple, "No." She could hardly explain she'd always put their need for a father, supportive or not, ahead of her own desires. Keeping up the pretence of a happy relationship was hard work. Maybe attempting to do so was a bad idea, especially since Mike's time-consuming silver obsession had resumed. In the last month they'd barely spoken to each other except to arrange practicalities. The only plus point was that it gave her the freedom to spend more time with Aunt May at the nursery and concentrate on her final project for her horticultural degree.

She watched Edward rummage through the box. A quick peep at her wound confirmed he was right. It was bad. She pressed the kitchen roll down.

"Can you find the steri-strips?" she said.

5

Edward plucked them out of the box. She'd used them often enough on his rugby injuries for him to know what she wanted. He found a large non-stick dressing and a roll of sticky tape and put them on the marble top. Then he took her hand in his and lifted off the blood soaked wad of kitchen paper.

"You should go to hospital."

"I can't go back. Patch it up. Those tapes will do the job. Get the edges to hold together," she said, hoping her panic would go undetected.

"Are you sure?"

"Yes," she lied.

Somehow Edward stuck criss-crossed strips over the cut sealing the two inch long gash which stung rather than hurt.

"Brilliant, stick one of those dressings on top and then a bandage."

She slipped off her wedding and engagement rings and placed them on the table. Edward bound up her hand. By the time he'd finished she looked ready for a one-handed boxing match.

Edward cleared up then peered through the glass door of the oven at the bubbling casserole. "What's cooking?"

"Chicken casserole."

"Smells good." He picked up the saucepan she had been filling with potatoes. "Shall I put these on?"

"Yes, please. They need twenty minutes."

"Vegetables?" he asked, as he cleared the potato peelings out of the sink and binned them.

"Already in with the chicken."

"Great. If you're okay, I'll go and check on Hannah."

"Can you persuade her to come down for supper?"

"Don't worry, I will." He wiped his hands. "I know she has to eat with her medication."

She sat with her eyes closed, savouring the peace and the comforting sound of the ticking clock and the bubbling pot, grateful for Edward's thoughtfulness.

When Hannah reappeared she dodged Clare's outstretched arm and sat opposite her. Edward took the casserole out of the oven, drained the potatoes putting both dishes on the table so they could help themselves. Hannah toyed with her food pushing the chicken pieces round the plate while Edward tucked in, chatting between mouthfuls about the school rugby team itinerary.

Clare struggled to suppress the desire to remind Hannah to take her pills. Hannah eventually reached out and picked up her pill box, downed all her tablets, then finished her meal without any sign of enjoyment.

Chocolate pie followed. No one was interested in second helpings.

Hannah pushed back her chair and stood up. "I'm off, goodnight."

"What about physio?" Clare asked.

"I had a long session at the hospital this afternoon." She pointed at the bandaged hand. "That might make it rather difficult."

Clare touched the bulky dressing. "You're probably right."

A patch of blood was seeping through the thick layers of the dressing. Clare hid the stain with her good hand and watched her daughter leave without her customary goodnight hug.

Edward wiped the table. "That's it. I'm off to do my homework. See you in the morning."

The empty kitchen felt clinical and heartless. So much for the cosy family supper she had planned. Her rings lay gleaming on the table. For eighteen years she had never taken them off. She picked them up and dropped them into her junk drawer.

Chapter 2

Clare registered a sharp shooting pain as she silenced the alarm clock. The effort not to disturb Mike was pointless. The bed beside her was empty.

Her bandage was tight and stiff, a hard crust of blood stretched from the palm of her hand out to her wrist. She rose and managed to dress without setting the bleeding off again.

It was unusual to have to wake Hannah for their early morning physio session. Today, Hannah lay still. She looked so peaceful, her puffy eyes and the old battered teddy bear in her arms telling a different story.

Clare gently shook her shoulder.

The reaction, a wheezy whisper, "Go away."

"Come on love, you know you must do this."

"Leave me alone." Hannah tugged the covers over her ears.

Clare had never encountered resistance before. How could Hannah reject such vital treatment so soon after a spell in hospital? The wheeze was serious. The clogging mucus in her lungs needed shifting.

She kissed Hannah's forehead and left the room, willing

8

Hannah to change her mind.

As she waited for the kettle to come to the boil, she started making plans. Mike shirking responsibility had been one of the most contentious issues in their marriage, but she couldn't let him get away with such a damaging accusation.

She sat down at the table and checked the diary to see what everyone had planned for the day. Mike had scrawled in a viewing for that morning. Normally a pending appointment would send her into manic cleaning mode. Not today. Mike's rude comment about the house being a mess had sparked the argument the previous evening. The ending of which cured her of the desire to continue with the housekeeping role she had fallen into when they moved into the first of many show homes he had built to sell. She'd played the good housekeeper long enough. If he needed the house to be gleaming for potential clients, he would have to clean it himself.

She had other priorities, heading the list was a morning with May at Dovedales Nursery to go over the expansion plans. May had been trying to get her involved with the offer of a partnership deal. She'd avoided accepting because of Mike, but his approval no longer mattered, if anything, his disapproval made the deal more appealing.

The timing was perfect too. Her horticultural degree course was over. Taking the course had been her lifeline to sanity, a distraction from the demands of living in a show house that never felt like a home. Their current abode was a stark mix of hard surfaces, marble, slate, glass and chrome, a perfect fit for Mike, but far from the character cottage of her dreams. Living in the show house of his current development project, made financial sense, but knowing it was only a temporary residence was for her a penance.

Edward padded barefoot into the kitchen in his pyjamas, hair standing on end, eyes half closed. He grunted, grabbed a mug and filled it with milk from the fridge. He peered over at her bandaged hand.

"Yuk, you should get that seen to."

She loved that he cared.

"Don't worry. I'll let Aunt May look at it later." May had been a nurse before she married Arthur Dovedale and started her love affair with plants and the nursery. "Are you staying in to do revision?"

"Yeah... unless you need me to do something else."

"Keep an eye on Hannah, she's still in bed. She wouldn't let me do her physio." His crestfallen expression made her add, "One day won't hurt. Perhaps you can persuade her to go for a run instead." Edward had seen Hannah struggling to breathe often enough to understand the importance of her daily exercise routine.

"Call me at May's if she changes her mind," Clare said, as she fumbled for her keys.

On the way to the nursery she mulled over the benefits of going into business with May.

Working full-time would give her financial security, a positive step towards independence. Something she must establish before she could look for a place to live, not just a roof over her head, but a home with a garden to nurture. She wanted stability. The old-fashioned idea of putting down deep roots appealed more than ever. Mike's nomadic life going from one impersonal property development to another was no longer something she could endure.

She drove to May's back gate. She liked this entrance best because she could walk through the vibrant red and orange leaves that carpeted the path in May's garden. An early mist had transformed the grasses and perennial seed heads into glistening sculptures in the weak October sunshine. The scent of a late flowering honeysuckle wafted over the border, and a bright cheerful splash of yellow from the winter Jasmine lit up the far wall. May's little terrier, Limbu, bounded up to greet her. She stopped for a moment to stroke him.

As Clare stepped over the threshold, May greeted her

with, "Morning. I'll put the kettle on."

The cosy kitchen with its worn and softened edges was a perfect counterbalance to the clinical hard shiny surfaces of the house she had just left. Her tension eased. This place had provided a refuge in the last few years as communication with Mike had become harder. Clare often wished May had been her mother instead of her aunt. Her mother lacked the art of listening and caring, something May did open heartedly. Clare hung up her coat and moved towards the warmth of the stove.

"I didn't expect you in today, let alone so early. I thought you'd stay at home with Hannah." May bustled about, filling mugs with coffee. "I'm glad you came, a batch of parcels for Mike arrived yesterday and I wasn't sure what to do with them. Silver, by the look of them. What happened to get him collecting again?" She handed a mug to Clare.

Clare shrugged, wishing she knew the answer. She reached out without thinking.

May spotted the stained bandage and withdrew the proffered mug.

"Let me take a look at that."

Fear flashed in May's eyes as she inspected the crusty dressing especially the brightest area around the wrist. Clare guessed what she was thinking and resisted the urge to laugh.

"I was peeling potatoes," she explained. "The knife slipped." She indicated the line of the cut.

May didn't look convinced. Clare was tempted to leave it at that but knew it wasn't fair.

"I was distracted. Mike accused me of wanting Hannah to die..."

May's eyes widened. "What?"

"He said I wanted to be able to gloat."

"That's insane."

May's choice of word fitted perfectly. "Yes, but it gets worse... Hannah and Edward overheard the whole argument. Now Hannah won't talk to me. She even refused her physio

11

this morning. I'm worried she might believe him."

May shook her head. "Nonsense. Let me check what you've done."

Clare edged her way to a chair as May undid the safety pin and started to unwind the dressing. The thought of the exposed wound brought her out in a cold sweat.

"This is deep. You should go to hospital."

"I'd rather not," Clare said, knowing May hated them too. Years as a nurse had put her off.

May peered over her glasses. "I'll do what I can. Is it painful?"

"Just a dull throb," Clare lied, afraid the truth would make May change her mind about the hospital.

May worked silently. Clare concentrated on studying her Aunt more closely. She never thought of May as old. True, she was in her early seventies, her hair was silver and she had her share of wrinkles but she still had a mischievous sparkle in her eyes.

"Neat work with the steri-strips."

"Edward's handiwork."

"I'm impressed," May said as she tidied up.

Clare admired the neat bloodless bandage that was less bulky than Edward's effort.

"I'm glad you came in early. I wanted to speak to you before Gary arrives," May said.

"Fire away." Clare wondered what new scheme for the nursery May had dreamt up while she had been absent.

"You know if anything happens to me, you have to make sure Gary stays on."

"For heaven's sake May, nothing's going to happen to you."

May raised her eyebrows. "Maybe not. Humour me anyway. We need to discuss the expansion plan."

"Good, because I've decided I want in."

"Wonderful."

"But I can't put much cash in."

12

"No need. We have a backer." May's eyes lit up with excitement that had been missing since Arthur's death five years ago.

"Who?"

"Gary's brother. With his help, I get to keep my garden, he says we can expand into the field instead."

May's garden was an extension of herself, and a memorial to Arthur. Clare's biggest reservation about expansion had been the need to sacrifice a part of this treasured haven. Space was tight, there appeared to be no other option. "Sorry May, you've lost me. I didn't know Gary was in contact with his family, let alone that they might be in a position to help save your garden."

"The brother he'd lost contact with, came back a couple of weeks ago. He's so impressed that Gary has been studying horticulture that he bought the land behind the nursery to enable us to expand. We'll have plenty of room for a big car park and space for new buildings so we can become a proper garden centre."

"I'm all for saving your garden," Clare answered, shuddering at the thought of a huge garden supermarket. All she wanted was a nursery where the plants were the stars and customers could be confident of getting expert advice. This new scheme sounded overambitious. "Do you want to expand that much? Who will have control?"

"Don't worry. I'll still be in charge. The design team is yours and Gary will carry on in the greenhouse. We'll have room to grow more interesting varieties and set ourselves apart from the competition."

"What does Gary think?" His passion for growing things was not in question. He'd come a long way since May and Arthur had offered him a home when they found him living on the streets with few prospects. They had transformed him from a disheartened teenager to a plant-mad workaholic. Learning the Latin names had somehow unlocked his early reading problems. Arthur's death hit him hard, but May kept him busy and boosted his self-esteem by putting him in charge of the greenhouses.

"His brother doesn't want to discuss the details with Gary until I give the go ahead. I said I had to wait until I had your decision."

"Why? Don't you trust him?"

"Of course I do. But I had to be sure you'd be willing to work with him." May proceeded to open a can of food for her mad-looking cat, Foggy.

"I don't see a problem. Why has he suddenly decided to come to the rescue? Where was he when Gary needed him most?"

"Seems he had issues of his own and had no idea how tough things were for Gary after he left. Gary's so thrilled he's back. I'd hate to spoil things with recriminations, which is why I insisted I had your answer first. I promised to try to let him know by tomorrow."

Clare was tempted to say yes immediately. She held back, knowing May wouldn't expect an impulsive answer.

Foggy jumped up onto the work surface, peered at the can in May's hand, gave a disdainful look, and slinked off to the far end of the dresser. The blue and white willow pattern plates wobbled as he passed and leapt onto the windowsill and out the cat-flap. Clare smiled, yes, when she finally got a home of her own she'd get a cat. Maybe a small dog too. The kids would love it, and Mike would hate it.

Chapter 3

Hannah sat on the side of her bed. Her mother was right. The mucus clogging her lungs needed shifting. She shouldn't let her parents' fighting mess with her routine. She must figure out a way to block it out.

Edward stuck his head round the door. "Fancy a run?"

She peered out the window at a grey misty scene. "Mum's suggestion?"

"No. But she did mention you'd refused to let her do your physio."

"Would you do it?" She'd never asked him for help before but Edward was always up for a challenge.

He hesitated for a second. "Your physio?"

She nodded.

"Sure, I'll give it a go. Tell me what to do."

Hannah stumbled out of the bed, and went to the tilting table used for her regime. She selected and positioned some wedge cushions to get the correct angle to deal with her lower left lobe. That was the one needing the most attention, shoved a CD into the player, pressed play and climbed up.

"You've seen the way mum taps." He nodded. She

twisted her arm round to point to the best place. "Start here, I'll tell you when you hit the spot. Keep tapping until I say enough."

"Here?" He gave a tentative prod.

"Higher, a bit towards the window." He tried again. "Perfect. Now follow the beat of the music."

"This is like playing the drums," he said, getting into the rhythm.

"Harder would be good."

The sensation of someone different tapping felt weird, apart from the physiotherapist and her mother, no one else had ever done it.

She hoped Edward wouldn't tire too soon. The track on the CD changed for the third time before she had a coughing fit and spat out the gunk causing the problem.

Edward hovered over her even though he was gagging himself.

"You okay?" he asked.

"Fine," she answered, trying to catch her breath. "It's disgusting, but really helps."

"Want me to keep going?"

She was tempted to accept, but shook her head, best not to be too demanding and put him off ever helping her again.

"Please don't tell Mum you did this. I'll tell her I went for a run."

"Why?"

"She might struggle with someone else taking over."

Edward shrugged. "Fine, but I'm happy to have a go anytime."

"Thanks. What are you going to do now? You don't have to hang around to keep an eye on me."

"Get out of here. Dad's due to show people round the house at eleven."

"Thanks for the warning. I'll cycle to the nursery and help Gary." She and Edward both hated being at home with strangers wandering through the house peering into their rooms. There was something creepy about it.

Edward seemed pleased. "Hurry and get dressed. I'll ride with you on my way to do some extra rugby practice."

Hannah piled on layers of clothes. She couldn't afford to get cold. She had a quick bowl of cereal and took her morning pills.

The ride over was hard. Two weeks inactivity had weakened her legs more than expected. Edward didn't push her. He even waited when she had to stop to cough out the muck from her lungs.

Aunt May and her mother were busy when she arrived at the nursery. She got a quick hug from May, an offer of something to eat and drink and was shooed off to the greenhouse. The missed morning session escaped mention, all she got was a relieved look from her mum at the news she'd cycled over.

Gary stood at his workbench stripping the lower leaves of rosemary shoots. These he inserted around the edge of the compost filled pots on trays, giving each little shoot the same tender care as the one before. She loved watching him work. He completed one batch and moved the tray onto the waiting trolley. When he spotted her, he stopped and smiled.

"Hi, I didn't expect you back here for days."

"Miss me?" she teased.

"Of course we did."

His use of we, was disappointing. Crazy to think he might fancy her. He was only nine years older than she was. That didn't stop the girls at school asking if he had a proper girlfriend. The thought of him with any of them made her want to laugh. None of them cared for the things he was passionate about, plants, the environment, or people. For now, she'd settle for friendship.

"Can I help?"

"Which, cutting or potting?" he asked.

"You know me ... potting ... got to get my hands dirty."

He cleared a space on the counter next to where he was

working, passed her a little bunch of prepared shoots. He watched as she filled the first pot, firming the shoots into the compost the way he'd taught her.

"Perfect," he said under his breath, then set to work on another batch.

His company was relaxing. There was no pressure to talk, though he'd listen if she wanted to chat, which she sometimes did. He never made her feel foolish, even if she rambled on about school.

Today silence was good.

Being ill was tough enough without having her parents fighting over her condition. It was crazy, after fifteen years, they ought to have come to terms with it. She had.

She filled pot after pot.

She didn't mind that her dad pretended nothing was wrong. Hell, she was guilty of the same thing, never willingly admitting to having a scary disease, especially since moving to secondary school. She'd even persuaded her mum to check with her before telling anyone about her problems. A couple of her teachers knew because of her frequent absences, but so far none of her classmates at her current school had found out. She hoped they never would.

It was different with Rosie and her friends from the hospital wards. Compared to them she was lucky. Rosie had been stuck in the hospital for three months waiting for a lung transplant, her face all puffed up. Everyone was in a panic because her medication didn't seem to be working any more.

"What's wrong?" Gary asked as he shoved a paper towel into her hand.

Tears blurred her vision. She hadn't realized she was crying. She wiped her eyes and tried to pretend everything was fine. Gary wasn't fooled.

"Come," he said, gripping her elbow gently he led her towards an upturned tea chest. "Sit down." He rummaged in his canvas bag, pulled out a thermos and filled a chipped stained mug and the lid of the flask. He plonked himself

18

down on the box directly in front of her and handed her the plastic cup.

"Thanks." She wrapped her hands around it for warmth, staring into the steam wondering what to say. She took a sip, unsure if it was tea or coffee.

"I meant to visit you in the hospital, but your mum said not to. She wouldn't even say what was wrong with you."

She stayed silent.

A tap dripped in the background. The earthy smell of the damp potting compost mixed with a slight hint of disinfectant filled the greenhouse. Rows of benches, covered with small black pots, surrounded them. Some had tiny sprouting shoots, others appeared empty, or had barren looking little sticks poking upwards, several batches were overflowing with lush leaves, flourishing the way Rosie never would. Her eyes filled up again. She hadn't cried at the hospital when Rosie told her she was unlikely to get a transplant in time. Hannah knew what that meant. She'd avoided breaking down then. She didn't want Gary to witness her do it now. Better to deal with his question.

"You needn't pretend you don't know." She wiped her tears away with the back of her hand.

"Know what?" He looked intently into her eyes.

"I have Cystic Fibrosis."

"Shit, Cystic Fibrosis. That's..."

His struggle for the right word left her wondering if she should fill in the gap. Choices were a death sentence, or killer disease. It soon would be for Rosie, but maybe not for her, not for a while yet.

"Life threatening...?" she said.

"I honestly had no idea." He reached out to touch her. It made her sorry she'd given her Mum a hard time this morning. Keeping her illness secret from Gary must have been difficult.

"I hate people finding out. It makes them treat me differently."

19

"No chance." He whisked his hand away. "Is that why you're crying?"

"Not for me... I'm worried about my friend Rosie, she needs a lung transplant. Without one she's going to die, and there's nothing I can do."

"You can be her friend. I bet she needs one more than ever right now."

"It's complicated. Cystic Fibrosis sufferers aren't encouraged to mix because they can pass infections to each other too easily."

"Tough. Can't you phone or text her."

"I do, but it's not the same."

"Tell your Mum how important it is. She'll understand."

Hannah doubted it. It didn't seem right to ask her mother for any favours, not until the fighting with her dad stopped.

"You don't look convinced." He dug into the bottom of his bag and produced a packet of chocolate biscuits. "Have one of these. Best cure for the blues."

His cheerful grin made her take one. If only chocolate biscuits could cure everything. At least talking about Rosie helped.

"How old is she?" he asked.

"A year younger than me, but her condition is much worse than mine. She's had a lot of complications. I'm lucky. I have a pretty normal life by comparison."

"Rosie's not your only problem?"

She wondered for a moment if her mother had said anything. No, she'd never talk about stuff like that.

"My folks have been fighting."

"Parents do that," he said softly.

"I know, but they're arguing over me..." The tears bubbled up again. Gary put his arm around her. Words tumbled out. The frustrations of being ill, the guilt that followed on all sides of the family, her parents for passing on the CF genes, Edward, for being normal, her for upsetting

20

them all.

When she finally ran out of words and tears, she became aware of the warmth of his body. The faint spicy smell of soap kicked in, making her feel awkward. So much for a trouble shared being a trouble halved. She had just doubled hers.

Gary didn't seem bothered by her sobbing. He waved the nearly empty packet of biscuits in her direction. "We might as well eat these before we get back to work. I take it you're going to help finish this batch of cuttings?" It was as if they had just had a normal tea break.

While they worked, Gary chatted about subjects unrelated to illness. Hannah hardly registered what he was saying until he asked her a direct question. "Has your mother posted her entry to the gardening competition?"

"She filled out the form weeks ago. I think it's still on her desk. My spell in hospital might have made her abandon the idea of entering, or perhaps she's just forgotten to post it."

"Shame to miss the deadline, it's a great opportunity. She pushed me to enter, but her garden design is far better than mine."

Hannah saw a chance to do something nice for her mum. "She worries too much about me and thinks she hasn't got the time. Don't say a word. I'll post it this afternoon."

"She'll get one heck of a shock if she wins."

"Let's hope she does. I'm sure she won't complain."

She settled back to her task, picturing her mother's reaction. The chance to build a garden at one of the biggest shows was a designer's dream. Doing the course with Gary had cheered her up and given her less time to fuss over Hannah's health, which was good. Hannah was trying to take control of her wellbeing herself. She couldn't rely on her mother forever.

Hannah finished the batch of cuttings, eager to get home to search for the form.

She tapped Gary on the shoulder and said, "Goodbye." He nodded and went on working in the same way he always did. It made her happy. At last she'd found someone who hadn't treated her differently after learning about her illness.

Chapter 4

Mike's accusation created a tense, uneasy atmosphere in the house. For three weeks he had left earlier each morning and come back later in the evening, which was his way of avoiding any opportunity for a meaningful conversation with the family.

Clare wasn't sure whether to be pleased or relieved. She still hadn't forgiven him and couldn't understand what had driven him to suggest she wanted Hannah to die. Could he be on the verge of a breakdown? At times, she felt close to one herself.

The desire to create an independent life was building momentum and the only thing keeping her sane. Until she reached that goal, she felt she must honour all engagements made prior to the fight. The charity ball at the Golf Club was going to be the toughest event. As a member of the fund raising committee, she had begged Mike to get his company to book a table, and felt duty bound to attend and maintain the charade of a united couple.

She put on the expensive green silk dress, chosen weeks ago when she had been trying to find a way to break the growing barrier between them. Mike had always liked the colour on her.

The large sticking plaster on her hand stuck to her hair as she tried to put it up. She somehow managed to twist the shoulder length, sun-bleached strands into a knot and clamp them with a comb clip. Then she applied her minimalist make-up and surveyed herself in the mirror. She had lost weight. The stress of Hannah being in hospital along with the tension in the house had been more effective than any diet she'd ever followed.

Allowing Mike to maintain the myth of a happy family man was foolish. None of his clients, or so called friends cared about his private life. They were only interested in what they could get from a deal, just like Mike. She slipped on her new shoes, picked up her bag and went downstairs.

Edward and Hannah were eating pizza in the kitchen. Hannah bit into a wedge, stringy cheese stretched from the portion in her hand to her mouth.

The phone rang. Edward tipped back his stool and picked up the handset. "Yes, Dad, she left a few minutes ago."

Clare hated that Edward had chosen to lie on her behalf.

"You'd better hurry," he said as he put the phone down.

"You look fantastic," Hannah muttered, wiping the greasy mess off her chin with a paper napkin.

"Classy," Edward added as he checked her up and down.

Their praise was a much needed boost. Since the fateful argument her self-esteem had slumped.

They shooed her out of the house and she drove to the club. Mike paced down the corridor outside the function room waiting for her. His agitation was a worrying sign that he'd already had a lot to drink.

"What took you so long? Everyone is about to sit down." His tight grip on her elbow hurt as he steered her towards their guests barely giving her time to survey the room. Pink and purple balloons bobbed about in clusters over each table, more hung in a huge net over the dance

24

floor. She shivered. She hated balloons. People stood around their tables, the floating decorations obscured their faces. Mike halted by two couples she recognised. They were the architect and the surveyor who Mike worked with most often along with their wives. Then she spotted Tom and Elaine Everley, a pompous duo, she struggled to like. Tom never stopped trying to impress everyone with talk of his wealth, while his snobbish wife, Elaine crowed about how much she spent on her face, hair and clothes. Clare forced a smile as she shook hands wishing the evening had already ended.

Mike squeezed her elbow harder, steering her to the left and said, "And this is Belinda, Tom and Elaine's daughter."

Clare hadn't seen Belinda since leaving school.

"Belinda. What a wonderful surprise." Clare ignored the outstretched hand and gave her old friend a hug. They had been inseparable while at school, but Clare couldn't think what happened to make them lose touch so completely. "We've a lot of catching up to do."

She wondered if the tall red head had overcome her habit of blurting out whatever came into her head with no filtering in between and no realization of the mayhem her unguarded comments created.

Mike tugged her elbow.

"And this is Belinda's fiancé, Adam." Clare twisted round with her hand automatically extended, thinking he needed to be a brave man to take on Belinda.

Adam Lang faced her, his penetrating sapphire eyes boring through her. Her heart skipped more than a beat. Nineteen years. Scary that she knew how long it had been since he went out of her life. His face had filled out a little, his unruly hair was shorter, but otherwise he seemed unchanged. For a few seconds she stared at him, speechless.

"Adam," she said trying to hide her shock and disentangle her tightly gripped hand.

He held fast and pulled her towards him, brushing her cheek with a kiss. "You look great."

25

Mike frowned. "You know each other?"

"We went to school together," Adam explained.

"Go on.... tell him, she was your girlfriend all through secondary school," Belinda announced, as she possessively hooked her arm through Adam's, confirming to Clare that nothing had changed.

Clare wanted to laugh, but Mike's thunderous expression at Belinda's revelation stopped her.

Adam flashed an apologetic smile. For being there... for Belinda's lack of tact... for his unexplained disappearance? It was hard to decide which.

Someone banging a knife on a glass deflected the awkward moment. The party focus changed as the guests hurried to their allotted seats for dinner. Clare found herself sandwiched between Adam and the grey haired architect responsible for the modern house they lived in. Mike was on the far side of the circular table, with Belinda seated beside him.

Clare put a lot of effort into generating a conversation with the mono-syllabic architect. It was particularly hard to fake enthusiasm over his designs. His total lack of humour didn't help. She found herself trying to listen to what Belinda was telling Mike. It sounded as if she had become the buyer for a gift store. Having failed to find a topic that would keep the architect in a conversation that lasted more than three sentences she turned to face Adam, acutely aware he'd been struggling to converse with the woman on his left. He needed saving too.

She was afraid to start. She had so many questions to ask, but none she could ask here. In fact, she wasn't sure she dared ask them at all.

"How long have you been back?" she managed, hoping to break the ice.

"A couple of weeks... I didn't think you still lived in the area."

"I never left." She poked at the smoked salmon on her

26

plate.

"Except for college?"

"No. I gave up that idea."

Adam peered at her looking stunned. "Your dream... I thought... she said... Oh... never mind." He shook his head and bit his bottom lip the way he used to when they were together and things weren't going right.

"What are you planning to do now?" She needed to break the thread leading them to the past.

"Several things, one of them is to help my brother, Gary, you must remember him. He's looking for a backer to expand the business where he works."

"Gary... Gary Fisher... the skinny little kid who used to follow us.... your brother?" Her voice rose. Memories flooded back.

"Yes. Is there something wrong with that?"

"I'm such an idiot... I never made the connection."

"Connection?" Adam echoed. "Hard to believe he's the same kid. He's changed a lot since my cowardly exit. He even changed his name. Not sure our step-father gave him much choice."

Clare sat in stunned silence registering answers to questions she had failed to ask. This explained May's concern about getting her approval before she agreed to him investing in the nursery. May knew Adam had broken her heart.

"Oh yes, I know Gary. I work with him." She struggled to believe she hadn't recognised him. When Gary first came to May's, she had been living on the other side of town, with two small children. By the time she moved nearer, Gary was the shy teenager who spent most of his time out in the greenhouse. It took ages to get him to talk to her at all. Now she understood, he probably blamed her for Adam's departure.

Adam opened his mouth to say something, but quickly shut it again.

"We graduate together next week."

"You?"

"Yes, May's niece... your new partner."

She reached for the jug of iced water. Adam lifted it and filled her glass and his own. He, like her, hadn't touched the wine poured out at the start of the meal while Mike was on his third if not his fourth glass since they sat down.

The discovery of their pending partnership hung between them. She was too shocked to gauge his reaction.

As she sipped the water she wondered how she failed to realise Gary was the boy who tagged along after his big brother all those years ago. Most of the other kids at school wouldn't have put up with having a five year old shadow. The fact Adam wasn't bothered was one of the things Clare loved about him. It was common knowledge their step-dad had a mean temper and that Gary was safer with them than at home, so she had become used to him trailing along wherever they went.

A waitress came to clear their plates, Clare realised hers was empty. She had no recollection of the food. Adam's nearness was far too much of a distraction.

The way he dumped her still hurt. His cowardly departure, made worse by his lack of response to her letters, had left lasting scars.

She studied Mike across the table and recognized that while she never had the burning passion for him she'd felt for Adam, she had loved him nonetheless.

Mike was deep in conversation with Belinda. Clare heard snippets, buyer, gift shop, new things, all spoken with Belinda's special enthusiasm. It was only when Clare heard the words garden centre, gazebos, gerbils and gnomes that panic set in.

Mike glanced in her direction, their eyes met before he quickly switched his focus to Adam. "Belinda tells me you've bought some property on the edge of town," he called across the table, loud enough that everyone at the table stopped to listen.

"Yes, Manor Croft Farm," Adam answered with a hint of pride in his voice. "Got the contract signed today, so tonight's a celebration."

An unhealthy red flush crept up Mike's face. He looked ready to explode. Mike had wanted to get his hands on that land for years.

"How the hell did you get Harry Weller to agree?" Mike slapped his crumpled napkin down and grabbed his glass of wine. "I didn't know it was on the market."

"I went and asked if he would to sell the field behind the nursery so Dovedales could expand. We talked, and he agreed to sell the whole farm, named his price, our solicitors did the rest."

"What interest do you have in Dovedales?" Mike demanded as he lifted his glass to his lips.

"My brother works there," Adam answered.

The tension was electric, everyone tuned into the exchange. Mike glared at Clare. "Why didn't you tell me?"

Clare had no desire to admit that until moments ago she had been unaware of Adam's involvement with the proposed expansion. She tried to make light of it and answered, "No one was certain it would happen."

Her response did little to placate Mike. She didn't know enough to expand on Adam's participation or the extent of his intentions regarding Harry Weller's land. May had only mentioned using the field next to the existing greenhouses, which allowed expansion without her losing her beloved garden. She'd never let on the new backer was buying the whole property.

Mike went silent as he concentrated on refilling his glass with wine. Clare was relieved when he turned his attention back to Belinda and conversations round the table resumed.

The band started to play making further discussion almost impossible. Adam put his hand on her back, indicating they should dance. His touch unnerved her. Her dreams of meeting him again were no preparation for reality.

A refusal might make him think the past was a problem. She'd hate him to know the truth. Mike had seen the gesture, his jealous glance helped her decide. She could survive a dance. She stood up and let Adam guide her from the table, acutely aware of his gentle touch on her spine, as he guided her between the tables and chairs to the dance floor.

Adam held her firmly. When the music changed to a slower number, Clare tried to draw back.

Adam pulled her closer. Bodies touched. Old memories swept back, destroying her will to break away.

They swayed in silence. As the music died away, he whispered, "Meet me at the park tomorrow at eleven." His warm breath made her shiver.

She pulled away sharply. "I can't."

His crestfallen expression made her regret her answer, but she couldn't do this. It was wrong. He was cruel to ask.

He straightened up, biting his lip again. "Sorry... insensitive..."

"It's okay."

"Will we be able to work together?"

She forced a smile.

"We don't have a choice, do we?"

He spun her back towards the centre of the dance floor.

Chapter 5

Being in Adam's arms again was a mixture of heaven and hell, which ended when Mike tapped on Adam's shoulder.

"My turn," he said.

Belinda stood beside him, embarrassed at being abandoned mid-dance.

Clare was conscious of Adam's arm tightening for a brief hug before he released her to take Belinda's hand. Clare barely had time to breathe as Mike pulled her possessively to his chest and led her away.

Dancing had never been one of Mike's strengths, drink didn't improve his ability. His first step crushed her toes. With each successive circuit, he trampled them more. She pleaded with him to stop, preferring to rejoin the party at the table, including Adam and Belinda who had retired from the floor.

Mike, having made his point, gave in and escorted her back. He sank into a chair next to Adam, leaving her to take the only other vacant seat on the opposite side. He lurched forward and grabbed a glass, sloshed red wine into it, splashing some on the white tablecloth.

"Cheers," he called out, "to old friends." He downed the

contents of his glass in one go. He quickly refilled it, made a show of waving the nearly empty bottle in the air, offering it to the other guests. Everyone indicated their refusal by putting their hands over their glasses. Adam included. Mike ignored his gesture and waited. The moment Adam took his hand away Mike proceeded to pour him a drink.

Adam caught Clare's eye and shook his head. Mike must have spotted the movement. He raised his glass again, "Perhaps we should toast old lovers?"

Adam didn't move. Mike wasn't ready to give up. "Not prepared to drink with me then?" A nasty edge had crept into his voice as he gestured frantically towards the others. "Come on, surely everyone has an old lover to drink to?"

The tension and disapproving glances did little to dampen his enthusiasm. He leaned back in the chair, focussed on Belinda. "You'll join me, won't you?"

Belinda nodded and took a sip of wine. Clare studied the group. Mike's attempt to impress his guests had failed. The architect and his wife made the first move. "Thank you for inviting us to join you." With a farewell wave to Mike, they hurried away.

Clare, compelled by habit, walked with them to the door, forcing herself to gush about the hated house. She wanted them to go home with a positive thought rather than remembering Mike's drunken state. Her award winning performance had the architect glowing with pride and his wife slightly mollified. Clare toyed with the idea of inviting them to dinner to see the house inhabited, but doubted they would want to spend time with Mike. She remembered their interest in gardening, so out of politeness offered to show them round the nursery, not expecting them to accept. But they did.

"That would be wonderful. But we can't make it until later in the month."

Clare said that was fine, she was at the nursery most days so no specific date need be set. She waved them off, and turned to go back to the ballroom. Her pace slowed, she asked herself why she bothered. It shouldn't matter what they thought of Mike, but it did. He was her husband, the father of her children. Loyalty ran deep, and eighteen years of marriage made supporting him second nature even if he was playing to a mysterious set of new rules.

She headed back to the table, straightening her shoulders hoping her unhappiness didn't show. The band members were packing up. At least she wouldn't have to dance again. The party had diminished further. The surveyor and his wife had gone. The Everleys were standing a few feet away, poised to leave. Beverley beside them, looking rather concerned.

Mike's voice carried across the room. "Someone tipped you off about that land. Mark my words, I'll make them pay."

"Hate to disillusion you," Adam answered calmly as he took Belinda's arm. "I happened to ask at the right time. Harry wanted a buyer. He named his terms and I was happy to agree. Deal done."

Clare wished they'd stop talking about Dovedales. The topic seemed to be winding Mike up and she had no idea how he'd react, she hadn't seen him this drunk before.

All she needed now was for Belinda to throw in a tactless comment to get fireworks going.

"Dovedales is a tin-pot nursery. You'll never make a fortune there," Mike said.

"That might be your opinion," Clare replied, "but if you really want to know, the nursery is doing so well that May needs to expand." Clare forced herself to smile at Adam, his future in-laws and Belinda. "And she's extremely grateful for Adam's input."

Mike glared at her until the need to top up his glass distracted him. The Everleys took advantage of the momentary lull to walk away. Belinda snatched up her purse and chased after them. Mike didn't seem to notice. He was too busy looking for an unfinished bottle. Adam came close, brushed her arm as he passed and whispered, "Sorry, never intended to upset anyone, I had no idea..."

She shook her head. He understood and kept moving.

Mike looked up, mumbled, "Good riddance." He drained the dregs in his glass with one gulp.

Clare watched with disgust. She had nothing against moderate drinking, but Mike was past that. He had been drinking more in the last few weeks and she noticed it made him more aggressive. She wished she knew what had triggered this change in him. Now was not the moment to try to find out, getting home without an argument would suffice.

He shook off her hand when she reached out to steady him. She walked to the car, slid into the driver's seat and closed the door, quelling the temptation to drive off without him. She pressed down the door lock on her side as he banged on the window demanding she let him drive. She was glad she'd made sure his car was still at home. She stared straight ahead and waited. Eventually he stumbled round to the passenger side of the car and got in.

"You're a bitch," he slurred. "A first class bitch."

Clare's teeth hurt from the pressure of keeping her mouth shut. She strapped herself in, and waited for him to put his seat belt on before she turned the key.

She refused to react to his tirade of abuse, but coping with his waving arms was another matter. When he grabbed the steering wheel, making the car swerve, she regained control then lashed out with one arm, catching him in the ribs.

With a grunt, he let go and bellowed, "How dare you hit me?"

She pulled over onto the grass verge, took a second to catch her breath, calmly reached over, opened the passenger door then pressed the button to release his seat belt.

"If you don't like the way I drive get out and walk." She kept her voice soft but firm. The interior light, which came on when the door opened, was bright enough to show his dazed expression. He knew she meant what she said.

The stench of alcohol that exuded from his skin turned her stomach. The fresh air calmed him slightly and he pulled the door closed and slotted the seat belt catch back into its socket and silently waited.

She slipped the car into gear, and resumed the journey.

When she reached the house, she hurried to their bedroom to get a few essentials. A night in the spare room appealed more than sharing a bed with Mike. He'd made it clear he didn't think much of her. Getting their marriage back on course would be tough.

She heard him lumbering up the stairs so hurried to get her things and escape before he reached the bedroom. Too late.

"Going somewhere?" he asked, his swaying body filling the doorway, blocking her exit.

"The spare room." She hoped he wouldn't sense how intimidated she felt.

"No... you sleep here." He pushed her backwards and kicked the door shut. Then to her surprise turned the key, pulled it out of the lock and shoved it into his pocket.

Her mouth went dry. "It's no good Mike. I'm leaving."

"Think you can go back to your old lover... think again. I saw the way you looked at him. You thought I wouldn't find out. You put him onto that property. Your eyes gave you away."

"I didn't."

"Was he a good lover? I bet he doesn't know how to rouse you as I do." He lunged towards her. Clare stepped backwards catching her heel on the rug. She put out her arms to break her fall. He grabbed her, his fingers dug into her arms as he pressed her body to his so firmly the wind was blasted out of her.

"This is where you belong, not with that thieving bastard." His hands ran over her. She'd rather be on the floor than in his arms. He touched her shoulder and hooked his fingers under the strap on her dress. "You don't need this." He yanked downwards shredding the delicate fibres.

Clare pushed against his chest, but couldn't match his strength. He shoved her backward onto the bed, and fell forward himself landing on top of her, his weight pinning her to the mattress. She stifled a scream. She didn't want the children to witness this. Mike fumbled with his trousers, Clare fought waves of nausea, knowing what he intended. Wife or not, it would be rape.

She forced herself to go limp, hoping to lull him into thinking she was going to submit, so she could try to escape. His struggle to free himself of his clothes offered her one last chance.

"Let me help," she offered with a false sense of serenity. Help being the last thing on her mind.

"Can't wait now?" he mumbled rolling a little way off her, letting go of one of her arms. She didn't hesitate as she closed her fist and aimed.

His yell was ear shattering, but his reflexes were too quick. He retaliated with a punch to her stomach before he doubled up and fell to the floor.

She couldn't let pain paralyse her, catching her breath she rolled from the bed. As her feet touched the ground, she remembered he'd locked the door. Could she get the key out of his pocket before he recovered? No, he was lying on it. Her only hope was to take refuge in the bathroom. She had to slip past him, but he caught her ankle with a vice-like grip.

"Let me go," she screamed, no longer caring if the children heard. In fact she was willing them to come and end this nightmare.

Mike pulled himself up onto his knees. "No, you're mine and I intend having you."

"No Mike..." She pounded his chest trying to shove him away. "You have no rights over me. Not now, not ever."

"I'll show you what rights I have," he said through his clenched teeth, as he threw her back onto the bed. She

36

kicked out. The heavy brass bedside lamp crashed to the floor, the bulb exploded. She screamed again. He silenced her by pressing his lips to hers. She bit his lip. He pulled back far enough to land a punch on her jaw. "You want to play rough. Fine."

He lashed out again, this time hitting her cheek.

"Stop... Stop..." she screamed, tears flowing. She was powerless to stop him on her own.

Hammering on the door made him tense up. He clamped his hand over her mouth and froze for a second, his weight pinning her down. "Go away," he yelled.

The handle turned making her almost cry with relief. There was hope. The knocking persisted. This time Edward called out, "Are you okay, Mum?"

Mike glared at her. She mumbled against his palm. Her words too muffled to carry.

Edward called out again. This time Mike answered. "She's fine."

Her lungs were on fire. If she didn't get air soon she would suffocate. She clawed at his fingers. How could Mike do this to her? The idea that her children knew what was happening was terrifying and humiliating. She'd done everything in the past to protect them. Now she needed their help.

A thud. A second, and then a third gave hope. The door finally flew open. Edward came in with it.

Mike rolled off her. She quickly tugged at the tattered remains of her dress to cover herself up, gulped in some air. On trembling legs she managed to escape from the room dragging Edward out with her.

Hannah was on the landing.

"He's crazy drunk. Let's leave him alone," Clare said, surprised at how calm her voice was.

Hannah ignored her and started to move towards her father's hunched form perched on the end of the bed, his head hanging down. Clare couldn't help thinking how broken he looked.

Tears trickle down Hannah's cheeks as she kept going calmly forward. Clare watched in terror, expecting Mike to react. Hannah scooped up the dressing gown and nightdress that lay on the floor, then turned and left, pulling the door closed behind her.

"Thanks," Clare whispered through her thickening lip. She reached out and wiped Hannah's tears away.

"Anyone want a cup of tea?" It sounded so silly, so normal, when there was nothing normal about the situation.

Chapter 6

Placating the children took longer than expected. Once reassured that their father was unlikely to do anything more they agreed to go back to their beds once she had locked the spare room door.

The incident played over in her mind and clarified her plans. The marriage was over, moving out was her only option.

In the morning, moments after the children came down for breakfast, Mike stuck his head through the kitchen door. Clare turned to face him to ensure he saw the purple rings round her eyes, and the split lip. Smiling was impossible, not that she had reason to try. The bruising on her body would stay hidden but she wouldn't hide her face to protect him.

His eyes never engaged with hers.

"I'll move into the flat over the office," he said before she had a chance to say anything. The small holdall and the spare suit on a hanger he carried made her breathe easy.

Within seconds he was gone. No farewell. No apology.

To mask her anger from the children, she stuffed bread into the toaster for toast she didn't want.

The level of tension in the house eased with his

departure. His going gave her time to find somewhere to live. The only downside was that it would delay discussing their future apart, but maybe it was too soon for that conversation.

Edward and Hannah took his leaving as a sign they could bombard her with questions.

"Will you stay at home today?" Hannah asked.

"Do you mean, hide away, and pretend nothing happened?" Hannah's blush told her she'd guessed right. Hibernation was tempting. Mike's handiwork would be hard to disguise. "No. I won't, but I promise not to turn up at school or anywhere embarrassing either."

She still couldn't get her head round the fact that Mike had turned violent. It was so out of character. Shouting, screaming, going off in a sulk she could handle, but she'd never give him a chance to hit her again.

She had a sense of guilt and sadness that their relationship had deteriorated to this level. She had never questioned why he'd started drinking, or why he stayed so late at the office, or why he'd avoided intimacy for so long. The warning signs had been there. Would she have been able to stop the melt-down? Probably not. Previous attempts to get him to open up had always failed, sometimes making matters worse.

"I need to go and discuss the expansion plans with Aunt May," she said. A huge understatement considering what she'd overheard Belinda telling Mike at the dinner table. May couldn't have agreed to the things Belinda had talked about. May and Gary were plants people, not shop-keepers.

The children stared at her, waiting for something more. "I'll start looking for somewhere else to live."

The relief to have it out in the open was huge. The prospect of returning to the marital bed made her shiver.

"He can't make you move." Edward said.

"No, he can't and I doubt he'll try. But I must go, I hate this house. I want somewhere cosy and permanent."

"Like Aunt May's?" Hannah asked.

"Yes, perhaps a bit less cluttered." An old farmhouse had always been her dream though the chance of finding an affordable one was slim.

"He's going to sell this place anyway." Hannah reminded them.

"Yes, but until he does, this is home, whether I'm here or not. Wherever he moves I'm sure he'll have rooms for both of you."

"He needn't bother," Edward muttered.

"He's your father, nothing changes that. Our fight is not your problem."

Mending the relationship between Edward and Mike would be tough. Preventing the break-up becoming more acrimonious was the only way she could help. She'd rather walk away with nothing than ruin the fragile bond of parenthood.

"I'll come to May's after school," Hannah said as she squeezed books into her bag. "See if Gary needs some help."

Clare was grateful for the change in conversation. Hannah looked well considering how little sleep everyone had managed. She had not needed as long on the physio table this morning, the drugs given in hospital appeared to be working, which was good, because the cut on Clare's hand was inflamed.

"Fine, I'll bring you home," she answered. Hannah's obvious enjoyment of time spent at the nursery greatly reduced Clare's guilt over the long hours she put in. "What about you, Edward?"

Edward mumbled something about rugby practice and letting her know his plans later.

When she got to Dovedales, May took one look at her face and hustled her into the kitchen, made her sit down beside the Aga, put the kettle on and waited for an explanation.

"Too much to drink... and, yes, I'm leaving him."

"You can always stay here."

41

Clare shook her head. "Thanks, but no. Mike's moved out for now."

May didn't press the invitation. The offer was heartfelt but impractical. May had only two spare rooms, one she used as an office. Clare was determined to find somewhere with rooms for each of the children and one for herself. Until then she had to stay put.

"May, I met Adam last night. I'm still in shock."

"Shock?" May queried, as she poured boiling water into the fine china teapot. Her silver charm bracelet jangling as she moved. Clare loved the way May used her treasured items. Arthur had given her the charms to mark special events. Occasionally she'd catch May fingering them like rosary beads. Once she had recounted the story behind each of the little tokens, milestones in their long and happy marriage. She never took the bracelet off regardless of whether she was elbow deep in compost in the potting shed or dressed for a party. She was the same with all her possessions. The beautiful old china teapot, inherited from her grandmother was in constant use, not saved for high days and holidays. Monetary value was unimportant, family memories mattered more. She'd have used the matching cups and saucers too, if everyone hadn't begged for mugs because they preferred the more generous size.

"Yes, shock," Clare answered. "I know you tried to prepare me, but I never twigged Gary's brother was Adam Lang."

"I thought you took it a bit calmly. How did it go?"

It was impossible to describe to May the intensity of emotion seeing Adam had stirred. Years of trying to bury the pain had failed. One second was enough to rekindle the agony she had endured when Adam vanished from her life. "Let's put it this way, it wasn't a relaxing evening."

"Sorry."

"Have you met his fiancée?"

"Not yet."

"Remember my school friend, the one who always managed to say the wrong thing?" May nodded. "That's her, Belinda. And, she hasn't changed. First she announced Adam had been my boyfriend. Then she let on about Manor Croft Farm. Thankfully, we were in a public place because Mike looked set to throttle Adam, because he's wanted to get his hands on that land for years. To cap that she announced Adam was financially committed to expanding this place."

"Hardly an excuse to give you a black eye?"

"Let's not discuss that."

"Fine," May answered as she poured tea into the mugs on the counter. She added some milk and pushed one mug towards Clare with a trembling hand. Clare had never noticed a tremble before. The prospect of May not being fit enough to embark on such a big project had never entered her head. But she couldn't say a thing. May wasn't the type to sit back and enjoy retirement. Keeping busy made her happy and busy with plants even happier.

"I know I agreed in principal to expansion, but with Hannah being ill I haven't been paying too much attention to detail. I overheard Belinda say a few things that got me worried. I can't believe you approved half the things she raved about."

"What don't you approve of? All he's doing is helping finance the big glass house, three poly-tunnels and extending the carpark. I still can't believe Harry sold him the house and all the land. I never thought Harry would ever move. I understand Adam has promised that only two fields will be used for the Dovedale expansion, the rest stays as grazing land."

"And you trust him?"

"Adam? Why wouldn't I? His plan saves my garden."

"What about all the gazebos, gnomes and gerbils? Did you discuss those?"

"What are you talking about?"

"Belinda's been enthusiastically researching suppliers. It

appears she will be helping Adam with his new venture."

"You didn't query it?"

"No. I couldn't show my ignorance about the deal, could I? And Adam didn't contradict her." The split lip made sipping tea without spilling any, rather difficult. "You need to double check the details. That's not something I want to be part of."

"You can't back out now," May said.

"I don't want to, but we need to clarify details."

"I will, as soon as Adam returns. He's away for a couple of days."

"That worries me. Having great ideas and not sticking around to back them. We need to be clear about what each of us, including Gary, wants out of the expansion."

"Are you sure you aren't having doubts because Adam's involved?"

"I can work with him, but I'm not sure I could survive Belinda's company at work without falling out. I'd rather keep her as a friend. Business is tough enough, no need to add stress."

"Leave it to me," May said, "I'll talk to Adam. I can't believe he'd be considering gnomes and gerbils."

Chapter 7

With Mike away from the house, routine at home settled down. Clare woke Hannah at six every morning for her hour long physio session. Next she did household chores before chasing the children to finish eating their breakfast so that they could all leave the house at the same time.

It didn't take long before she noticed their unusual interest in the post delivery. For the third day running, Edward had come downstairs half an hour earlier than usual and joined Hannah in the rush to greet the postman. When she asked what the excitement was about, all she got was wide-eyed innocence.

The postman's van drew up. Hannah dropped her spoon into her cereal bowl and rushed to the door. She bounced back clutching a large white envelope.

"It came."

Edward pushed his plate away. "Stop messing, hand it over."

Clare dreaded to think what mad scheme they'd been hatching as Hannah presented the letter to her with a flourish and a bow.

The Garden Show logo on the back flap allowed her to

relax. An early birthday present, tickets for the next event.

"Go on. Open it." Hannah said.

Clare checked the clock. Their eager faces indicated delay wasn't an option. Edward handed her a knife to make certain. She sliced through the top end of the envelope, pulled out the thick wad of pages. The covering letter bore her name and the single word heading, "Congratulations" printed in bold gold letters.

She read on.

"You've won the opportunity to build your own show garden in the small gardens section of our summer show."

The two happy faces peering over her shoulder distracted her from the lengthy instructions that followed. She ought to be cross with them because she'd decided not to enter, having neither the time nor the energy to cope with such a huge commitment. A decision made long before house hunting and expansion plans had taken over her life.

"I need an explanation."

"Hannah and Gary are to blame," Edward said, as if that was supposed to make everything fine.

"Do you realize how much work is required?"

"Yes. I thought you didn't enter because I'd been ill," Hannah answered. "I'm better now, so you can't use me as an excuse. The design was ready and you'd filled out the forms, all I did was post them."

The Fairy Pond Garden design was part of her third year project, and definitely her best. May and Gary both loved it, which meant more than her tutor's praise. May had persuaded her to take the course to make up for never having formal training herself. Not that anyone would know. May's passion and practical application had taught her more about plants than Clare could ever hope to learn.

"Did Gary enter?"

Hannah nodded. "Yes, but he thinks your design is better."

"I don't agree."

"Who cares? You won. Aunt May will be thrilled for you," Edward said.

They were right. It was a fantastic opportunity to fulfil a life-long ambition even if the twenty-page guide looked terrifying.

The idea took a little adjusting to, but on reflection, the pressure of a show garden would give her plenty to distract her from her problems with both Mike and Adam.

Perhaps she had been a fool to turn down Adam's offer to talk after the ball. What was she afraid of, making matters worse by letting her true feelings show?

On the few occasions they'd met up since, May and Gary had been present and she'd proved working together was possible. He'd even solved the Belinda problem by encouraging her to open a gift shop in the High Street.

"So will you accept?" Hannah pestered.

"Do I have a choice?"

"No!" they answered in unison. Hannah hugged her and Edward smiled. The first smile she'd seen since the night Mike moved out.

Their triumph had consequences. Searching for a place to live must be resolved fast, coping with moving and organizing a show garden at the same time as expanding the business would stretch her to the limit.

She chivvied the children out of the house, anxious to visit the estate agents to check if there were any three bedroom properties for her to view. She had reached the point where she didn't care if they were old or new. They had nothing to offer.

A big cheer went up when Clare reached the Nursery. Hannah had spread the word.

May greeted her with the biggest grin she had seen for years. "I'm so proud. I'm glad you entered."

Gary sat looking pleased. "I knew you'd win." He handed her a coffee.

Before she had a sip, Adam arrived. "Gary told me the

good news. I had to come to congratulate you." He crossed the room and hugged her. "What fantastic timing. Think of the publicity your win will generate."

Clare wanted to protest she didn't want publicity, but held back. He was right, she'd have to get used to promoting herself if she wanted to build a career as a garden designer.

Adam helped himself to coffee, and sat down next to her. "Count me in as a helper. I bet the next few months will fly."

Clare managed a feeble, "Thanks," though she dreaded the prospect of accepting his offer. The last thing she needed was to spend more time in his company. Old memories kept surfacing.

"Any joy with your house hunting?" May asked, as if she knew the subject needed changing.

Clare shook her head.

Adam put his head to one side. "House hunting?"

"Clare's trying to find somewhere for her and the kids to live," May answered.

"Maybe I can help. Are you hoping to buy or rent?"

"At this stage I'd take anything with a roof and three bedrooms."

"Still hankering after an old farmhouse oozing with character?" He stared into her eyes with an intensity that made her uncomfortable. An intangible hush enveloped the room. "What about Manor Croft Farm," he added, "it's big enough, though it'll be a few weeks before anyone can move in."

Clare's mouth was dry. He remembered their fantasy of setting up home together. His look confirmed he was thinking about that time too.

"Manor Croft Farm?" She could barely get the words out. "Are you serious?"

"Yes, I have builders lined up to start renovating it, after that I had planned to let it. You'd be the perfect tenant, if you're interested."

Clare managed to nod.

"Great, problem solved. Manor Croft Farm it is." Adam raised his mug and added, "To your new home. Cheers."

This was madness. He'd bought the place for himself.

"But... I understood... don't you want to live there... after the wedding?" Clare stuttered.

"Belinda at Manor Croft Farm?" He laughed. "Sadly not. Her politest description was 'a dump'. We have rather differing tastes regarding cosy habitats. Her heart is set on a brand new modern home with a designer kitchen."

His disappointment was obvious, but Clare couldn't help being pleased Belinda's dislike of the house worked to her advantage. "How much?"

"We can work out a reasonable rate. To be honest, having you as a tenant, would be a blessing. I didn't relish letting to strangers, and I can't afford to leave it empty."

Clare was afraid to agree until practical issues that might have an impact on Hannah's health had been resolved.

"Harry will be pleased. He said the house needed a family to revive it," Adam continued, "Don't you think so May?"

"I'm certain he will." May's grin couldn't have been wider. "And I'd love to have you as my neighbour. What about furniture?"

Trust May to be ever practical.

Adam smiled. "Apart from the basics Harry took for his new flat, the rest of his furniture stayed as part of our deal."

"What on earth did you pay him?" May asked, as she topped up his coffee cup.

"Nothing. Don't look so shocked. I realize he owned some lovely old pieces, but he threatened to burn the lot. I offered to take the place as it stood, furniture and all. Harry was happy not to have to clear the premises."

Adam faced her and added, "You needn't keep anything you don't want. I'll find somewhere to store it."

"The furniture isn't a problem..., but I'm ... I'm... I'm not sure I can live there..." Clare stammered in a fit of indecision. The speed of events had taken on a frightening momentum.

"Why not?" Adam asked, chewing his bottom lip, perhaps already regretting his offer. "Check the place out before you turn me down."

"Good plan," May responded. "Why don't you go now?"

Clare put her hands up in defeat. It seemed there was a major conspiracy taking control of her life.

Chapter 8

Clare buttoned her coat, shoved her hands deep into her pockets and braced herself against the biting north-easterly wind. The icy blast encouraged a brisk pace, too brisk to talk, which suited her fine. She had avoided being alone with Adam for weeks and was still afraid of the intensity of her feelings for him. She couldn't risk voicing them.

Adam stayed close behind her as they edged round the prickly leaves of the mahonia bush burgeoning out over the pathway.

As soon as they were out of May's back gate, and on the grassy track leading to Manor Croft Farm, Adam came alongside, his arm almost touching hers.

"Belinda's been trying to get hold of you. She wants to meet up." His reminder made her guilt escalate.

"I've been meaning to call her," Clare lied, wondering if she could endure being teamed up with Belinda again. Belinda had left over a dozen messages which she'd ignored to avoid coping with the blow by blow descriptions of the two divorces she had been through. Or worse still have to contend with endless descriptions of Belinda's wonderful relationship with Adam.

51

"She's lonely. None of her school-friends are still in the area. You're the only one she's met so far."

How could he not guess their past was the reason she kept her distance. Maybe she'd worked too hard to give the impression of indifference, making him think marriage and motherhood had wiped her memory.

"Gorgeous rosehips," she said pointing towards the overgrown shrubbery that hid the farmhouse from May's house. She hoped he wouldn't notice the change of subject.

"Will you ring her?"

He deserved full marks for persistence. "Yes. But I might wait until next week." Adam nodded as if he knew why. He'd not commented on her bruised face, but Belinda would demand the gory details.

"What are you going to do with the land? Take up farming?"

"No, I've renewed the lease with the farmer who's used it for the last five years, all part of Harry Weller's terms and conditions when he sold."

The sun broke through the billowing clouds bathing the old farmhouse in soft glowing light. The silvery grey thatch overlapped the walls like an overstuffed feather-duvet. Windows peeked out from under its folds. The pink plaster had faded to a muted, pale rose. From a distance it was the picture postcard house of her dreams.

There was one major obstacle to overcome. The inside had to be a safe environment for Hannah.

She hadn't realized she had stopped to stare at the house, until Adam cupped her elbow, and said, "We can turn back if you want. I never wanted to bulldoze you into taking the place."

"No, no," she muttered, "it's so beautiful. I can't believe you're serious about renting."

"Don't get too excited. You haven't seen inside."

"I've been into the kitchen a few times. May sometimes sent me over with a pot of stew for Harry. She's been worried about him."

"I'm not surprised. He told me he hadn't ventured upstairs for a long time and some rooms haven't been touched since his wife died ten years ago. He was embarrassed he hadn't maintained her standards."

"Dirt I can handle. Damp and mould are my major concern."

"No shortage of all of those things. The place needs an airing, and a coat of paint from top to bottom, inside and out."

"You won't change the colour, will you?"

"You like the faded pink?"

"Love it."

"Good." He looked pleased with himself. "I don't believe in over-restoration," he continued. "Sympathetic repairs and a few concessions to modern living should do."

"A jacuzzi?" she asked, thinking Belinda would expect one as a standard fitting.

He raised an eyebrow and smiled. "Absolutely not. Plumbing for a dishwasher and a washing machine was all I planned."

The fact he'd considered these improvements told her a lot. "You wanted to live here, didn't you?"

He shrugged. "Some things are not meant to be."

Clare knew he was trying to hide his disappointment. His loss was her gain. She couldn't help being pleased Belinda hated the place. Belinda's adaptations would have broken his heart.

"Where will you live?"

"We're going to stay on in the flat at her parents until we find the perfect house."

"Are you happy about that?" Clare instantly regretted the question. His situation was not her business.

"It depends on how long it takes for the right place to come on the market."

The sun disappeared again, making her shiver. She

moved on, picking up speed, eager to be inside. Adam opened the gate into the garden. Weeds poked up through the path, and the lawn had a layer of suffocating dead grass and leaves on it. Harry hadn't mowed for a long time. The flower beds were a jumble of tangled stalks showing similar neglect. Adam led her round the back. He fumbled with a bunch of keys strung together on a piece of orange baler twine, eventually finding the right one. He eased the door open, ushering her out of the wind into the cold kitchen.

He set about relighting the old solid fuel stove. First he balled some paper, then lifted the metal lid, pushed the paper in, struck a match, after a moment he shovelled in some fuel, making the task appear to be simple. Clare wondered where he had learnt this particular skill. She'd watched May attempt to do the same thing often enough before she installed a more reliable oil fired version.

The prospect of renting gave Clare a fresh perspective. The comfortable room with its huge beams didn't disappoint. The wallpaper and paintwork though yellowed had charm. Everything was reasonably clean apart from the muddy footprints on the greenish slate floor. The old sink, with wooden draining boards wouldn't suit everyone. The stove set into the large inglenook fireplace had a clothes drying rack with a rope pulley system hanging from the ceiling. She loved the well-worn, pine table that was big enough to seat about ten people and the matching dresser that filled one wall. To the left of the fireplace was a huge walk-in larder, shelves groaning with the weight of dusty jam and pickle jars with faded labels.

A startled mouse scurried behind a pile of newspapers making her wonder how many other unwanted creatures had established residence.

She peered into a cloakroom, complete with racks of boots and a whole array of moth-eaten coats and overalls that Harry had worn on the farm. Maybe Harry should have had his bonfire. These were prime candidates for burning.

She turned back to face Adam.

"I think I've won," he announced with a triumphant grin. "It'll be good to have the new oil fired replacement up and running. You wouldn't want to be doing this every day." He picked up the battered looking kettle. "Not sure how long the water will take to boil but I'll put it on and hope for the best."

She hadn't the heart to tell him he had an enormous soot smudge on his cheek.

He ushered her through the door leading to the main part of the house.

"I hardly had more than a quick glimpse of each room before I bought. I thought Harry only wanted to sell a couple of fields. When I realized he was selling the whole thing it seemed more important to chat to him than to explore the place."

"Wasn't that a huge risk?"

"No. I love everything. Belinda thinks I'm mad but I'd have been madder not to buy, even if the land for Dovedales wasn't a consideration. Only a fool would have let this opportunity slip by."

"And now?" she asked, half afraid of the response she might get, when really all she wanted to do was delay stepping through a doorway into a pitch black space.

"I'm happy to think someone as passionate about old houses will make a home here. Don't worry. I'll make it habitable, starting with letting some daylight in."

Clare ran her hand over the wall, searching for a light switch. Adam stepped forward and opened the door opposite, allowing enough light in to show boarded up windows at either end of the passageway.

"Uncovering those will make a big difference," he said as he flicked a switch. A naked bulb lit the way.

His enthusiasm was infectious. He'd be a great landlord, as long as their past relationship didn't complicate things.

Clare peered through the open door to the dining room,

which had an impressive fireplace, low beamed ceiling and two windows with window seats. A thick coating of dust dulled the heavily-carved oak furniture. Clare struggled to contain her excitement fearing Adam might change his mind and revoke his offer.

The further they went the deeper the layers of dust and the more musty the air. Mildewed stains on the walls, a sagging rose patterned sofa, threadbare Persian rugs, overcrowded china cabinets, desks buried under yellowing papers, distracted from the wonderful proportions of the rooms and their potential.

"Did Harry go through the cupboards before he sold?" she asked.

"I think so, he was adamant he'd taken all he wanted."

"Those cabinets are treasure troves. Reminds me of a place I went once that had a real cabinet of curiosities, this one is nearly as good," she said pointing to the crammed display.

Adam shrugged. "I did my best with Harry."

Clare believed him. Adam's honesty frequently got him into trouble with his peers at school, several of whom had ended up in jail.

"I'm more than happy for you to sort through them, I wouldn't have a clue about what is worth keeping or what needs to be thrown out," he said.

Clare didn't dare answer, she was afraid to show her excitement at the prospect of spending time in this magical space, in case she jinxed the deal.

He moved on. The room where Harry slept was cleaner. Through the murky glass Clare caught a glimpse of an enclosed garden. Creepers rampaged over shrubs leaving trails of stems like giant cobwebs over everything. Whorls of silvery clematis seed heads caught the late afternoon sunshine brightening up the arched gateway. She longed to explore in more depth. She checked for Adam's reaction to the garden, only to find him fingering the edge of the desk in front of the window. He slid open the middle drawer. Papers spilt out onto the floor.

"Ten year old receipts," he said, as he shoved them back in. "That bonfire might be a necessity."

"You wouldn't want to burn that?" Clare asked unable to bear the thought.

Adam turned towards her. "Not the desk...you didn't think I'd destroy something like that, did you?"

Her cheeks got hot.

He laughed. "You did, didn't you?"

"Not really..." she stammered feeling a fool. "Will you take it?" she asked, desperately hoping he wouldn't.

"It stays."

"Oh thank you, the furniture is fantastic."

"All of it?" Adam queried with a hint of a smile.

"Well, maybe not all... there are a couple of chairs beyond repair."

"No problem. I wouldn't want to have nightmares about your being swallowed alive by that flowery sofa."

Clare chuckled, he'd read her mind. "A great prop for a horror movie."

"You're right. Don't rush into choosing what you want to keep. Start with essentials, the rest can be stored while you make up your mind. Come on, let's check upstairs." His enthusiasm worried her, reminding her of the hours spent planning their dream home together all those years ago. It was the past, no going back.

Upstairs was less cluttered and she only glanced briefly through the doorways mentally allocating one room to Hannah, and one to Edward, trying to imagine how a coat of paint and new carpets would transform them.

Adam took her along another passage and down a second narrow staircase, back to the pantry side of the kitchen.

"There's another wing which needs a lot more work. Once you're settled we can discuss the options." She couldn't believe he was offering her such freedom with his property.

The stove had warmed up the kitchen. After the tour of the icy rooms it felt good. The kettle was boiling and the windows misty with steam.

"Perfect timing," Clare said as she pulled the kettle to one side. She spotted a selection of battered tin canisters on the old pine dresser. An array of mugs hung from cup hooks along the bottom shelf. She picked the least cracked pair, and inspected the contents of the tins. One contained half a packet of teabags with a foil wrapper which gave her confidence they were relatively recent purchases. The sugar looked fine too. Adam opened a couple of cupboards and produced a packet of biscuits still within their sell by date, and a carton of long life milk. Clare filled the cups, putting two sugars into his without consulting him.

"Sugar?" he asked as she handed him a mug.

"Two, in already, I hope that's right?"

"Yes, no change there." Adam sat in the big old carver chair at the head of the kitchen table. "Ok, what's the verdict? Can you imagine living here?"

Clare laughed as she sat down. "Try and stop me." The simple task of making him a cup of tea had given her a sense of belonging.

"Good. Tell me when you want to be in, and I'll do my best."

"Today would be fine, but somewhat unrealistic." She took a deep breath. He needed to know about Hannah. Not the whole truth. "Hannah's prone to chest infections and can't be exposed to damp or dust."

"No problem. The builder is coming tomorrow. He'll need a week or two to fix the roof and deal with the damp. The electrician is booked to completely rewire the building and a plumber lined up to replace the Aga with a more modern version. He'll also sort out the bathrooms and the heating system."

"I didn't know you were that organized."

"I don't waste time. All the furniture can go into the big barn out the back. Choose the things you really want to keep. The rest can be sorted later when the pressure is off."

"You make everything sound so simple."

"It is. Deal?" He stuck out his hand. She grasped it, and immediately felt a surge of emotion. Could she cope with the strain of being so close to him without her feelings showing?

"I'll get the chimneys swept too," he said, still holding her hand.

"Dare I mention the mouse problem?" she muttered, trying to ignore his touch, but unable to pull away.

His grasp tightened, "Clare, we can't avoid the subject forever. Why did you refuse to talk to me after your accident?"

The question confused her. She'd never refused to see him. What made him think that? He was the one who took off, never responding to her letters. She didn't know how to answer. The way he chewed his bottom lip told her his question was serious.

"You're wrong." she blurted out in a strange squeaky voice as she pulled her hand away from his.

A swish of a car on the rough driveway outside and a repeated hooting of the horn drowned his response. Adam moved to the door. From where Clare was sitting, she had a clear view of who was responsible for the noisy entrance. Belinda, her timing, as always, perfect for maximum disruption.

Clare braced herself for a tactless inquisition. She estimated three seconds. Almost worse, was the prospect of having to listen to Belinda's rude remarks about the house that she found captivating. No amount of dirt or neglect could mask the magic of the place. She grabbed the empty cups, swished them under the tap and put them on the wooden draining board while she planned her escape.

Adam came back with Belinda, whose enthusiastic greeting increased Clare's guilt over avoiding her.

"Oh, Clare, you're so difficult to get hold of. We have so much catching up to do."

Clare didn't even attempt to answer, she knew what was coming, Belinda didn't disappoint.

"What the hell happened to you?" Belinda inspected the swollen lip, black eyes and bruised chin.

Adam fidgeted, seeming to be uncomfortable with the line of questioning.

Belinda charged in again. "Adam tells me you're planning to move in. How did you persuade Mike? He thought this place was a dump, told me given half a chance he'd bulldoze and rebuild."

"He won't be joining me." Clare wondered how long it would take for the implications of her reply to sink in.

Belinda stared at her, eyes wide, put her hand to her mouth. "Your face... No, he couldn't..."

Adam intervened. "Sorry, have to rush off, got to sort out Belinda's new shop premises." He placed the ragged looking bunch of keys on the table. "Take your time. Lock up when you're through," he added, as he ushered Belinda out the door.

"We can continue our discussion tomorrow," he said quietly as he left.

She could hear Belinda as she got into the car, "Sorry, did I interrupt something?" She wondered what reply he gave.

Chapter 9

All her fuss about staying in bed for an extra couple of hours didn't stop Hannah waking at her usual time. She listened to her mother going downstairs and was tempted to follow, but embarrassment stopped her. Their argument had been about taking control not extra sleep.

No one gained from her selfish action. The six o'clock regime created less disruption to the family especially during term time, ensuring she got there on time and didn't need to invent excuses to hide her illness.

By seven, guilt got the better of her and Hannah tip-toed down to the kitchen. The ironing board creaked, a sure sign her mum had begun her endless list of daily chores. When she wasn't at home she would be equally busy at the nursery, or this week at Manor Croft, scrubbing and painting. Hannah was cross because she wasn't allowed to help because of the danger from the mould and dust.

"Morning." Her mum looked up, smiled and continued ironing and folding pillowcases. After a while she stopped and rescued her cup from the windowsill behind her. "Bad night?"

"No. Sorry I made a fuss."

"Don't be silly, you're entitled to a lie in. There's no law to say physio has to be done at dawn. I should apologise for being inflexible."

"You're not. The plan worked for both of us, and I'd like to stick with it... if that's all right?"

"Thanks. Let me finish up these." She put down the cup and plucked another pillowcase from the wash basket.

Hannah, mesmerised by the motion of the iron smoothing out the wrinkles, wished life's wrinkles would vanish so easily. First she'd fix her lungs and digestive system. Then get her parents to make up. No maybe not. Her mum would be a fool to forgive him for hitting her, drunk or not.

"You look serious. Want to share your thoughts?"

Hannah's face got hot. Blushing was the pits. She might as well ask. "How will Dad cope when we all move out?"

"Are you suggesting I give him a second chance?"

"No... No... Not after what he did. I mean, what will he do about the house?"

"He'll move back in so he can spend time with you."

"Us... here... with him?"

"Yes, he's your dad. Our fight had nothing to do with you."

"Edward's never going to agree. He's still spitting mad."

"You'll need to help me talk him round."

"I don't know how. He's always off somewhere, either playing rugby or helping you at Manor Croft."

"Funny, he complained he never saw you because you practically lived in the greenhouse at Dovedales."

"He said that?" Edward missed her. That had never occurred to her.

"Yes." Her mum's tone indicated the solution was in her hands.

"Anyway, that's why it's important to keep enough things here so the place still feels like home. And I'll organize a cleaner, so you don't get landed with the job."

"What if Dad sells the house?"

"Don't worry. I doubt that will happen for quite some time." She took the last item out of the wash basket. "Nearly finished, then I'm all yours."

Hannah tried to imagine being here without her mother. Her father wasn't likely to start doing her early morning physio sessions. He'd never been involved and always gave the impression he thought the whole thing a waste of time and energy. Sometimes Hannah was inclined to agree, but deep down knew the difference the exercise made to her overall fitness.

"You're worried about something."

"My physio. Who will do it? Dad won't."

"We'll work out a different schedule. Come on. Let's get it over and done with." She put her cup in the dishwasher. Picked up the pile of ironing, and led the way upstairs.

First Hannah did some exercises while her mum listened to her chest. She was feeling good and hoped for a short session.

"I don't like the sound of that."

"But I'm breathing better than I was when I came out of hospital."

She hated the way her mother would pick up problems when she was sure her lungs were clear. It made her doubt her own ability to detect a build up of mucus, and it was important that she should monitor her own condition.

Her mum tilted the special massage table into position to tackle the lower lobes. Hannah selected one of her mum's favourite CD's, stuck it in the machine, pressed play and let her mother work her magic. Before long a load of mucus dislodged and Hannah had an effective coughing fit.

The steady rhythm was comforting, the music soothing. Hannah stared at the pictures of Rosie that she'd pasted on a board. She didn't see Rosie often enough. The risk of cross-infection of bacteria was too high, especially now Rosie was on the transplant list.

Hannah sat up, breaking the rhythm, catching her mum by surprise.

"What's wrong?"

"I want to visit Rosie." The fear in her mother's eyes made her add, "I can ask Gary to take me." She hadn't forgotten how upset her mother had been after the last time with Rosie. "I know you're extra busy with the farmhouse."

Her mother's hesitation made Hannah certain she was trying to find an excuse to refuse.

"I'll wear a mask and a gown, and wash my hands. I'll clear it with Rosie's parents and the ward nurse first."

"If they agree, I'll take you."

Hannah flung her arms round her mum's neck. "Thank you."

"Now get back on the table. We need to do the other side. Have you thought about what you'd like to do for your birthday?"

"I know what I don't want."

"A posh dinner with all the oldies, like you had last year?"

"It was nice, but..."

"It would be a disaster. The "Grands" are difficult enough without our problems in the mix."

"Why don't you and your mum get on?"

Her mum stopped tapping, making Hannah wish she hadn't asked the question.

"She tried to control every single thing I ever did. I rebelled, which wrecked our relationship, remarrying very soon after my dad died didn't help."

The tapping started again, firmer, in fact so firm, Hannah could almost feel her mother's tension coming out.

"I wondered about having a party at the stables?"

"Sounds interesting."

"I'd love to include Rosie too."

The expected comment that Rosie wouldn't be fit enough never came.

"You like to set a challenge." Her mum said. "Let's work on it."

"You'll probably think I've gone mad, but I wanted to give Rosie a chance to interact with the horses. Maybe try a carriage ride." Hannah could tell her mother was struggling to picture Rosie being so active after being wheelchair bound for three years.

"Do you really think she'd want to?"

"She's so envious when I go riding. I hardly dare tell her when I'm going."

"Isn't she permanently attached to an oxygen tank?"

"Yes. Don't worry, I'll check with Sue at the stables. If she says it's possible, then I'll ask Rosie's parents and Doctor James."

"You seem to have thought of everything." Hannah had expected more resistance. Her mum was terrified of horses, not that she'd let her fear prevent Hannah from riding. She always encouraged any activity that improved her lung function.

Hannah hugged her. "You're the best. Thanks."

Clare pushed her gently away. "Whatever you do, don't say anything to Rosie. You mustn't set her up for a disappointment."

"I won't."

"Once we have it fixed you can decide who else you want to invite."

"I suppose I have to include the Grands?"

"I'm afraid so. Dad's parents are coming as usual for your half term break. And my mother would never forgive me if she was left out."

"Oh, I thought that with dad moving out his parents wouldn't come."

"He's written their visit on the calendar, so they must still be coming. It'll coincide with the first week I'm gone. I thought having them around would make the changeover easier for you and Edward."

Hannah wasn't sure about that. Gran Hilda and Grandad Denis were hard work, they spent most of the time quizzing her and Edward about their school work and telling them how important their exam marks were. Not much fun at all.

"Why can't we move with you?"

"I have to be sure everything is working properly."

"Gran Hilda will have a fit about your leaving," Hannah said, hoping to make her mother change her mind. She and Edward were going to need to have plenty of activities planned to escape Gran's endless rants. Grandad was okay, not that he ever got the chance to speak.

At least she had the greenhouse and Gary to escape to. Her computer skills were handy for helping Gary to source plants for the show garden and to plot timetables for planting seeds, taking cuttings and buying plants. They'd sown the first batch of seeds, but still had hundreds of cuttings to pot up. There was more involved than Hannah had expected when she posted the entry for the competition. Now she understood why her mother had been hesitant about entering.

Working with Gary was easier since she'd told him about her illness. No need to be sneaky about taking her enzymes, or mentioning her physio sessions, or her medical check-ups. Time with him had made her think of the future. She wanted to enjoy living not studying. A university degree was her parents' dream not hers. After her birthday she'd tell them her plans.

Chapter 10

Clare's palms sweated as she rang Mike's mobile number.

"What's happened?" he asked.

"Nothing, but we must make plans for the children's sake."

"Okay, I'll come to the house."

"No." The response was silly. She should be able to cope.

"Sorry." His tone was softer, almost apologetic. "How about lunch at the café in Bath Place, next to the bookshop, you know the one I mean?"

His choice of a café rather than a pub was a good start. Maybe he was cutting back on drink.

"Fine, what time?"

"One o'clock? Oh, by the way, Mrs Haig enjoyed her tour of the nursery."

"No need to thank me," Clare answered once she had remembered who Mrs Haig was. "May took care of her." The architect's wife had turned up the week after the ball, while she and Adam were exploring the farmhouse. May, assessed the situation and to spare Clare the embarrassment of showing off her black eye and split lip, had taken the woman on a rapid tour of both her garden and the nursery, ending the tour with a gift of a couple of plants.

As Clare ended the call she wondered if civil communication would continue once she broached the subject of divorce and her intention to move into Manor Croft Farm. Mike was bound to comment on her new landlord.

Clare told May her plans.

"I hope you're going to change," May said, looking her up and down. "Paint-splattered jeans and a jumper won't do. Wear something sexy." Her eyes twinkled with mischief. "Remind him what he's losing."

"We're meeting in a coffee shop."

"You're joking. Sorry, I didn't mean it to sound so..."

"Don't worry, my reaction was the same."

"I'll come if you need moral support."

"Thanks, but I must do this on my own. And don't fret, I'm still leaving him."

"Quite right."

"Anyway, I thought I'd spend an hour here doing some paperwork."

May's eyes lit up. "Good. If you're here, I'll go and help Gary."

"Please, pace yourself," Clare begged.

May should be putting her feet up, not trebling her work load. The expansion plan was moving too fast.

"I will," May said as she changed into her heavy outdoor shoes. "I've asked Gary to try to find someone to help in the greenhouse." Clare noticed how May fumbled with her laces and struggled with the poppers on her coat. Moving close by would make keeping an eye on her easier. She wondered if May's health had anything to do with the desire to take on an extra employee. Asking would imply concern, which would not be appreciated.

She dealt with some outstanding bills before taking out the plan for the Fairy Pond Garden. The thrill of organizing the show garden had turned to panic. Anything less than perfection was not an option. At odd moments like this she wished she could back out. The move, the expansion, May's shakiness were all potential excuses.

Gary and Hannah were doing great work on sourcing plants. But Edward's initial enthusiasm for helping at the farmhouse had dwindled. That alone wouldn't have bothered her if he hadn't started lying. His enthusiasm for rugby appeared to have vanished. He used rugby as an excuse, but the lack of dirty kit had her wondering where he went and, more difficult, how she should react. All that and the prospect of lunch with Mike made concentration impossible.

She went home to change, found a pink silk top, a pair of once tight jeans, which now fitted perfectly, and a multi-flecked knitted jacket. She surveyed the results in the mirror. Perhaps not sexy enough for May's approval, but a look she was comfortable with.

The painting and scrubbing had taken their toll on her hands. The deep cut, a constant reminder of Mike's hurtful comment, wouldn't heal. She'd lost count of the number of sticking plasters she'd used. She filled the basin with hot water, and immersed her hands. The softened plaster peeled off easily, the inflamed wound oozed a rather nasty coloured liquid. Not healthy at all. She must ask May to look at it later. She put on a fresh dressing.

She parked her car and walked through a narrow alley to Bath Place. She loved this little pedestrian lane. The diverse collection of shops always kept her enthralled. Being early was not a problem. She wandered round the art gallery then bought a cake at the Women's Institute shop. She was about to go book browsing when she saw Mike enter the Café. She couldn't decide if his being early was a good sign or not. She followed him in. No point in delaying.

Mike was trying to cram his long legs under a table by the window. He attempted to stand up when she arrived nearly knocking over the chair behind him. Clare guessed he intended to kiss her and backed away. The prospect of intimacy was unthinkable. Being in the same room was difficult enough.

"Don't get up." She peeled off her jacket, slipped it on the back of her chair and sat down.

The waitress brought them menus. Mike ordered a baked potato and a cappuccino. Clare sensed impatience and made her choice, not that she was interested in eating.

She smiled at the waitress. "The chicken salad." Her mouth was dry with nerves. "And a glass of water, please."

Orders placed, they were left alone.

Clare was determined to let Mike open the conversation. His tone would indicate his mood, but not alter what she intended to say.

He leant in towards the table, sliding his hand across reaching for hers. She delved in her handbag for a tissue to avoid contact. She didn't want him to touch her, not now, not ever. She hated the fact that one outburst of violence could end what had up to then been a fairly sound marriage.

He acted as if he hadn't noticed. A tiny twitch of a muscle above his left eyebrow, told her he had. He said quietly, "Clare, I was out of order. I don't know what came over me. I want to start again."

The admission he'd behaved badly was unexpected. The lack of sincerity in his tone made it meaningless. Clare swallowed. He couldn't think she'd have him back as if nothing had happened.

The waitress returned with their order. Gratefully, Clare took a sip of water.

"You can move back on Thursday, the week after next, when your parents are visiting," she answered, her voice coming out as a squeak. She took another sip. "I'll stay until then. Your parents can help with the children while you settle back into the house."

Mike choked on his coffee. "You can't leave."

"Sorry. We can't fix this."

70

"We ought to try." She sensed desperation in his voice. Was it more to do with being stuck in the house with his parents? She felt mean for thinking it.

"No Mike, it's over. I've found a place to live, but the builders and decorators won't be out until the end of the month."

"You can't take the children." His tone came over as somewhere between angry and pleading.

"I know. That's why I'm here trying to make a workable plan. I'll have space for them to stay with me. The rest of the time they will be at the house with you. It's up to them to decide how to divide their time. But the important thing is that you'll have to make peace with them. It won't be easy, especially with Edward."

He glared at her. She waited for the accusation she was poisoning them against him. Instead he picked up his knife and fork and sliced into his potato.

"You think they won't want to live under the same roof as me?"

"They're not happy with the prospect. Hannah misses you. Edward's still angry. You need to regain their trust."

"What do you suggest?"

"You could start by helping Edward with his family history project. He's asked you often enough. You've always fobbed him off in the past. Now would be the perfect time."

Mike fidgeted in his seat. He bore the same panic stricken look that he'd shown at the beginning of the school year when Edward announced a family tree was to be the main element of his history project.

"He's desperate for information about your side of the family. He's done my side." She wasn't prepared to give up yet, even though she could see Mike's jaw tighten. "If you won't help, he'll have to ask your parents when they come down."

The suggestion made Mike look more stressed than before. Could it have been the trigger for his odd behaviour or was she just imagining things?

"No." Mike put his cutlery down firmly. "No. Whatever happens, he mustn't do that. I'll deal with it."

Clare knew from his tone he had effectively ended the discussion. He might think he'd closed the topic, but all he'd done was arouse her curiosity. Best not to mention she had already ordered some birth and marriage certificates. She remembered hiding the envelope in the kitchen drawer. She ate a few mouthfuls of food and changed the subject.

"Hannah's rather preoccupied with her birthday plans. She's trying to include her friend Rosie." Mike's frown made her add, "The girl she met in hospital, the one waiting for the lung transplant."

"Rather an odd request."

"Not really. If it makes Hannah happy we must agree. She wants to have a picnic lunch at the stables. That way everyone can come and Hannah can show off her dressage skills."

She wanted to add Hannah seemed to be growing up or more accurately growing away from her, and how much she had changed in such a short time.

Mike nodded, finishing his mouthful of food. "You haven't said where you'll live?"

"Manor Croft Farm."

He closed his eyes for a second. She waited for an outburst. Instead he carefully cut and prepared another forkful.

"That dump? Surely a dirty, damp place like that isn't ideal for a Cystic Fibrosis sufferer."

Clare nearly dropped her fork. After all those years denying Hannah had a problem he had the cheek to lecture her on the quality of Hannah's living space. He'd even uttered the dreaded words, "Cystic Fibrosis".

"The builders are working overtime on the renovations. I know Hannah can't move in until the dust has settled and the paint fumes have cleared."

"It'll take more than a lick of paint to fix that place. Am I expected to pay for this?"

She shook her head. "No, it's the landlord's responsibility."

He muttered, "What's in it for lover-boy?"

Clare chose to ignore the comment. Let him think what he wanted. It was more important to maintain a civilized relationship for the benefit of the children.

"What about rent?" Before she could answer, he added, "Oh, don't get me wrong, I'm happy to pay. It won't be long until you come back home."

"Mike, I'm not coming back."

He shook his head and almost smiled, as if he wasn't sure he'd heard right. "Of course you will."

"No, Mike. Never. I want a divorce."

His semi-smile evaporated. He opened his mouth to speak, closed it again, took a deep breath then carefully put his fork neatly on the side of his plate.

Clare pushed her plate aside, reached for the water glass. She had expected this moment would be difficult. Whatever hopes and dreams they'd ever had had faded long ago. There was nothing left to salvage.

"Because of Adam?"

"No, he has nothing to do with it."

"I find that hard to believe," he said, looking unconvinced. "Let's go slowly, make sure the children are settled before we get into the legal stuff."

Clare sat back in her chair in amazement. Mike showing concern was a new concept. His normal indifference to their well-being was the main reason their marriage had failed. She bit her lip to stop herself making a scathing comment.

"You're right, their needs come first."

"Don't move out. I'll stay in the flat."

"No. It's all arranged, and better for the children because they have their rooms set up and therefore minimum disruption to their lives when they are with you."

73

"Yes, but if you take half the furniture..."

"I won't be taking anything, the farmhouse is fully furnished, and I don't want to destroy the family home."

"You say that now. How long before you demand a half share of everything I own?"

"Don't push me, Mike. I don't want anything."

His brow furrowed. He ripped open a sachet of sugar, poured the contents into his cappuccino, opened another, and another, and was ready to attack a fourth packet when she reached out to stop him. "I'm serious. I don't expect you to sell your silver collection, the house, the business. Just let me go. I'll have a home where the children can come when they are not with you."

"Okay," he said as he drew his hand away from hers.

She couldn't help wondering if saying he needn't sell his precious silver was the main reason for his agreement.

"Oh, by the way, Mother's upset you didn't let her know Hannah had been in hospital."

"Why didn't you tell her yourself?" Clare refused to accept the blame.

Even on a good day Mike's mother could cause friction. He'd soon discover how much. Clare had chosen her date of departure specifically to avoid listening to her spouting on about the sanctity of marriage. If the house wasn't ready she'd move in with May to escape her mother-in-law. The woman had perfected the art of complaining, finding fault with everything, from the brand of tea to the difficulty of sleeping in a strange bed. Every sentence she uttered contained some barbed remarks about Clare's standard of housekeeping.

Mike's father usually ignored everyone, his focus firmly fixed on his next round of golf or whether his car had enough water and oil.

"You can't go until after they've left." The panic in his voice made her want to laugh. She bit back the desire to say their pending arrival had speeded up her departure. She

74

would probably have done the same thing if her own mother had been planning to come and stay. She was even harder to handle.

The waitress stopped to enquire if everything was all right. Clare noticed for the first time the café was full. She checked her watch. One hour since she arrived, and he hadn't raised his voice once. She'd love to leave before that changed.

"Shall I come over to see the children?"

"I think you should phone them and talk to them first. How about going to the school concert on Friday, or going to watch Edward play rugby on Saturday. You could offer to take them out for a pizza afterwards," she added. "Better still, get started on Edward's family history project."

"I told you before, I'll deal with that," he snapped back, confirming her suspicion of a family secret.

"Fine, I'll leave it to you to think of something else to win them over."

Mike waved impatiently for the bill. Clare had said enough for now. She didn't dare ask what he would tell his parents about her departure. She doubted they would ever ask for her version of events.

Chapter 11

The meeting with Mike had gone better than Clare expected. At least they were communicating again.

When she got to her car she checked her phone. There were two messages from Adam. He needed her input at Manor Croft. She wished she could ignore the request, the tension of her lunch with Mike had left her with a headache and cold sweats but, having given Mike a moving date, she needed to clear it with Adam.

Spending time with Adam was not getting any easier. If anything it made her question her sanity. With her life falling apart around her, adding him as her landlord was a huge complication, but the chance to live in her dream house made it all worthwhile.

Vehicles filled the courtyard of the farmhouse. One, a yellow van, belonged to a specialist furniture polishing and restoration company. Adam was getting ahead of himself again. He didn't seem to understand her lack of funds to splash out on that sort of thing. Independence from Mike would give her a very limited budget.

Adam was in the kitchen, filling some mugs with tea, looking pleased with himself.

"I dealt with the pest control company. They'll be finished tomorrow." He never gave her a second to query if he had checked what chemicals they intended using. He put the four mugs of tea on an old tin tray, added a packet of biscuits, a bag of sugar and a teaspoon. "Be back in a second. Help yourself."

On his return, he announced, "The electrics have been tested and passed. The new boiler goes in tomorrow."

She didn't know what to say. Half of her loved his determination to get the work done, the other half was terrified the controlling behaviour would continue after she moved in.

"Is something wrong?" he asked.

"Nothing... no... not really." She had to speak up. "Adam, you're taking over my life. I know you love this place, but it isn't going to be your home."

"Sorry, but it has to be safe before you move in. I can't rent you a house in an unfit state and have you turn round and sue me if something goes wrong."

"I wouldn't."

"Good. I promise I'll become an elusive landlord who's impossible to contact."

"You know I can't afford perfection." She pointed to the van outside.

"I'm only doing what needs to be done." He raised his hands in surrender. "Enough, time to eat."

"You must stop. Belinda might start to think something's going on."

"Isn't there?"

His casual tone took her by surprise.

"Don't push your luck. Landlord, business partner and friend, that's your lot."

He smiled. "I'm glad you threw in friend. As for Belinda being worried, she's so thrilled with her shop in town she's not bothered about what I'm doing." He put a huge Danish pastry on a cracked plate and pushed it across the table.

"I should call her."

"She'd love that. She was disappointed not to be working with you, but the town centre shop suits her better."

Clare wanted to hug him, happy his solution for the Belinda problem was a success.

"Thank you, but I still think you ought to spend more time with her. She is your fiancée remember."

"Yes, but she needs to make the shop her project. If I'm around she'll look to me to make decisions. She needs to believe in herself."

True, but Clare doubted boosting Belinda's confidence would change anything.

"Anyway," he continued, "she accepts I must get the house sorted before you move in. She thinks I'm motivated by self interest. The quicker the house is in order, the sooner you'll be able to concentrate on the expansion and I'll be rewarded."

Clare shook her head. Belinda and Adam made an odd couple, so odd they might actually suit each other if the relationship survived.

"You never did tell me how you made your fortune."

He shrugged. "Do you really want to know?"

"Of course."

Adam added an extra spoonful of sugar to his coffee and stirred slowly. "I had some lucky breaks when I was in Bristol."

She was tempted to butt in and ask why he'd gone there in the first place, but was afraid to reopen the conversation Belinda had interrupted the first day they had been at the farmhouse.

He took a sip from his mug and continued, "The builder I worked for encouraged me to save and invest in property. He worked out that employees who invested in the developments put more effort in to protect their share. It was true and a sort of co-op developed from that. It grew, moving from student flats to big office developments."

Clare picked the cherry off the top of her Danish pastry, trying to summon up the desire to eat. She struggled to focus. She wanted to hear his story but felt so odd that she wished Adam would hurry up so she could go home.

"The boss retired, a few of the others dropped out, I took over."

"Sounds impressive." It was so like Adam to make light of what must have been a huge struggle.

He shrugged. "Rubbish. Enough of that, how are the Show Garden plans coming on?"

"Fine, apart from a little trouble sourcing some of the plants, Gary will have to get them from a nursery in Wales."

"Is that a problem?"

"No, except Hannah wants to go with him."

"What's wrong with that? Don't you trust him?"

"Of course I do. But if he has to stay overnight, he doesn't need a fifteen year old in tow."

"No, I suppose not."

"That reminds me, I've a big favour to ask. Mike's parents are coming down to visit the week after next, for Hannah's birthday..."

"Go on," he answered, looking wary.

"I need to move in before they arrive. I'm happy to camp. I don't care if the builders are still here."

"A tight deadline..." He raised an eyebrow. "You still like setting challenges, don't you?"

Clare was touched that he remembered the crazy challenges they used to set each other all those years ago.

"I'll do my best, not sure about guests though."

"Oh, no panic... I'm the only one needing a bed," she answered quickly. "In fact, it would suit me better not to have room for the children. I'd rather they had a whole week with Mike's parents in the house when I move out to make the transition easier. I'm the one in need of an escape from his parents."

She could feel her face colour with embarrassment,

unable to believe she had implied a dislike of Mike's parents to Adam of all people, so added, "Sorry, all too dramatic sounding."

Adam smiled. "Don't worry, I understand. Families, always difficult."

That coming from Adam was an understatement. Maybe she should consider herself lucky in the lottery of parents. Hers might be awful but were angelic in comparison to his. All this talk about parents, reminded her she hadn't informed her mother of her planned move or the plans for Hannah's birthday.

"How are they?" he asked. She gave him what must have been a blank look, because he qualified it with "Your parents? Do they still live in the area?"

"Father died, Mother remarried, and moved up to Exmoor a few years ago. I hardly ever see her."

"Good or bad?"

"Good. Mother still tries to interfere when she can."

He nodded, obviously remembering her efforts to keep them apart. For a fleeting second she wondered if they had something to do with his sudden departure. No. It was stupid to try to lay blame for the way Adam had left. He'd dumped her. Simple. Right now she didn't want to spend time thinking about parental disappointments.

Adam broke her train of thought. "Sitting around talking is not getting anything done. Best get on, or it will be Christmas next year before you move in."

"What needs doing? I thought you had everything under control."

"Colour choices," he said handing her a big box file which had scraps of fabric sticking out the sides. "Sorry we're limited to this range, but the decorator wants to use a lime based wash because of the structure of the house. These are the best."

The weight of the box on her injured hand was so painful she nearly screamed. The file slipped, landed with a thud on the table, knocking her cup over. She took a deep breath and kept up the pretence of being in control. There hadn't been much liquid left in her cup and Adam was so busy mopping up he didn't spot her nursing her hand. Somehow she lifted the lid to find all her favourite colours inside, along with a tick list for the rooms. She made an effort to work through the choices without showing her pain.

When she finished Adam dragged a folded paper out of his pocket and slapped it on the table. "Snap!" His list was identical to hers. He pulled out swatches of curtain fabric which matched the agreed colours. She was impressed. She couldn't have done better, even if she had spent weeks scouring every shop in town.

"Good, now you can concentrate on the business and the show garden, while I get this lot sorted. I'll also get a couple of chaps in to clear up the garden, but I don't think that will be ready by the time you move in."

"Don't you dare..." she said, slamming her hand down on the table. An agonizing jolt shot up her arm, making the rest of the sentence come out as a gasp, "touch the garden."

She needed to put her head down between her knees. She had to stop herself from fainting. She must not pass out. Not in front of Adam.

Chapter 12

Clare's fainting had consequences. Adam rushed her to the doctor. Blood poisoning from the infected cut was to blame. He took her to the chemist to collect the antibiotics to stop the infection and drove her home. She didn't ask him in, she needed time alone.

For two days she felt so ill she didn't care about anything, even getting out of bed was a struggle. Edward and Hannah supplied cups of tea to wash down her medication. They tried to tempt her to eat by bringing platefuls of buttered toast to her bedside. She ate the odd mouthful to please them and listened as they reassured her that pizzas and fish and chips would keep them from starvation.

Once she started to feel that she could and should stir herself and get back to work, she found out that Adam had banned her from going anywhere near Manor Croft Farm. He had persuaded May to ban her from Dovedales too.

The only place permitted seemed to be the doctor's surgery, where she could get her dressings changed by the nurse.

The time at home gave her a chance to try to work out what she needed to do before she moved. Paperwork was the easiest to handle. What documents did she need? Should she take all the stuff related to the children? Or should she take copies. She started with her desk, found a big box file and began to fill it. Passport, birth certificates, she should keep those. Putting them in the box reminded her of the envelope from the records office which she'd ordered in an effort to get Edward's project underway. It should contain a selection of certificates for Mike's parents, and grandparents. She checked the kitchen drawer where she'd put it on the day it arrived. All she found was the unopened anniversary card from Mike, and a scrap of a brown envelope.

Someone had found it and removed it, even though it was addressed to her. Who? Mike had access, he often came into the house when he showed people round, but she had never known him open any drawers, let alone this one. The only other option was that one of the children had taken it, but they never opened her post, she was sure they'd have checked with her first.

She was stuck. If she accused Mike, and he hadn't taken them, he would get angry that she had gone ahead and asked for copies of his family's documents. If she asked the children they would feel she didn't trust them, a no win situation. The best solution was to request another set of copies to discover what they revealed.

Banishment from the farm and the nursery had another knock-on effect. It removed excuses to avoid Belinda's repeated invitations to join her for lunch.

Her reluctance to renew the childhood friendship had more to do with fear than anything. Belinda would expect an intense relationship which would lead to extra time with Adam. She found it hard enough working with him, but continual contact in a social context filled her with dread, especially with Belinda clinging possessively to his arm.

Belinda's excited response to her call added to her guilt. Clare managed to interrupt Belinda's non-stop chatter long enough to suggest they meet at the new shop followed by lunch.

"It'll be just like old times," Belinda answered. "Bring Mike. I've some lovely things I'd like his opinion on. We had such an interesting chat the other day about silver. He told me you loved going antique hunting with him."

Clare couldn't believe Mike had said that. True, she'd enjoyed the antiques fairs for a while when Edward was a baby, but once Hannah arrived she'd been more than happy to let Mike go on his own. Mike's silver collecting had become obsessive and she hadn't wanted to be a part of it.

"Belinda, you've forgotten something."

"What?"

"We've split up. All we're discussing right now are divorce details."

"Sorry, I forgot... your face... moving out... I'm forever sticking my foot in. He seems such a lovely man," Belinda said, "and a wonderful father."

Trust Belinda to apologize with one breath and counteract the effort with the next. Clare resisted the temptation to blurt out he was a lousy father who couldn't deal with the fact his daughter had a cruel genetic disease.

Belinda didn't seem to notice the lack of response. "I envy you being surrounded by silver treasures."

Clare managed to interrupt. "Sorry to disillusion you. Mike keeps his silver locked away in the safe." She didn't elaborate on the fact that the safe was a strong room at his office, the building having previously belonged to a jeweller and that she had no idea how big or small the collection had become.

"Oh, that's not the impression I got."

"No. It's his private collection." She nearly added, private to the point of obsession, but stopped herself.

"Not on display?"

"No, with moving house so often, it was difficult to find the right place. And the insurance became a problem too."

"That's a shame. I bet he hates not having them on

84

show."

Clare wasn't sure. There were times when she thought he was happier that they were not. Secrecy seemed to suit him better. She wanted to end the discussion, talking about Mike felt wrong. She fixed a time and hung up.

Belinda's reminder of the early years of her marriage when the silver had been a shared interest, brought timings into focus. Mike began his christening mug collecting after Edward was born. She had found it odd that he could be so passionate about old silver when his taste was for ultra modern things. She put it down to his being a proud father. His interest waned after Hannah was born, which was a relief. They didn't have spare cash, and life was easier without having to attend antique fairs with two children in tow.

Soon after Hannah's birth they moved house again, this one more modern than before with even less space to display personal possessions. The silver collection went into the safe in the office. His collecting enthusiasm appeared to dwindle as golf became the new passion.

Occasionally a flurry of parcels would arrive in the post. Instead of going to antique fairs, Mike bought on the internet. He'd spend hours at the kitchen table cleaning and polishing the new treasures, with obsessive fervour. This was the only time she saw his purchases and could see the range of objects had widened, but with the maker and age being the focus. Once cleaned to his satisfaction the items disappeared into the office safe.

The coincidence that a fresh bout of collecting started about the time Edward asked for information for his family tree needed checking.

With this in mind, she approached Mike's desk where the family papers were stored. She took a sheet of paper from the printer tray, found a pen to make notes and opened the drawer with the key which he kept hidden in a silver inkwell. She systematically went through the papers, jotting down everything that might provide a date or place to help her with an online search.

She'd already found their current passports, and her marriage certificate and the children's birth certificates. She made copies, which she'd leave behind. Determined not to miss one shred of family history information, she scanned every photo she could find, including a few unfamiliar ones that she discovered, wrapped in browning tissue paper, tucked inside a tarnished and battered christening mug that lay abandoned at the back of the drawer.

The initials LS were inscribed on the mug. It was a similar shape to Mike's own Irish silver christening mug, which had been the inspiration behind his collection. What didn't make sense was that he allowed this one to become tarnished. Still there was a lot about Mike's behaviour of late that made no sense. She put it back where it had come from, wondering if the photos were perhaps more to do with the mug than to Edward's project.

It was time to leave for her lunch with Belinda. She put all the scanned files onto a memory stick, and slipped it into an envelope with the documents she had chosen to take, and put it into her bag for later.

Belinda's shop was a joy to enter. Bright and uncluttered, but stocked with an extraordinary range of objects, an eclectic mix of gimmicky and practical gifts. Kitchen gadgets and pretty household utensils sat alongside outdoor things, unusual door mats, boot scrapers and the like. All of which Clare would have been happy to give to friends. Perhaps Belinda buying for the garden centre would not have been such a bad idea.

Lunch turned out to be more fun than expected. Clare hadn't laughed so much in a long time. Not since they'd teamed up at school, them against the world, Belinda was as entertaining as ever. Surprisingly, Adam barely got a mention.

Chapter 13

"Mum, please let me go to Wales with Gary."

"I've already said no. If Gary can't find the plants he wants, he may head across to Derby, which means spending longer away."

Hannah watched her mother turn the pastry round on the floured board and roll it the other way.

"I don't mind." Hannah began to eat sultanas from the jar.

"I'm sure you don't, but I can't expect him to look after you. Also your grandparents will be down for their half-term visit."

"A couple of nights wouldn't hurt," Hannah said in an attempt to wear her mother down.

"What about your physio sessions? You can't afford to skip them with exams looming next month."

"I'll go for a run instead, same as I did on the days you were ill." It was a mean argument.

Her mum stopped mid roll. "I don't want to spoil your fun, and I understand that you want to check where the plants come from. But you can't go. You're too young."

"I'll be sixteen by then, or had you forgotten?" Hannah

wasn't ready to give up.

"As if I could ... right now fifteen or sixteen doesn't make any difference." She put the rolling pin down and pulled a dish over and attempted to lift and fold the pastry. The pastry stretched and tore, even a knife failed to coax the mess off the board. "I need to start again."

"How do you think Gary will feel when I tell him you won't let me go?"

"Don't push me, Hannah."

"It was his idea."

"Well it's not a practical one."

"Who needs practical? I'll be old and grey before you let me out of your sight." A hurtful comment, but one she needed to voice.

"Rubbish, I'm not that bad." Her mum wiped her eyes with the back of her floury hand. "If I had time, I'd go myself."

"You never have time."

"Whose fault is that? Who entered my name for the Show Garden Competition?"

"Ok, you win," Hannah said. "What are you trying to make?"

"Lemon meringue pie, if I can get this into the dish."

Hannah looked at the shredded mess and at the flapping plaster on her mother's hand. "I'll finish this while you sort out that dressing."

Hannah was struck by the oddity of the caring role being reversed. She loved cooking and often helped out, with enjoyable results. She dipped her hands into the flour and set about kneading the overworked pastry.

Edward was due home soon. He'd been frustratingly quiet, refusing to talk about anything, let alone what it would be like when their father came home. She heard a car door slam. His friend must have given him a lift which might have put him in a better mood. Rugby practice made him hungry so it was a good thing supper was nearly ready.

One look was enough for her to catch the stagger and the bright eyed look. He'd been drinking. Was this the cause of his bad moods, the silent shifts at the nursery and his new enthusiasm to rush off to rugby practice at every opportunity?

She'd overheard Aunt May making a comment about his going through the grunt stage, dismissing it as normal behaviour for his age, especially with the tense situation at home.

Hannah wanted to tell her mum that Edward had sworn never to speak to his father again. Stress seemed to have destroyed her maternal radar and Hannah didn't want to make matters worse. Not even when she'd been asked to talk to Edward about the move. What a mess! Still, that was no excuse for Edward's behaviour.

Edward stumbled again as he sat down. Hannah watched for her mother's reaction. For a fleeting second her mother's eyes screamed fear.

"Supper's ready," Hannah said. "Shall I dish up?"

"Yes, please." Her mother pulled out her chair to sit. Edward nodded. Hannah mouthed, "Say something," to her mother and got a firm, 'Don't interfere' look in return.

Edward took the plate Hannah passed to him. At least he was capable of that.

"Did you go for a drink after practice?" her mum asked, trying to give the impression of being completely relaxed about the question.

Edward answered with a guilty sounding, "Yes."

"I hope your friend hadn't been drinking."

After a slight hesitation he managed, "No, he's careful."

"Good. Next time, ask him in. I'd like to meet him and I bet Hannah would too."

Edward mumbled, "Sure." Eating seemed to require intense concentration.

They ate in silence. The two courses took ages. Edward moved first, muttered something about homework and left the room.

Hannah waited until he'd left before tipping his sports bag over. His spotlessly clean kit tumbled out.

"You knew he hadn't been to practice. Why didn't you say something?" She regretted the question. Fear was the key. Clearly her mother hadn't forgotten their father's drunken violence.

"I will. Hannah. But I'll pick a more effective time." She pushed her chair back. "Is that a problem?"

Hannah reached out for the empty plate. "No. As long as you promise you'll do something. He's been really odd lately."

"Trust me. Now, what shall we watch tonight?" She reached for the weekly television programme.

Hannah wanted to be alone to think. "I've some revision to do, pick whatever you want."

"Fine." She blew a kiss in Hannah's direction and made a big thing of opening the programme magazine. The gesture didn't fool Hannah. Instead it increased her guilt about abandoning her mother. Maybe she'd stay for a while, do some extra clearing up.

"Find something good?" she queried.

"No, but I've plenty of other things to do."

Hannah was going to offer to help when the door bell rang. Her mother went to answer it.

"Belinda. What a nice surprise!"

The surprise was genuine enough, but Hannah sensed a lack of joy in the greeting. When she saw their visitor it was easy to guess why. Belinda was dressed in a sexy figure-hugging dress while her mum was wearing loose sweatpants and a baggy jumper. Not exactly the ego boost her mother needed.

"I was passing by and thought I'd drop in to show you the silver I mentioned," Belinda said.

"I told you yesterday. Mike's moved out. Surely you remember?"

"Yes, but can't you give me your opinion." She held out a small silver jug.

Hannah's mum ducked backwards, as if the thing was contaminated. It was no secret the silver collection created a lot of tension, but even so the reaction was extreme.

"I wouldn't know," she said stepping even further away from Belinda. "Mike was exaggerating when he mentioned my interest. To be honest it is one of the reasons I'm leaving."

"Oh, when I saw the "For Sale" sign I assumed he'd be moving at the same time as you."

"This is the show house for the estate and has always been for sale. He won't move out until all the others are sold."

She might as well not have bothered explaining. Belinda wasn't listening.

"It's wonderful." Belinda stepped forward, heading towards the lounge in a daze. "Adam must come over. I'm having trouble getting him to consider a modern house. He's determined to find some quaint old place. I nearly died when he suggested we live at Manor Croft Farm. Such a dump! Don't you think so? Oh God, I forgot you're about to take refuge there."

Hannah couldn't work out if the lack of response was because her mum considered the comment an insult. Belinda was spot on with calling the farm a refuge. Anywhere would be paradise compared to this place. No one had been happy here.

Belinda peered into the lounge. "What perfect dimensions," she commented. "I'd prefer a subtle shade of sage, you know the soft tone I mean, don't you? What's the kitchen like? Can I?"

Hannah could tell nothing would stop Belinda. She was already heading towards the kitchen with unstoppable determination.

"Did Mike design this?"

"What?"

Belinda who never listened to a word anyone told her seemed indignant that Clare wasn't following the conversation. "The kitchen, did Mike design it?"

"No, he just sells them. The architect you met at dinner at the club designs them all." Her mum sounded tired.

"He's good. I love it. Mind if I call Adam? I want him to check this over."

"Sorry Belinda. Not now." Hannah picked up real panic in her mum's voice. Why was she so upset? They were supposed to be old friends, inseparable by all accounts.

"I need an early night, got a terrible migraine." A blatant lie as her mum had never had a migraine before. The desperate bid to get Belinda out of the house included steering her back to the door. "Sorry to be so unwelcoming. Perhaps some other time, it would be best to call Mike at his office."

Belinda didn't seem to mind eviction.

When she left, Hannah questioned her motives. She had an air about her that screamed, flirt. Had the stunning silk dress been for her dad's benefit? Had that been why she left so quickly? She hoped her mother hadn't come to the same conclusion.

Chapter 14

As the day of the move approached Clare double checked the house to make sure that she didn't leave anything behind that had any sentimental value.

The frequent moves from one house to another made collecting keepsakes impossible. Her personal treasures were crammed into a single box. Her clothes and shoes filled a couple of suitcases.

Dismay on Hannah's face as she loaded the car made her briefly question her actions. No, it wasn't selfish to expect to feel safe in your own home. Staying for the children's sake would benefit no one.

Her discussion with Edward about drinking had been awkward. Embarrassment and contrition appeared to lead to a swift reversion to his normal thoughtful self, with a promise that he would get back to work on his history project, using the census material he'd found in the library. Clare was pleased and offered to help him as soon as she was settled at the farmhouse. She didn't mention the missing documents, or that she had put in a request for another set of certificates from the records office. No need to let him know about his father's reluctance to discuss his family.

The disruption to Hannah's daily routine remained her biggest worry. The extra long session of physiotherapy done that morning should suffice for now. Hannah promised to fit strenuous activities into the days when her early morning sessions were missed. If the exercise wasn't enough then Clare would give her a session after school.

Three mornings without the responsibility of those vital tapping sessions would require adjustment on both sides. Perhaps the experience would be good for Hannah and make her better able to pick up the subtle changes in her lungs, the warning signs of infection taking hold.

The children would cycle to school every day. Today, she waved them off and went back inside for one last tour of the building. No happy memories lingered. All that marked her existence at the property was a faint brown stain on the kitchen floor.

She arrived at her new home after a two week absence with no idea what to expect. Adam was pacing up and down outside waiting for her. He rushed over, brushed her cheek with a kiss and handed her an enormous bunch of keys.

It was the same bunch he'd taken from her earlier, which now had a new gold-plated key-ring in the shape of a thatched cottage, almost identical to Manor Croft, attached. She mumbled thanks, slightly overwhelmed by the enthusiastic welcome.

"I hope you'll be happy." He led her round to the front door and gestured she should use her key. She fumbled for the right one, feeling awkward about going in. His choice of the front entrance made her wonder what was wrong with the kitchen.

Since banishing her from the house he'd refused to give her progress reports. Even with an army of craftsmen working full time she didn't expect the renovations to be complete and was determined not to show any signs of disappointment.

The door opened to reveal glowing floorboards. Sunlight

flooded in from the previously blocked up windows. The walls, painted a soft buttery yellow, gave the area warmth and a vase of lilies standing on a heavily carved dark oak chest added a heady aroma, the impact was breathtaking.

She took a deep breath, smiled to show approval and stepped in to her home. Adam opened one door after another. The same layout and furniture, but everything gleamed invitingly. Only the pictures were missing. She was about to ask, but Adam got in first.

"Harry's pictures are clean but rather gloomy. You can choose which, if any, you'd like put back. They're in the store with the boxes of china. Sift through them and decide what you want."

"I can't believe the work you've done," Clare said, finding it hard to comprehend the transformation that had occurred in her absence.

The man-eating sofa had vanished replaced by an inviting cream, deep-cushioned settee, big enough for about five people. The other chairs had been beautifully re-upholstered using neutral toned fabrics. All the furniture gleamed with fresh polish. The china cabinet was bare, for a fleeting second she imagined what it would look like if it were to house Mike's silver collection. She quickly dismissed the thought. Harry's treasures were more in keeping, maybe Adam would allow her put them back.

"Come on," he said, obviously eager to show off the rest, each room better than the one before. The bedrooms and bathrooms far exceeded expectation. The biggest shock was the room filled with a specially adapted tilting massage table, perfect for Hannah's tapping sessions, an array of wedge shaped cushions in varying sizes, just right for the different positions Hannah had to lie in during her daily sessions. He even had speakers set up for her music.

Clare spun round to face him. "Who told you about Hannah?"

"Hannah."

"But she never tells anyone."

"I asked her for special requests. This was hers."

Clare brushed away a tear, overwhelmed by his thoughtfulness. She didn't deserve so much. Renting from him made everything complicated.

His arm went round her shoulder. "Come on, time to explore the kitchen."

One glimpse threw her into a panic. How could Belinda not want to live here?

Adam prodded her arm. "Go on say something."

"Has Belinda seen this?" His puzzled expression was enough to indicate this wasn't the expected response.

"No, she's not interested."

"Are you sure?"

"I don't follow you?"

"With this transformation are you sure she won't change her mind?"

"No chance!" She sensed disappointment. "Relax, she's found somewhere she's crazy about."

"Did she say where?"

"No, but she's managed to organize for us to view this evening."

"Do you want the bad news?"

"Bad news... you hate what I've done?"

"No, I love it. The house Belinda loves is the one I've just left." It was Adam's turn to be speechless. "She called round the other night, and loved everything she saw."

Adam found his voice. "You think I'd hate it?"

"Not think... I know you will."

"What excuse can I use?"

"Too close to the main road, traffic noise. Or appeal to her snobbish side. Say, you need something more of a statement, one that a bigger garden would provide."

"That last excuse sounds like the best angle," he said with a rather wicked smile. "Now, are you going to make your landlord a cup of coffee to thank him for his efforts, or not?"

Clare moved over to the newly restored Aga. To her amazement the battered old kettle was in its customary place to the left of the hot plate.

Adam registered her surprise. "I hadn't the heart to get rid of it."

"I'm glad. A new one wouldn't have been nearly as nice." She filled it and moved back to the Aga. She put the kettle down and hung onto the rail along the front, keeping her back to him to hide how overwhelmed she was.

"Adam, I... I don't know how to thank you enough. To be honest, I'm embarrassed, it is too much... I don't deserve this... worse still I can't repay you." Her eyes welled up. God she must get a grip. His kindness was getting to her, bringing back the reasons she had loved him so much all those years ago. Without the children to take into consideration she would run rather than be in debt to him. The prospect of watching Belinda flaunting their relationship didn't bear thinking about.

"I don't expect anything from you," Adam said softly, moving close behind her.

"That doesn't make a difference."

"Difference to what?"

His breath tickled the back of her neck. Far too distracting, she ought to move away, but she wanted to sink into his arms instead.

"Being near you," she whispered.

Silence engulfed them. What would he make of her response? He stayed still. The noise of the kettle grew louder, eventually the lid rattled. Clare pushed it to one side to silence it. Adam put his hands on her shoulder and turned her to face him.

With barely an inch between them, he trailed a finger over her lips. The heat of his body seared across the gap.

"It is hard for me too. Tell me what to do."

Her mind raced over the possibilities. Run like hell.

97

Don't let him out of your grasp. Don't let him hurt you again. Let him kiss you. She so wanted him to make the decision for her. She longed for a kiss. But was terrified one kiss would never satisfy her needs.

His phone buzzed in his pocket.

The intimacy instantly shattered. No need for an answer. Not now, perhaps never.

His hand left her face to dive into his pocket to rescue the vibrating gadget. He stared at the screen, stepped away from her and headed towards the door putting it to his ear, then talking. "Yes Belinda..."

Clare was glad she didn't have to listen to any more. Hearing the name was enough to realize she'd nearly let a difficult situation become an impossible one.

She made the coffee, placed the cups on opposite sides of the table to put a solid barrier between her and Adam. She must never let him get that close again.

When he returned, she was already sitting. He spotted where she'd placed his cup and sat opposite her, seeming to understand their earlier intimacy was a mistake. He looked serious. "You were right about your house. Mike's lined up to show us round later."

"Not wasting time then?"

"No. How will it work? I thought the children were going to carry on living part time with Mike?"

"If he moves, they do too. It isn't the first time they've had to accept a change of house. And if he doesn't find somewhere suitable for them all, then the part-time arrangement would fall by the wayside."

"Would he let that happen?"

"I don't know. He's never been a close father, especially in the last year. I sometimes wonder if he'd notice if they weren't around." It felt wrong being so disloyal about Mike to Adam of all people.

"Well, he's the one missing out, they're great kids. A credit to you, you should be proud of them."

"Thank you."

"I've a confession to make." Adam's guilt ridden expression and brighter tone made her less concerned about what might follow.

"Go on."

"Remember we agreed I could do what I wanted to the house as long as I didn't touch the garden. I had to break my promise."

Clare glanced out of the kitchen window. Nothing seemed amiss. She'd been so busy exploring the house she hadn't even peeked out of the windows as they went round.

"What?"

"The painter needed to cut back the plants touching the wall. I got Gary to come and supervise what he did, but the result is a bit drastic. Gary swears the plants will survive and be better for pruning in the long run."

Clare was relieved, but not convinced that was all Adam had done. "And what else?"

"I got the lawns cut and the farm boundary hedges trimmed hard for the winter. May suggested it, so if you're not pleased, blame her."

"You're forgiven."

"Thank you, I didn't want you mad at me." His sad eyes made her smile." Oh I nearly forgot, May sent over a small fork, she said to put it with the collection of gardening tools Harry left in the shed. She thought Harry's might be too big for you and that you'd probably want to get stuck in the minute you arrived."

"She knows me too well."

"In that case I'd better get out of your way. Can I carry anything in for you?"

"Yes please, if you don't mind. I've a couple of cases and one heavy box in the car."

"Is that all?"

"Two cases can hardly be classified as travelling light." Her response instinctive, a reaction to the promise made to each other when planning their big adventure, to travel light and never accumulate more than one medium sized rucksack each. If Adam remembered, he avoided showing it by slipping out the door to collect her bags and taking them upstairs.

She listened to his footsteps. She loved the squeak of the landing floor boards, thrilled by the prospect of living in a house with a voice of its own, learning to unravel all the secrets of its sounds would be a treat.

She worked out when he reached her room, heard him deposit the bags. On their tour she had been too stunned to comment on the room. The soft peachy toned walls complimented the mellow wood of the furniture. The huge bed dressed with crisp white bed linen had a quilted silk throw which reflected the colour of the walls. What a waste for a single woman. She imagined he had almost planned it for himself. She must stop letting her imagination get out of hand. Of course he'd buy a big bed. In such a big room anything smaller would have looked lost.

He returned with the box, placed it on the kitchen table and left.

Alone at last, she slowly retraced the route she had taken with him. This time savouring his attention to detail revealed with every step she took. Tiny personal touches, left her in no doubt, he remembered their teenage dreams. Now destiny chose to have her live alone in their fantasy house.

Chapter 15

Clare didn't want to mull over past dreams. Better to do something practical like unpacking. She flipped open the catches on her suitcase, but the urge to explore the garden took over. She hurried outside to inspect her new surroundings.

The freshly mown grass and the trimmed boundary hedges improved the initial impression and reduced the look of neglect. The structure and lay-out of the shrubbery was good and would have been spectacular when first planted. The plants were either overpoweringly bushy or choked with dead wood or had grown too tall seeking light. She identified several unusual plants and was excited at the prospect of discovering more. The garden deserved restoring to its original design.

The well maintained vegetable garden, behind the shrubbery, was full of plants groaning under the weight of their produce.

The best discovery was the entrance to the small enclosed garden, previously glimpsed from the study window, where an intricate tangle of creepers masked the walls. Honeysuckle, wisteria, clematis and roses fought for light and space, tendrils enveloping the taller perennials and shrubs in the borders on all four sides. Moss covered steps led to a pond in the centre, so full of water-lilies, marsh marigolds and irises, that the water was invisible.

The physical energy required to pull this garden back in shape would be enormous, but every back-aching moment would be worthwhile. First she had to find out what hidden gems in the way of bulbs and corms lurked below the surface waiting to flower.

The need to wait was an advantage as work on the show garden must take precedence. She paced out a flat space between the vegetable garden and the path to May's house. This would be the ideal location with regard to the north south aspect to test the layout of her design. The show garden needed to be perfect, for the sake of the business and her self esteem. Mike had undermined her to the point where she almost ceased to be a person in her own right. This would allow her to redress the situation and prove the late night studying was worthwhile.

In the shed she found a pruning saw and a pair of loppers and went off to the furthest point of the shrubbery to start. Even though she didn't technically own this magical space, she was going to pretend she did.

She hacked one bush down to ground level, a hardy one that would regenerate from the base. The next she thinned out, removing dead wood and lowering some of the tall shoots to encourage new stems to sprout.

Time to stop. She couldn't risk opening the cut on her hand again. She'd need a shredder to deal with the heap of branches she had removed. She heard May's gate bang and waved to greet her visitor.

"I tried phoning," May called out, as she crossed the lawn. "You didn't answer so I guessed you'd be out here." "I've brought you some lunch."

Clare glanced at her watch. "I didn't realize I'd been out for so long." May's basket looked full of tempting things.

"That smells good, I'm starving. Come on in."

"Will Adam have to get the big diggers in?"

"Diggers, you must be joking. All this needs is tender loving care. Who did the planting? Harry?"

"No. His wife Daphne. Harry hated not being able to keep it up. I know he tried but missed her too much and he was terrified of doing more harm than good. And his veggie patch kept him busy enough."

"Maybe his neglect did the garden a favour. I'd like to restore what's there rather than make changes. Can you help keep me on track by telling me what she had growing so I can replace as near the original as possible? I've already found some intriguing plants hidden in the undergrowth."

Clare put her tools back in the shed and took the basket from May.

"I hope Adam got the house clean enough," May said as they approached. "Gary and I offered to come over and help but he wouldn't let either of us in."

"It's immaculate. So good it's embarrassing, especially with our history. I don't know how I'll ever repay him. He won't even let me pay extra rent."

"Maybe this is his way of thanking you for helping Gary to get so far with his studies."

"Nice thought, but the credit belongs to you."

"Nonsense, I couldn't give the encouragement you gave."

Clare followed May, soaking up her approval. "Harry will be so pleased when I tell him. Maybe you could ask him over one day."

Back in the kitchen, Clare put Harry's battered old kettle into use while May unpacked the lunch, a quiche, a bowl of salad and some fresh fruit. Clare hadn't even opened the cupboards to check for crockery, or cutlery or cooking utensils. She went to the one nearest her, and found three shiny new saucepans. The next revealed a set of four white dinner plates, four bowls, and four small plates. The cutlery drawer contained a set of four of everything, all new. Her heart sank. Sad that Adam appeared to have disposed of all Harry's things except the kettle. She didn't want May to know, so she quickly grabbed two plates and some cutlery, and put them on the table.

May still hadn't answered her question about Harry coming over.

"Perhaps we should wait until I've done some work on the garden?"

"Yes, later might be better."

"Do serve up while I wash my hands."

May's glance fixed on the grubby plaster.

"Don't' worry, it's healed. I keep this on for protection while the skin hardens.

She washed her hand, showed May the healed wound, before sticking on a fresh dressing.

"What did Harry do with all the vegetables he grew? Tons of produce is just going to waste. I think even if we all become vegetarians we'll never eat that lot."

"He used to distribute them to his neighbours. It gave him an excuse to visit old friends. I bet he's missing those visits. Growing vegetables was his passion, particularly the old varieties."

"I don't suppose he'd consider looking after it like an allotment and stop that area from becoming a wilderness."

"I'll ask."

"At least get him to come and harvest his crops. It's such a waste to have them rotting on the plants."

"I'll go and see him later. The worst that can happen is he turns down the offer."

May's quiche was delicious. Clare was surprised at how hungry her stint in the garden had made her.

"What time are the children coming over?" May asked.

"After school, but they're not moving until after the weekend."

"They're okay with that?"

"They're fine, not that I gave them a choice. Mike's parents are staying all this week. I thought it would make the transition, from my leaving and Mike moving back, less tense." She wondered if May had guessed that Mike's parents impending visit had given her the impetus to push Adam into an early completion date.

"I bet they wanted to move with you."

"Yes, they did."

"I hope you stocked up with house-warming treats. You know how hungry they are after school."

Clare hadn't given food a thought. The well-stocked freezer and groaning larder were no longer at hand. She'd have to start all over again.

"This move has seriously affected my brain. Food never entered my head. I'd better go shopping."

May nodded and packed her dishes back into the basket ready to take them home.

By the time Clare had done a grocery shop for essentials, it was late. Marking out the show garden would have to wait.

She had barely unpacked the food when Hannah burst into the kitchen, eyes wide with expectation.

For a moment she said nothing, then a big grin formed. "Wow!" She turned towards the door, "Come on, Edward. This is fantastic."

Edward stuck his head in and muttered, "Not bad."

"Can I see my room?"

Clare waved then on and followed, revelling in their excitement as they explored, peeking quickly into each room. Hannah squealed with delight. Edward seemed less keen.

"Now I understand your wanting an old house. Such a cosy, lived in atmosphere, even though everything is new," Hannah said.

Edward perked up at the sight of his computer desk and the space reserved for a television. No accounting for children's reactions. He'd never given her much cause for concern before, which made his subdued behaviour more noticeable.

"Hannah, there's something else you need to see." She held open the door to the room Adam had set up for her physiotherapy. "I hope you like it."

The happy smile disappeared for a fraction of a second. "Great." But she didn't cross the threshold.

Clare guessed the table was a reminder of her illness. In time she'd appreciate the space. For now, she wanted to forget. Clare understood and pulled the door closed.

"What time are Gran and Grandad arriving?" she asked. "I'll run you home so you can be there to meet them."

"No need. Dad's going to collect us from here on his way back from the station."

Clare shivered. She didn't want Mike or his parents coming anywhere near her new home, and certainly not on the first night. She wanted to change the arrangement without making an issue of it. The best alternative was to watch for his arrival, and not give him a chance to step out of the car. Make some excuse about being in a muddle, and not up for visitors.

"Can you be ready to leave the minute he gets here? I don't want to ask him in and have to explain to Gran and Grandad why I've moved out."

Both the children nodded. They seemed to understand her difficulties. "Thanks."

"Now, is everything sorted for Sunday?" she asked.

"I think so. I spoke to Rosie today. She's really looking forward to getting out of hospital for a few hours." Hannah's beaming smile, made all the planning worthwhile. "The weather forecast looks alright."

Clare sliced the cake she'd bought and handed it round. "And you haven't even hinted about the chance to ride in the trap?"

"No, I promise. I remembered your warning about setting her up for a disappointment."

"Good."

Their discussion about dividing their time between homes and what was needed to make swapping between the two houses easier was interrupted by the sound of car wheels crunching on the newly laid pea-gravel. Mike had arrived.

"Hurry and get your things," she said to the children as she stepped outside. She moved quickly round to the driver's door, standing so close Mike couldn't open it. She bent down making it obvious he should lower the window. She greeted his parents through the opening.

"Hello Hilda and Denis. Lovely to see you again." They responded with rather weak smiles. "Mike, you didn't need to come. I was going to drop them home."

"No bother," he mumbled. Bother my foot, she thought, all he wanted to do was inspect the place and find fault. And she didn't intend to give him the opportunity, not tonight, not ever if she had her way.

The children had followed her out and were already buckling up their seat belts, distracting his parents.

Mike was reaching to turn the key when another car pulled up. Everyone turned to look. Adam and Belinda. Clare stood still. She daren't give Mike the chance to step out of his vehicle.

Hannah shattered her calm. "Can you invite Belinda and Adam to come to my party?"

Clare didn't have much choice with her response. "Of course I will. The more the merrier, don't you think, Mike?"

The tight white knuckles on the steering wheel were the only indication he gave of his displeasure.

No escape now. Explaining to her daughter the complications of her past relationship or her present confusion regarding Adam and Belinda was far too difficult to contemplate.

Mike, to give him credit, managed a barely audible response, "Yes."

"Bye, see you tomorrow." She pulled back, stepped away from the car and raised her hand in a wave. Mike's tight lips the only visible reaction to her taking control of the situation. Tough, he'd have to get used to her new independent status.

Now, she must deal with her second batch of unwelcome visitors.

Belinda brandished a large bottle of champagne. "We've come to help you celebrate."

Clare had no option. She had to invite them in.

Seeing the size of the bottle she said, "Shall we ask May and Gary over to join us?"

Adam nodded and pulled out his phone to pass on the invitation.

Clare ushered them in, dreading Belinda's reaction. What if she loved the transformation and wanted to move in? Now she was being selfish. It was Adam's house and if he wanted to live here, then she couldn't stop him from evicting her.

Her fears were short-lived. Belinda cast her eye over the room and gave her verdict. "Much better than last time I came. I still don't get the attraction of an old fashioned stove. How you can bear to leave that beautiful modern house is beyond me. I persuaded Adam to view it with me, but couldn't get him enthusiastic about it at all. He says the garden is too small. But I don't want anything bigger."

"The surrounding space matters." Adam answered. "I want a house with a view."

"This one doesn't have a view and you love this place."

"That's different. This one isn't overlooked by near neighbours. One day we'll find the right place, but Clare's old home isn't it." The firmness in the final statement made Belinda pout. Clare guessed she hadn't totally given up on the idea, in spite of Adam's veto.

"Come on, Clare, show me the rest. Adam, be a darling, find some glasses."

Clare wanted to chuckle. Be a darling! How did he put up with her? She felt sorry for him, Adam was too kind to protest, but how long before he snapped. Then guilt hit, she wanted that to happen, the sooner the better.

108

Clare showed Belinda the transformed rooms and was delighted with her polite reaction, quite an achievement for Belinda. They explored everywhere except Hannah's exercise room. Clare blocked the way, and encouraged Belinda onwards. She didn't want to discuss Hannah's illness.

By the time they got back downstairs May and Gary had appeared.

"I'll probably live in this room but on this occasion, we should head to the lounge for our drinks." Clare waved them towards the other room. As they filed out, she grabbed a bag of crisps from the cupboard, filled a bowl and followed them.

Adam raised his glass. "To your new home."

Everyone joined in.

"The nursery and the show garden," Gary said, raising his glass for a second time.

Clare was glad Gary had brought up the subject. "I found the perfect spot to lay out the show garden. I'd like you to tell me what you think."

"I'll come over first thing. Oh, what time should we be there tomorrow?"

Clare gulped as she remembered Hannah's last minute request. "Twelve."

She turned to Belinda and Adam, "I nearly forgot. Hannah is having a lunch out at Hilltop Stables to celebrate her birthday. She'd like you to come." Belinda's puzzled expression over the venue made her fill in the details. "Hannah wants to give a sick friend the chance to be near some horses. So we organized a fancy picnic lunch at the stables. If Rosie is well enough, she may get to ride in one of the little carriages. The stable owners are so helpful."

"We'd love to join you, wouldn't we, Adam?"

After a slight hesitation he answered "Yes, thanks."

May, with her usual tact, got up and suggested it was time to leave. "Let's give Clare a quiet evening to finish unpacking. She was too busy gardening to get much done

109

earlier." May put her glass down and asked, "Is your mother coming to the party?"

What an odd question! Did she intend it as a warning for Adam?

Clare nodded. "Yes, of course?"

Having both her mother and her parents-in-law together for a celebration, with her ex-boyfriend and her soon to be divorced husband and a moody son was the sort of scenario a script writer would delight in. But nothing, not even a tactless remark from Belinda was going to spoil Hannah's day.

Gary stood up to go too. "Let me know if you need a hand with anything."

Adam followed his example, "I look forward to meeting your mother again," he said quietly. A wicked glint in his eye told her more than his words did.

Clare didn't dare respond. Shame Hannah was unaware of the animosity that her maternal grandmother harboured against Adam when she issued the invitation.

Adam pressed a small bunch of keys into her hand. "The keys to the big store out the back, I forgot to give them to you earlier. All the pictures, china, glasses and kitchen stuff from the house is there, help yourself to whatever you can use."

Half of her wanted to turn down the offer, but she didn't have spare cash to waste. Crazy not to make use of the things that had done service in this house for so long, just because of guilt over his generosity.

Belinda muttered about not insulting her by offering her rubbish. The barbed comment made Clare happier to accept the gesture.

Chapter 16

Hannah found doing physio exercises on her own unsettling, but not seeing her Mum until lunch time on her birthday was even odder.

Sunshine reduced the chance of Rosie cancelling. Hannah had tried to block out the possibility, though she was sure her mum probably expected it.

Hannah hurried with her breakfast. She wanted to get out before the "olds" woke up. Gran Hilda hadn't stopped fussing and moaning about everything since she arrived. Grandad Denis had been hiding behind his newspaper more than before. She'd decided to cycle over to the stables early, which was good exercise and so that she could help get the horses ready. She wanted her horse, Tinker, and the docile grey mare, Dulcie, that pulled the trap that Rosie might be able to go in, groomed to perfection

Sue welcomed her and they fed the horses. Hannah never got to help cleaning the stalls, the straw dust made it too dangerous. But once the horses were outside, she could brush them until they gleamed in the sunshine, and plait their manes and tails with ribbons to add a festive touch.

Hannah wanted to show off her new dressage moves to

her mum, Rosie, Gary and Aunt May. None of the others would appreciate the effort needed to control the horses to get them moving in time to the music.

The horses were ready when her mum arrived looking happier than Hannah had seen her for a while. She offered to hold Tinker's reins while Hannah put the brushes away. It was the first time Hannah had seen her stand this close to a horse without showing any sign of fear.

Rosie and her parents arrived. Rosie's huge smile diverted attention from the oxygen feed that ran across her face. Getting out of the ward was working its magic.

Her parents wheeled Rosie down to meet the horses. Her initial response was even better than Hannah had expected, sometimes she wondered if other people made mental snapshots of special moments. This was a special one. That first joyful reaction was eclipsed when Sue told Rosie it was possible for her to take a ride in the trap.

Rosie checked with her parents, expecting them to refuse. They didn't. Hannah watched as Sue helped Rosie climb the step up and into the seat and as soon as her oxygen tank was wedged in securely, took the reins and led the grey mare round the ring. The other guests had arrived and were leaning on the railings in the late autumn sunshine to watch.

Hannah mounted her horse and rode alongside. "Want to go faster?" Hannah asked.

Rosie smiled and nodded. Sue handed her the reins, and explained how to flick them to signal the horse to go faster. Rosie nervously had a go, flicking the reins gently. The horse responded, picked up speed and began to trot. Rosie laughed. Seeing her so relaxed and happy was the best present Hannah could have.

As they circled the ring, Hannah checked where Rosie's folks were. The pleasure they got watching their daughter having fun could never quite blot out their look of concern.

Hannah noticed how pale her friend was. She had tired more quickly than expected.

"Had enough?" she asked.

Rosie nodded and Sue took over the reins again, slowed the pace and led the grey back to the mounting block and helped Rosie back into her wheelchair.

Now it was time for Hannah to demonstrate her newly perfected dressage skills to her awaiting fans. Tinker was ready and keen to play to the audience, obeying every nudge, performing an almost perfect routine. Judging from the applause the onlookers were suitably impressed, especially Rosie. Hannah would have liked to do a few more circuits, but cut the last section of the routine out so that everyone could get on with lunch.

Sue insisted on taking her horse back to unsaddle him, leaving Hannah free to join the party.

The food had been laid out on tables, surrounded by hay bales to sit on.

Her father was talking to Belinda. Gary and May were chatting to Rosie's parents. The change of scenery was good for them too. The carers fiddled with the mechanics of Rosie's chair, positioning it at the same level as everyone else to make it easier for her to join in. Even Edward appeared at ease as he and his friend Jamie said something to Grandma Irene that made her laugh. A little later Hannah noticed her dad head towards her mum, cornering her at one end of the food display.

Hannah moved nearer, picked up a plate, and dithered over the vast array of dishes. She wanted to listen to their conversation, hoping it wouldn't end in a fight.

"Well done," he said as he dolloped a spoonful of chicken onto his plate. "Rosie's happy and you look as if you're enjoying yourself."

"Thanks. It does seem to have worked well," her mum answered.

"I know this isn't the best time to bring this up, but I'd like to know if it's true, Hannah's thinking of quitting school."

Hannah wanted to shout out that Grandad Denis had no business telling anyone what she was thinking. She'd only been sounding out the possibility. Today's success with Rosie had helped her make the decision. She wanted to start working full time at the stables.

"Are you sure? Last week we discussed university options. I'll talk to her. Must be a misunderstanding. She might have mentioned a gap year or something similar."

"Gap years are a waste of time. I'm not funding either of them to swan about doing nothing."

Her mother didn't react. He shrugged and marched off in Belinda's direction.

Hannah knew both her parents were keen for her to go to university to get a degree but she had other plans. She wasn't going to let that discussion wreck her birthday.

She took her full plate and sat down on a hay bale as near to her friend as she dared and began eating.

"You okay?" Rosie asked with her usual sensitivity to mood.

"Fine," Hannah answered. "Parent stuff." She knew about the big fight so understood.

Rosie's parents had been brilliant, but Hannah could tell they were getting a bit twitchy and were anxious to get Rosie back to the hospital. The wait to get her on the transplant list had been tough. Now they had to ensure that she kept as fit as possible in case a donor was found.

As soon as Rosie finished her food Hannah took her plate from her.

"Thanks for making the day so special for me," Rosie said, her breathlessness triggered a cough. Rosie's parents stepped in, said a quick farewell to Hannah. She wanted to give her friend a hug but knew it was not safe so she walked alongside her chair as Rosie took a long, lingering look at the horse that had helped fulfil one of her lifetime wishes.

As Rosie was wheeled up the ramp into the specially adapted car, Hannah felt her mother's arm go round her shoulder. Hannah was sure she'd be wondering how Rosie's parents managed to stay brave all the time, especially now that her condition was so rapidly deteriorating.

"Maybe we can arrange for you to come back another day," her mum suggested.

Rosie smiled. "I'd like that. Thank you for letting me share Hannah's special day."

Hannah doubted Rosie would be fit enough to take up the offer if she didn't get a transplant soon.

Everyone stepped back as the carers and Rosie's parents settled her in the car. The others had joined them to wave goodbye.

"Thanks, Mum." Hannah said as they disappeared out of view.

"I'm so glad it worked well. Come on, there are lots of puddings left."

While they walked back to the food, there was no escaping the conversation going on behind.

"God, I don't know how I'd cope if I had a child with that illness," Belinda said.

Hannah wondered who Belinda was talking to. Her mum checked her reaction. Hannah decided to pretend she hadn't heard, though Belinda's voice carried so well she'd have to be deaf not to.

Gran Hilda's response was almost as bad as Belinda's comment.

"It's the same illness Hannah suffers from," she announced, as if it was something to be proud of.

Hannah said, "I'm going to check if Sue needs a hand before I eat any more." She hoped that this would fool her mum.

"I'm sure Sue would appreciate the offer," her mother answered. Hannah knew she wanted her out of earshot.

"What?" Belinda gasped, "I thought she was anorexic?"

"No, the illness makes her skinny." Gran Hilda answered.

Hannah kept up the pretence of being oblivious to the conversation and strode on towards the stable.

"For God's sake, will you two shut up. Hannah hates people talking about her illness. I am not going to let you spoil her day."

"How dare you tell me what I can or cannot say," Gran Hilda snapped back.

Hannah glanced round and caught the angry stares bouncing between her mother and Gran. Adam gripped Belinda's elbow, and was edging her away.

Grandma Irene joined in as peace maker. "Hilda, it's been a long day. I think we should go home."

Hannah didn't listen to any more. Sue let her help put the saddles back on their rack, and feed the horses. Then with no further excuse to stay away from the food table, she rejoined the party. Edward and his friend were tucking into a trifle and offered her a plateful. Edward's friend had been at the wine. Edward hadn't. Adam and Belinda came to say farewell. Hannah noticed he came back alone to speak to her mother. Hannah concentrated on watching his lips. No one knew she'd learned to lip read.

"She didn't mean to upset you," he pleaded.

"I know, but she's always saying the wrong thing. Sometimes it drives me insane. You'll have to get her to understand Hannah hates people knowing about her condition and treating her like an invalid."

"I'll try."

"Make her understand unless she can keep her mouth shut to Hannah or anyone else, she can consider our friendship over."

Adam backed away, "I will. Thanks for a great treat." He winked at her. "I'll make sure Belinda wears more sensible shoes if we get asked out again."

Her mum smiled.

Hannah was impressed at his ability to use humour to ease tension. Belinda's five inch heels had made walking on

116

the soft grass by the paddock rather hard. In fact her whole outfit was more suited to a day at Ascot than mucking about at the stables.

Their slightly cryptic conversation made Hannah wonder about their past connections. Aunt May might be able to help solve the mystery.

Chapter 17

"You must stop Hannah canoodling with your handyman."

Clare looked up from the accounts spread out in front of her on May's kitchen table. The interruption annoyed her for a start, but mainly because her Mother hadn't bothered with any sort of greeting before launching into her latest vendetta. Only her mother would come up with a word like canoodling.

"What are you talking about?"

"Are you blind? Didn't you catch the way she flirted with him all day yesterday?

"Flirted? Hannah? Who with?" Clare pushed her papers to one side.

"The scruffy lad who works here."

"Gary?"

"Yes, him. Can't you see he's taking advantage of her?" She rambled on. "Good thing we're all going to Cornwall for Christmas."

"Cornwall?"

"Yes, we fixed the details at Hannah's party. Hilda and Denis have booked a huge house on the coast for a fortnight. We'll all go together, get her away from here and keep them apart. He's far too old for Hannah."

"He's twenty-four, and not taking advantage of anyone." Clare could deal with defending Gary, but she couldn't cope with some mad scheme regarding Christmas. She had no intention of going anywhere with Mike or his parents regardless of who else was invited. Even if the guests included her mother.

"She's just like you were at that age. If you don't put an end to it like we did with you and Adam, you'll have regrets."

Clare felt every muscle in her body tense. "What do you mean?"

"Oh... nothing... that's not important now. I'm just warning you she'll get hurt."

"Not important to you, but it is to me." Clare couldn't believe that her mother had admitted she'd interfered.

"Face the truth, he ditched you."

Clare wanted to drag every detail out of her mother. The doorbell rang, halting the questioning she intended. A parcel delivery, more silver for Mike, by the time she had signed for the goods, her mother had slipped out, with a vague wave to indicate she was going to talk to May, but went instead to her car and drove off without bothering to say goodbye.

When May came in from the greenhouse, Clare didn't mention her mother's comments about Hannah and Gary. Instead she asked, "Did my mother do something to drive Adam away, all those years ago.

May frowned and after a moment answered, "Most likely."

"Come on, spit it out."

"After you got married to Mike she said something that made me suspicious. I asked for an explanation but she clammed up. She knew if she told me I'd probably tell you."

"Never mind, I don't suppose it matters now." Clare said, more to let May off the hook than anything. May didn't deserve the blame for something her mother might have done nearly twenty years ago. She put the kettle on while

May washed her hands.

"When did you see her?" May asked as she wiped them dry.

"Oh, she popped in for a moment this afternoon."

"How odd. I'll bet it wasn't to admit to something she did years ago."

"No, just sticking her nose into something she shouldn't."

"Let me guess, Gary and Hannah?"

"Becoming psychic in your old age?"

"No, but cut the age jokes." May chuckled. "She phoned earlier today. I told her to quit being a busy-body."

"Nice one."

"I doubt she'll be calling me again for a while. Not that I mind."

"Should I be worried about Gary and Hannah?"

"Of course not, you know Gary. He'd never take advantage of anyone, especially Hannah."

"I agree."

"Good. I'd hate to see you interfering like your mother did."

Clare had often puzzled over the relationship between her mother and her aunt. They had such different temperaments. May was kind, thoughtful, huggable, and her mother, Irene, was cool, aloof and constantly disapproving.

Her father, who she'd adored, had spent too much time at his office. He ought to have been a millionaire. Instead, he had a fatal heart attack when she was only ten. Within six months her mother had remarried, while Clare still grieved.

Clare never worked out if her mother loved her, or just loved the idea of being a parent. She showered her with toys, the more showy the better. A walk in the park to play on the swings was an opportunity to parade her perfect child, dressed in her best, never about having fun.

May was her saviour. She would talk about her father the way her mother never did, and would let her mess about in the garden without fretting about spoiling her clothes.

May's comment about not interfering with Hannah's life was a well aimed warning. She still wanted to find out the truth about how her mother came between her and Adam, but she wouldn't pressure May with questions. No need to burden her with guilt.

Clare tidied up the papers, finished her coffee and left May to get on with her own tasks.

Clare had several urgent issues to think about. Top of the list was Christmas. In her panic to move out, she'd never considered how the split would destroy family routines. What the children wanted was more important than meeting her desires. If they chose to go to Cornwall, she'd deal with the consequences, but nothing would entice her to spend Christmas with her soon to be ex-in-laws, let alone with her mother and her latest partner. She didn't care what excuse she had to invent to get out of it.

The other thing she had to check was Mike's comment that Hannah wanted to quit school. With luck Mike had misunderstood about her wanting a gap year, she didn't think Hannah would make such a drastic decision without consulting her first.

She tried to push the thoughts away so she could enjoy a couple of days of solitude in the house before the children moved in. The adjustment to being alone was odder than expected. Being part of a family made solitude a rare commodity. The welcoming atmosphere of the house made the transition easier, enveloping her in a way no other property ever had.

The phone rang a few minutes after she reached home.

"Hello," Mike said, "Congratulations on organizing such a good birthday celebration. Hannah can't stop talking about it and says Rosie being able to join in made it extra special."

She ought to be pleased he was making an attempt at civil communication, but she was sure he had a more serious motive for calling.

121

"Thanks, but I can't take the credit, the idea was Hannah's and she did most of the planning."

"If you say so." he said. "Now, about Christmas..."

Clare gulped with surprise. Christmas had been a taboo topic all their married life, with every detail left to her, from the decorations to the food and also buying and wrapping all the presents, including her own.

"Christmas?" she asked, wondering why he should so suddenly be thinking so far ahead.

"I thought about taking the kids skiing. Do you think they'd like the idea?" The uncertainty in his voice was new to her. She could only guess that the threat of having to spend time with his parents had prompted this sudden interest in winter sports.

"Skiing, versus Cornwall with the grandparents, no contest," she answered. "Have you asked them?"

"No. I wanted to check with you first. I'd like you to come too."

"Sorry, Mike, I won't be joining you, but I'm happy for the children to go if that's what they want."

"They might not, without you."

"Had you anywhere in mind?" she asked, her mind running through a long list of things that needed consideration. How Hannah would cope with her exercises and medication was one thing, trusting Mike with the responsibility, quite another.

"Possibly France."

"Well before you commit to anywhere make sure there are good medical facilities nearby, in case Hannah has a problem."

"Shit, Clare, can't you ever accept that she is fine?"

"No, and I never will. The reason she's so well today is because I refused to stick my head in the sand the way you do." Clare stopped and took a deep breath. She didn't want to aggravate the situation but at the same time she'd put up with his ostrich like stance on Hannah's condition long enough. "Without all those exercises, she'd be in the same position as Rosie, needing an oxygen mask, waiting for a lung transplant. That's what I have been trying to prevent, so don't think for one minute I'm sorry if my efforts upset you."

"If you're going to make a big production of the whole issue, I'll scrap the idea."

"You're kidding. Just because I expect you to ensure good healthcare is available is no excuse to back out, and certainly not one you can use to blame me."

"Ok, I'll ask them, and I'll make sure to meet your overprotective needs."

Clare decided to let him end the call to avoid giving him the chance of accusing her of being hostile.

"Anything else?" she asked.

"No, that's all."

"Let me know what the children decide and don't forget to tell your parents your plans. I think they're expecting you all in Cornwall for Christmas."

"Don't worry, I will." The relief in his voice confirmed this was why he had suggested the skiing trip.

He ended the call without a farewell. It didn't surprise her. Communication with him had become so unpredictable, varying from friendly to abrupt, and now civil.

The children would find the skiing option too tempting to turn down, but she must find a way of removing any guilt they might have about leaving her alone for the festive period. Staying behind was not a bad thing as it would allow her to spend more time with May and dispel concerns about her frailty. Meanwhile she and Gary must speed up the search for extra help at the nursery.

Clare settled down at the kitchen table and started making endless lists of things to do, wishing the children had never posted her entry for the competition.

But as they had, she had a duty to create a garden to make them proud and be a tribute to May, who inspired her in the first place.

To help keep the magic alive, and not let the project become a chore, she propped the picture that inspired the garden on the dresser in front of her to refresh her enthusiasm.

The picture, painted by her godmother, had hung in her bedroom throughout her childhood. An old gnarled willow tree leant across the page, casting shadows on a collection of red toadstools with white spots, on which sat a leprechaun. Several animals peered out from behind mossy rocks and branches, tempted to come out and play.

Clare still hadn't found a suitable willow tree for the show garden. May had a friend who was grubbing out old apple trees to make room for new varieties. He'd offered to let her go over and see if one of them would suit. An old apple tree might be a good substitute.

Large red garden umbrellas with floppy scalloped edges and appliquéd white spots would represent the big toadstools, mosaic topped tables with matching stools, the smaller ones. Willow sculptures of birds, deer and rabbits peeking through the flowering borders would complete the scene.

The least fun part was working out the quantities of rock, shale and other materials for the hard landscaping, as was the task of finding a supply of mossy logs to line the paths. Later she could pay more attention to the finer details of the planting.

Gary and Hannah had been sourcing the main plants and had started sowing seeds at the nursery. Several batches were already underway. The bigger plants they'd bought would need pruning to the right shape and size to fit the plan. They also had to consider reserves, in case the weather conspired against them. Maybe she was being over cautious, but for sanity's sake knowing a selection of earlier and later blooming substitutes would be available was vital.

She pushed the papers away. A vision of the next few

weeks flashed by, the children adjusting to a disrupted lifestyle, a few days in one house and the next few in the other. It was hard for her, what it was like for them had never been discussed. Would it help? She doubted it. The biggest challenge was going to be establishing a routine for Hannah's physiotherapy. She could either drop in early on her way to school or on the way home. Hannah ought to be able to manage on her own, but it was too easy to skip sessions, to test the system and discover how fit she really was. It frightened Clare, but at some point she had to let Hannah take control of her health. She could only hope Hannah wouldn't take unnecessary risks. Especially if the skiing trip were to become a reality.

Hannah called, asking if she minded if they went skiing.

"Of course I don't. Check the dates don't clash with school events or anything like that." Mike was unlikely to consider commitments the children had made were worth bothering about.

"Don't worry, we discussed dates with him. He's going to try to get flights the week before Christmas, so we'll be back by the New Year."

"Good, we can celebrate together when you get back."

Their decision to go prompted a new list. She would have to get extra medication for Hannah to take with her in case she fell ill. She didn't care if her actions made her look like a worrywart. They could joke about her as much as they liked.

On top of everything else she must add Christmas presents to her list. She'd have to find things that were easy to pack so they'd have something to open on the day.

Chapter 18

Hannah had made a good effort to keep up with her physio. She did all the exercises she could without help and appeared to have added extra runs and longer cycle rides to her routine, which she thought would replace tapping sessions. Clare tried to persuade her otherwise, without success.

As the day of departure approached, Clare was worried because, after an hour of intensive tapping, she knew she hadn't managed to shift the mucus that had lodged in Hannah's lungs. Hannah refused to acknowledge there was a problem and bounced off the table saying she felt great.

Clare knew it was a monumental lie. Hannah needed an x-ray.

Maternal alarms screamed, do something, but she couldn't force Hannah to listen to her advice.

At the airport Edward put his arm around her shoulders and said, "Stop fretting, Mum. I'll keep an eye on her."

Normally, Edward's promise would have been reassuring, but Hannah's determination to go on this skiing holiday had perhaps distorted her judgment of her capabilities.

As they loaded their bags onto the counter at the airport

Clare regretted turning down the invitation to join the ski party. She should never have let a silly assumption that Mike's invitation was a plot to get her to reconsider her request for a divorce put her off.

She wanted to alert Mike to her concerns about Hannah's health. But he managed to avoid her. She decided it would be a waste of time anyway, he'd never understood the signs, or the dangers they presented. Her only hope was Edward. She'd have to trust him to make sure Hannah didn't overdo things and took all her medications on a regular basis. She hated lumbering him with the responsibility.

The baggage was cleared and she watched them all head into the departure area. She sat on a hard bench watching for their flight to disappear off the screen, wondering how she'd fill the time while they were away.

When she got back from the airport Gary was waiting for her.

"Can we talk?"

"Yes. Come on in, I need some company."

"Problems?" he asked.

"Maybe, I think Hannah is pretending to be fitter than she really is, and there's nothing I can do." It was strange to be discussing Hannah with Gary.

"She said you'd packed a ton of emergency medication."

"I'm struggling to accept she's able to manage her own health. But I guess she has to learn. What did you want?"

"You know May's plan to rescue someone from a life on the streets. I might have a potential candidate."

Clare nodded. "Do we really want the responsibility of training someone from scratch?"

"Probably not, it terrifies me too." He picked at a callous on his thumb. "But I know the difference May's help made to my life. I'd like someone else to have the same chance and some help might enable May to ease off."

"Good point."

"My friend Joe thinks there's a new kid on the streets

who fits the bill. I'm meeting Joe this evening to check."

"Do you want me to come along?"

He nodded. "I hoped you'd offer. I'll pick you up at half past ten. No point in going earlier. Homeless people don't settle until the pubs close and the streets go quiet.

"I'll be ready. Should I bring anything?"

"Arm yourself with cigarettes and you'll be popular."

"Food?"

"A few bars of chocolate, but only what fits in your pocket. You don't want to look like a charity worker. Let me do all the talking." As an afterthought he added, "And don't wear anything fancy."

Clare smiled. He looked embarrassed. "Sorry, that sounds stupid, but trainers and jeans won't stand out."

Dressed as requested, Clare waited for him to collect her in his battered Volvo.

"Do you think we'll succeed in finding the right person this way?"

"No idea, but it has to be worth a go. The kids on the streets are desperate."

Gary parked and led the way through an alley into High Street. She had expected the area to be deserted, but several clusters of people stood in doorways, a mix of men wearing t-shirts, the girls in skimpy tops and short skirts. Some were rowdy, others enjoying a quiet smoke. Gary skirted round them and headed to a seating area occupied by a scruffy pair of men, the sort she'd normally have avoided. Empty beer cans littered the ground around them.

She wanted to run. Thinking they could pluck someone up off the streets was madness. Too late, Gary was shaking hands with one of the men. Gary gestured to her to come forward for an introduction.

"This is Joe," he said, "a mate from way back."

"Hi, I'm Clare," She stuck out her hand. If Gary knew him, he must be okay. He had his back to the light, his hood blocked his features. He pushed the hood back, revealing his bent nose, a jagged scar on his chin and a sizeable tattoo peeking above the edge of his t-shirt.

He smiled and said, "Hi."

The man next to him stuck out a nicotine-stained hand. Clare shook it while he mumbled his name, "Simon." His glazed eyes barely focussed on her, more concerned with the serious business of draining the last dregs from the can clasped in his other hand.

Gary handed Joe a packet of cigarettes.

"What's the connection?" Joe asked, looking towards her. His scrutiny made her uncomfortable.

"We're at college together."

Joe chuckled. "You at college! God, I remember how you could barely write your name to fill in those bloody forms. There's hope for us all yet."

"Come off it, Joe. You won't change how you live. I've offered you a job often enough."

"You're right. I'm not cut out for a so called normal life. Been there, done that, and didn't like it. Anyway who else is going to keep an eye out for the likes of him?" he said, pointing towards the other man, who had slumped sideways in a drunken stupor.

A black and white collie stirred at Joe's feet. He stooped and fondled the dog's ears.

"Is he friendly?" she asked.

"Yeah, took a while. She had a tough start before I rescued her."

"What's she called?"

"Shep, after the dog on TV." Joe stroked the dog ears tenderly.

Clare knelt down and put her hand out for the dog to sniff, glad of a distraction while Gary talked to Joe. The dog rolled over on her back to expose her tummy for a tickle.

"Tell us more about the kid."

"Far too young, to be out here. Help now would be the best thing, if you're serious."

"Do you think he'd be suitable?"

Joe went quiet for a while. "Depends, on what you expect." He rubbed his chin.

"Guess we'd better get on," Clare answered. "Where do we look?"

"Not sure, but they shouldn't be too hard to find. First let me get someone to keep an eye on Simon." Simon, slumped in the seat, was snoring loudly. "I'll be back in a minute." He stood up, patted the dog and said, "Stay."

Shep wagged her tail, and stayed still, her eyes followed him as he set off down the street.

Clare and Gary stayed with the sleeping drunk and the mongrel. "You never told me you offered Joe a job."

"Yes, Joe was good to me when I found myself out here. He made sure I had a dry place to sleep, and taught me the rules of survival."

"What's his story?" Clare asked.

"Ex-marine, post traumatic stress stuffed things up with his family. His wife threw him out. He had a flat for a while, but when his children stopped coming to visit, he ended up back here. He sells the Big Issue and cares for others, some are old comrades. He reckons he couldn't help them as much if he had a decent home to go to."

"That's sad."

"Yes. This lot are his family now."

Joe returned with another dishevelled character who greeted Shep like a long lost friend. "I'll keep an eye on them both," he said, showing gaps between his teeth. Joe handed him the packet of cigarettes Gary had given him earlier.

"I won't be too long," Joe answered, nodding to Gary and Clare to follow him.

Clare had no contact with homeless people before, and hadn't realized how independent minded they were. Pity was not what they wanted. To show any might cause offence. They walked past a few people begging outside pubs. Joe acknowledged them all, but didn't stop to introduce them to

Gary and Clare.

"Druggies," he muttered when they passed a trio huddled together on a filthy sleeping-bag. "Can't do much to help them." They went round one block, then another. At one point, he checked with Gary, "Any more cigarettes?" Gary handed over a packet. Joe made them stop. He crossed the street and joined a group of youngsters. He offered cigarettes all round. The light of the match gave Clare the impression the average age of the group was about fifteen, Hannah's age, what a scary thought.

Joe didn't talk much. He nodded occasionally, said a few words, and then listened again.

Clare and Gary huddled in a doorway to escape the icy wind funnelling down the street. At last he moved, he handed over a few more cigarettes and came back.

The church clock struck one. They'd been on the streets for a little over two hours and Clare was frozen.

"They're sleeping under the bridge."

"They?" she queried.

"Yes, a brother and sister," Joe answered, "they haven't been on the streets long. He's protective of his sister and wary of trusting anyone, which is a good thing. I think he'll leap at an offer of a safe place to stay. That is what you had in mind, isn't it?"

The enormity of the mission started to sink in. Rescuing one person was all she had considered. Would two be a step too far? Joe was right to ask the question.

"Will they trust us?" Gary asked.

Joe shrugged. "I think so, if you can't handle it, say so now, I don't want to dangle a carrot only to whip it away. They've been through enough already, but going home is not an option. Not ever."

Clare pushed her doubts aside. "Two will be fine."

She wanted to ask how old they were. Age could complicate matters, but she didn't care. If these youngsters needed help, nothing should stop her giving it. The legal and practical issues could wait. Joe stared at her in the dim street light. "Are you sure? No going back?"

"If you can get them to accept us, we'll do our best."

"Ok, let's go."

Music blared out of a pizza place. Joe stopped outside. "Reckon one of those would go down well." Gary joined the queue. Joe stood by Clare, and asked, "How do you fit into this?"

"My aunt helped Gary. I got roped in by Gary, mainly because anyone working at the nursery will be working with me too."

"Sounds like a good place."

"Sure is."

Gary came out armed with two pizza boxes and cans of Coke. Joe nodded approval. When they got close to the bridge, he made them stop. "Let me talk to them first. See how they're doing." He took one pizza and two cans and disappeared into the shadows.

Gary broke the intense silence that engulfed them. "If they're as young as I think they are, can we handle the complications?"

"May is sure to find a solution." Her confidence scared her, but maybe the truth was scarier.

"What if they're awful?"

"Joe wouldn't lumber you, would he?"

"No, you're right. He's a good bloke."

"So I see. Pity you can't get him on board."

Gary balanced the pizza box on the wall beside them. "We might as well eat."

Clare took a hand out of her pocket and took a slice, hoping hot food might warm her from inside. The food helped, but one slice was enough. She couldn't wait to get her frozen fingers back in her pockets. She tried to imagine sleeping out in the open at any time of the year, let alone on a freezing damp night like this.

"Have you heard from Edward and Hannah?"

132

"Yes, Edward phoned earlier. The snow's perfect for skiing. They've sorted out their equipment and passes and can't wait to get on the slopes."

"I bet you miss them."

Miss them. What an understatement! Having both lower limbs severed and losing her crutches might be close. What a sad case she had become, being grateful that she had so many things to keep her occupied. With May to fret over, show garden plans to tweak, the nursery development to watch over and now coping with these youngsters there wouldn't be time to spare.

Joe saved her from having to answer Gary. "Come over here," he called. Gary led the way. Clare prayed they were doing the right thing.

Joe introduced them to Pete and Abby. Pete eyed them with suspicion. Abby cowered behind him.

Clare longed to reach out and put her arms around the pair. She guessed that they were closer to fourteen than sixteen. Age didn't matter. Protecting them and getting them off the streets to somewhere warm and safe did.

Pete spoke first. "He says you want to help us."

Clare and Gary nodded.

"What's in it for you?"

Clare liked his up front approach, and wanted to match it. "We need help. Greenhouse work, nothing too heavy, some outside work too, you'd be like an apprentice. How old are you?"

"Sixteen," he snapped back.

Clare didn't believe him, but she liked his determination. She was prepared to overlook the lie about his age but she wasn't so sure about Abby. "She isn't."

Pete's shoulders slumped, hope vanished from his eyes. "No," he answered his voice dropped to a whisper, "but she can work too."

Clare hated the sadness in his eyes. Abby shivered. Age became insignificant. They needed shelter. All they had to do

133

was accept the offer.

"Honestly, I wasn't expecting you to be so young. It complicates things, but we can find a solution."

Pete's eyes widened in disbelief, and he looked to Joe for reassurance. Joe gave him the thumbs up signal.

"We'll provide somewhere warm and safe to sleep, food and hot water. In the morning we can discuss the work."

"You want us to come now?" Pete asked, looking less sure about the whole idea.

Joe piped in. "I can vouch for them. I know Gary. He was like you once. He knows how hard living out here is. Someone gave him a lucky break and now he wants to help you. If there's a problem, you come back and find me, I'll sort them out. I'd come back to their place too, except I have to keep an eye on Simon."

Clare put her hand on Joe's shoulder. "Thanks Joe, I promise I'll look after them." She reached out her hand to Abby, "Come on, you look frozen."

Abby checked with her brother. He gave her a nod. "I'll get our stuff." He shot back into the dark den they'd called home, and pulled out a black bin bag.

When Abby moved into the light, Clare saw how much younger than her brother she was. A few decent meals wouldn't go amiss. Abby kept her distance as they slowly made their way across town, passing the Christmas displays in the shop windows, back to where Joe had left Shep.

Joe's friend Simon was still out cold, as was his minder Jim. Neither of them moved.

The only greeting came from Shep.

His wagging tail transformed Abby, who smiled for the first time since they'd met. She sank to her knees and gave the dog a big hug. Clare had a sudden flash of the future, a vision of Abby hugging Limbu under a Christmas tree with May smiling happily. She was going mad. This crazy scheme was getting completely out of hand. What would Edward and Hannah think when they got back to find these two

134

youngsters living with May?

Gary and Joe were talking. Clare heard him invite Joe over yet again. Joe used the excuse he didn't want to let his other friends down, but promised he'd come and check the place over to make sure the kids settled.

With nothing else to organize Clare reached down and tapped Abby gently on the shoulder. "Shall we go?"

Abby's reaction took her by surprise. The youngster darted off, disappearing down a dark passage way.

Pete dropped the bag containing their possessions and shot off into the darkness after her.

Clare looked at Joe, unsure what she had done to get such a reaction. "What happened?"

"You touched her." Joe answered. "I knew things had been bad at home, but I had no idea that she was that jumpy."

"Should we go after them?" Gary asked.

Joe shook his head. "No, give them a moment. Pete knows what he's doing. He'll talk her round."

"I hardly touched her," Clare said, afraid that the others would think she had done something more. "Will they come back?"

"Yes, if only to pick up his things." Joe pointed to the pathetic black bag lying on the ground beside them. "Tell you what. When they come back I'll come with you as long as Shep's welcome."

"What about this pair?" Gary asked.

"Jim can keep an eye on him." He prodded Jim, got a grunt for his trouble. He prodded again, this time Jim sat up and opened his eyes. "I'm heading off with these folk. Look after Simon." Jim nodded, and slumped back down and closed his eyes.

Joe picked up Shep's lead, and Pete's bag, and moved away from the sleeping pair to another bay of seats.

"Let's wait, they may come back."

The church clock struck three. How much longer should

135

they wait? Gary cupped her elbow. "I'll run you home if you want. We could always leave things for now. Come back tomorrow and see if they have changed their minds."

"No. Let's wait," Clare muttered. "Give them an hour." Her feet were frozen, her fingers numb, but she couldn't go home to a warm bed, knowing Abby and Pete were out here in the freezing cold. She focussed on a flickering festive light trying to imagine being fifteen and facing a life on the streets. It put facing her first Christmas without her children into perspective. It would be different, but she had May and Gary for company, and she knew Hannah and Edward were happy.

Gary and Joe swapped information about friends they'd encountered on the streets. Clare closed her eyes, trying to imagine what it would be like to try to sleep in a place like this. Noise never ceased, if it wasn't a raucous crowd passing by, there was the wail of a police siren, or the roar of a revved up car speeding along the main road, a distant burglar alarm, a car alarm, banging doors or the beeping of the pedestrian crossing, enough to drive her insane.

She had no idea how long it was before Pete reappeared with his arm firmly round Abby's shoulder. Her tear streaked face and puffy eyes made Clare long to hug her but she now knew to keep her distance while trust grew.

"Abby's sorry," he said.

"It's okay," Clare answered, "I didn't mean to give her a fright. Listen, Joe will come too, if that will make it less scary coming to somewhere strange for the night."

Abby didn't look particularly reassured. Then Clare remembered her reaction to the dog. "He'll bring Shep."

At the mention of the dog Abby's shoulders relaxed. Joe handed her Shep's lead, picked up Pete's bag, and said, "Come on, it's bloody freezing out here. Where's your car?"

Gary led the way, Clare followed, her head spinning with the practicalities of what they had achieved. May had the spare room that Gary used when he lived with her before moving to the little cottage on the other side of the road. It had two bunk beds which would be fine for Pete and Abby. But housing Joe was another matter.

Gary must have read her mind, because he chipped in with the suggestion that Joe could sleep at his place. Clare wasn't sure Abby would accept the arrangement. Much depended on whether Limbu welcomed Shep into his territory.

They hadn't told May their plans because they hadn't wanted to raise her hopes. Now they were going to have to wake her up to introduce her to her new lodgers. When they drove into the yard May's bedroom light came on. She got to the door before they did, and stood in the open doorway, wrapped up in her fleecy dressing gown in the same warm welcoming way she would have greeted Edward and Hannah.

Her unflappable response to three total strangers arriving on her doorstep in the early hours of the morning seemed to win over the two youngsters. In the bright light of her cosy kitchen, Clare was even more shocked. Pete couldn't be more than fifteen, and Abby closer to thirteen.

May bustled about making everyone hot drinks, showed the children their room and where the bathroom was. Abby was reluctant to be separated from Shep. May had an answer for that too. "I'd ask Joe to let Shep stay the night, Limbu won't mind as he and Shep have already made friends, but I'm not sure my cat Foggy would be very pleased.

Abby studied Foggy who was pacing up and down the dresser, eyeing Shep with a certain amount of hostility.

She released her grip on Shep's lead. Joe hastily retrieved it. He might be ready to abandon the streets, but not to have his dog, his only treasured possession, stolen from him.

Chapter 19

Clare overslept and by the time she got back to May's with a selection of clothes Hannah and Edward no longer needed, a transformation had taken place.

Joe, minus his scruffy stubble, sat at the head of the kitchen table, Pete and Abby were on either side tucking into plates loaded with bacon, eggs, sausages, fried bread and tomatoes. May loved cooking and having an appreciative houseful to feed made her happy. She was all set to start cooking more, but Clare shook her head. She'd eaten a bowl of cereal at home.

"No thanks, a cup of tea will do me." May didn't press her, and passed her an empty cup. She went to join the others round the table.

Abby seemed to be having difficulty with her food. Clare soon spotted the reason. She was busy trying to keep Foggy on her lap by stroking him so she didn't have a spare hand for her knife.

"Where's Gary?"

"At the shops. We needed more milk and something for lunch and some food for Shep," May answered. Shep, curled up near the Aga, reacted to his name, his ears perked up, but he didn't move.

Clare wanted to suggest that instead of cooking, they all go out, but realized it would not work. This pair needed to get comfortable first.

"Joe's agreed to stay," May explained. "The promise of roast beef and Yorkshire pudding sealed the deal."

Joe, in the process of transporting a forkful of sausage to his mouth, managed a wry smile. He obviously didn't object to bribery, especially with food cooked by an expert.

"Have you decided on pudding?" Clare asked, looking directly at Abby.

Abby smiled and whispered, "Ice cream."

Clare, thrilled to hear Abby speak for the first time, answered, "Good, my favourite too."

Pete kept his eyes down, concentrating on his meal as if it might be the last meal ever. Now the plate was empty, he had a slightly concerned expression on his face.

Clare locked eyes with him. "Problem?"

He pursed his lips. "What work do you want done?"

Work? Did he think she'd forgotten? The purpose of the exercise was to get help. But how could she employ this pair? The rules made it impossible. She pictured the banner headlines "Local nursery exploits children," or "Child slaves in the greenhouse."

May gave her an odd look. Joe stared at her, looking as anxious as Pete for her reply. Only Abby didn't seem bothered, she was far too engrossed with Foggy.

Clare couldn't say she'd changed her mind, there was no job. She had to think of something to allow Pete to accept their hospitality. If she didn't, he'd take off and drag his sister with him.

"I have to discuss details with May and Gary when he gets back. Why don't you go for a wander round the nursery while we decide what you can do?"

Talk about a feeble attempt at buying time, but Pete smiled, reached out for another slice of toast and once more set about the important business of breakfast.

Joe drained his cup. May reached out to pick up his plate. He snatched it away from her. "No, no, you relax, you've done the cooking, the least we can do," he said looking pointedly at the children, "is clear up."

May looked ready to protest. But the speed with which the two children gathered up their plates in response to his comment deterred her. Instead she refilled her cup and did as instructed.

Joe seemed in his element as he mustered his troops. He filled the sink, gave Pete and Abby a tea towel each and started washing up, handing items alternately to the two children. All May had to do was point out which cupboards the clean dishes lived in.

Gary came back laden down with bags of shopping. He took a packet of cigarettes out of his pocket and handed them to Joe. "Figured you'd appreciate these. I know you gave away the rest last night."

"Thanks," he muttered stuffing them into his pocket, "I think Shep's ready for a walk."

"Can we come?" Pete begged.

Joe seemed happy with the suggestion so Clare felt safe to respond with, "Good idea."

Getting the children out of the house served two purposes, firstly the children could talk to Joe without anyone listening in, and secondly it gave May, Gary and herself a moment to work out a plan.

"Go up to the shed at top of the orchard, and bring back some of the big apples so May can make an apple crumble. There's a basket on the hook in the porch. When you come back we'll show you round the nursery." Clare added.

The minute they had left, Clare apologised to May. "We didn't have a choice. Once we knew they were sleeping rough we had to step in."

"Of course you did. I'd have done exactly the same thing myself."

140

"They're so young. What is the legal position? Is there anyone who should be informed? I don't want anyone thinking we've abducted them." Clare was out of her depth.

"Did they say what they had run away from?" May asked.

"I didn't ask," Clare confessed. "Joe mentioned an abusive step-father, but Abby was so scared I thought if I asked any questions she'd run off again."

"We should just let them stay, no questions, no pressure for the next week," May looked thoughtful. "Let's get them through Christmas. They might let slip scraps of information as they get more comfortable with us. After the holiday we can explain that they must contact their parents, not necessarily to go home, or we'll have to approach someone in authority, so we don't get into trouble. Then arrange for them to go back to school."

"For God's sake, don't mention school, it's far too soon," Gary said, obviously remembering his dread of the place. "I don't think they have any good memories of the last one they went to."

"What about Joe? How long will he stay?"

"Not sure, he won't go until he's happy they're settled. I promised to take him into town tonight. He's worried about Simon, one of the rough sleepers, who's not well, but won't stop drinking."

"Joe has a heart of gold. He doesn't deserve to be on the streets."

"I know, I've offered him a roof over his head often enough, but he's got a thing about helping others, like Pete and Abby."

"Try harder. If they need him here it will give him a reason to stick around." May put away the shopping Gary had brought in earlier. "I'll just get myself organized with the lunch." She got out the ingredients for Yorkshire pudding, measured out the quantities she needed, and set to work beating up the batter mix by hand. Clare knew better than to

141

offer to take over. This was one of May's favourite occupations. No new fangled short cuts, like a quick whiz in the liquidizer for her.

"Are you sure you can cope with two youngsters in the house?"

"Of course I can, especially with you two as my back up. You saw how good they were about washing up. I'm sure they'll do all they can to be helpful, especially with Joe whipping them into shape."

It wasn't long before Joe brought Pete and Abby back clutching an armful of apples each and the basket filled to the brim.

"Shep went after a rabbit." Abby said. Her cheeks had taken on a rosy glow, which suited her.

"Did he catch it?" Gary asked. Abby shook her head and smiled.

May put her batter mix to one side, and pulled the bag of potatoes out of the cupboard. Joe moved in beside her, took the knife out of her hand. "Let me do those, it was one of the useful things they taught me in the army."

Who could argue with that? May didn't even try.

"As soon as Joe's done the potatoes we'll have a look round the nursery and the new buildings," Clare said, with a feeling that things were going to work out better than anticipated the night before.

"Better listen to the weather forecast," Gary said. "I caught a bit on the radio on my way back. Doesn't sound good."

May switched on the TV in the kitchen. The news was nearly over, so they sat and waited for the weather report.

Winds would be picking up over the next few days, increasing to gale force with heavy rain and possibly snow to follow. By Christmas Eve the country could be suffering severe conditions for a prolonged period. Transport problems were expected over the holiday week. They urged everyone to stay tuned to their local weather reports for updates.

It was the worst possible combination of weather imaginable. With the greenhouse expansion work in progress, a gale could cause havoc.

"Sounds as if you might need extra help," Joe said. "I'll stay if you'd like, but I do need to go and make sure Simon has checked into the temporary Christmas shelter."

"Thanks, with that storm coming, we'll need every bit of help we can get."

"Will I get a Christmas dinner too?" he asked, with a cheeky grin.

"May, what do you think?"

"Most certainly, I'd better get shopping before supplies run out."

Chapter 20

Hannah knew the minute her bags went on the scales at the airport she had made a huge mistake.

She'd thought the skiing trip with her dad might be the best way of getting him and Edward together and ease the tension between them. It would also save her from spending Christmas cooped up in a strange house with the grandparents, all of whom had been behaving so oddly since her birthday.

The thing she hadn't considered was her health. The tightness in her chest was getting worse. She should have started taking antibiotics days ago, but knew if she told her mother she'd have stopped her from travelling. As it was, she knew her mum had packed extra medication in case she got an infection. Now her bag was on the conveyor belt giving her no chance of rescuing the pills she needed until they landed.

She gave her mum a quick hug and hurried through the departure gate. The real reason she rushed away was that she felt a coughing fit building up and didn't want to throw her mum into a panic. Security was her next hurdle, she prayed no one would expect her to talk, talking might trigger the cough. Phew, no delays, now she needed the privacy of the cloakroom. She made it into a cubicle as the suppressed cough hit. When the choking cough subsided she waited while her breathing eased. She attempted to do some energetic exercises to shift more mucus. Not much was possible in the confined space. She did her best, a bit dislodged, but not enough. Two weeks managing without her mother helping to clear her lungs were going to be hard.

Edward was waiting for her when she emerged.

"You okay?" he asked. She nodded, not wanting to talk in case the coughing started again.

"Dad's in the café with the owner of the chalet we're staying at." His lack of enthusiasm made her wonder what to expect. Best not to add to his glum mood by announcing she was feeling rough.

"Those are her kids." He pointed to two young boys who were tearing round the lounge seating area throwing sugar sachets like darts at each other. Their mother was too busy flashing her eyelashes in her father's direction for her to notice what havoc they were causing.

Her dad's impatience to stick with their new found travelling companion, Jennifer, meant Hannah never got a chance to slip her medication out of her case at the airport after they landed. She had to wait until they got to the apartment, by which time she was desperate to begin the course of treatment. She barely had time to find and swallow the pills before her father insisted they head out to get lift-passes, boots, ski equipment and to enrol them at the ski school. Hannah would have preferred a long sleep, but went along to keep the peace. To her relief, the friction between her dad and Edward had eased. Their tasks completed, they found a cosy café, round the corner from their apartment block, which served the most delicious hot chocolate and gooey cakes. While they ate they decided on the basic groceries needed for breakfasts. No one wanted to cook, so they agreed to make the most of the little café as their meeting and eating place.

The fresh air, altitude and travelling gave Hannah an excuse to plead exhaustion and go to bed, leaving Edward and her Dad playing chess.

In the morning she learnt her father had abandoned Edward within minutes of her leaving the room. Jennifer had popped round to invite him over for a drink.

Hannah sensed they might be seeing rather a lot of Jennifer over the holiday, together with her out of control, whinging twelve-year-old twins. Pity, because she had taken a dislike to Jennifer from the start. Not just because of her odd coloured spray tan, a shade that would look better on a handbag than a person, but more because she sensed this woman would monopolise their father, and destroy the aim of the trip. They were supposed to be reconnecting with him, not watching him make a fool of himself.

Jennifer as expected wasted no time in butting into their plans.

"You must celebrate on Christmas Eve, it's the custom round here."

Her father, of course, agreed, and suggested they join forces and go to one of the grander restaurants in the resort. Neither Edward nor Hannah or the obnoxious twins had any say in the matter.

Edward seemed happy with the fact that Jennifer diverted their dad's attention away from him. It freed him to spend more time helping with her physio. Hannah needed extra help so couldn't complain. She wished she could ask Edward to be more vigorous with his pummelling, the gunk on her lungs was building up faster than usual and his efforts weren't shifting enough. Fear stopped her. If she demanded more, he might freak out and drag her off to the doctor.

The ski school instructor moved Edward to an advanced group. He was reluctant to leave Hannah alone, but she convinced him her new friend, Meg, who was a year younger and rather timid, went at a pace more suited to her needs.

146

She didn't tell him she was happier at a less competitive level and preferred not having him watching her every move.

Their dad spent almost no time in their company. He and Jennifer seemed to have a lot to talk about. She collected silver too, but Hannah suspected there was more to the friendship than silver.

Parental contact consisted of brief encounters when he came back to change, or to check if they had enough cash for lunch or supper before he'd vanish again. Sometimes they'd be included in an invitation to dinner with Jennifer and the twins. Edward and Hannah often ate at the cafe early to have a good excuse to avoid having to join them.

Hannah sucked another cough sweet, in a desperate attempt to suppress her cough. Edward had offered to do her physio, but she didn't want to hold him back.

"Don't worry. Later will be fine. I'll call mum." She and Edward took turns to phone their mother. Today was his turn, but he had a chance to go on one of the harder runs. The sun was out, there was blue sky overhead. She pushed him out the door determined not to deprive him of this chance. He could always do her physio later. "Go on, enjoy yourself. I'm too stiff to go far today and I'm meeting Meg later." A lie because Meg had other plans for the day.

Edward shot off, a blast of cold air flooded in to remind her of what to expect if she stuck her nose outside.

She made the call home, intending to keep it short by saying she had to go and meet someone. Luckily her mum was in a hurry too.

"We're expecting a gale. Gary, Joe and the kids are trying to cover up whatever we can, and put all the loose pots and things away."

She couldn't wait to meet Pete and Abby and Joe who sounded a fascinating character.

"Is Adam helping?"

"No, he's gone to London."

"Wish I could lend a hand," she said, even though right

now she wasn't fit to do anything except go to bed. "Edward sends his love, he's already gone. The snow is fantastic."

"I'll call tonight."

"Don't, we're going out for dinner." No need to mention that they would be celebrating Christmas eve, continental style, rather than on Christmas day.

"And how are things with Dad?"

"Fine. I'll call tomorrow." Best not to mention he'd been away at a silver sale, leaving them on their own for a night. Her mother would have a fit if she knew, but both of them agreed to keep his vanishing act to themselves. No need to stir things up.

"Bye. Miss you both."

"Miss you too." Hannah ended the call.

While she did some exercises she thought about the two kids Gary and her mum had rescued off the streets. She envied them because they would spend Christmas with her mum and Aunt May, doing all the things that made Christmas perfect, making mince pies, choosing and decorating the tree and icing the cake.

The chalet's fake tree, even with a few wrapped presents her mum had packed under it, didn't add much of a Christmassy feel. She and Edward agreed to open their presents on Christmas morning regardless of Jennifer's suggestions.

The effort of tugging off her outdoor socks triggered a coughing spasm which left her dizzy and hardly able to stand. She dropped the socks and crawled to bed. She had been a fool. Her lies were catching up with her. She searched for more antibiotics, ones powerful enough to make a difference to her breathing. There were none left. She somehow had to survive a few more days, long enough to get home and get help. Until then bed seemed a good option. She drank a glass of water and took a banana out of the fruit bowl. She swallowed her regular medication, forced down the banana and lay down convinced she'd be better by the afternoon.

148

She woke to disorientating darkness. Alone and scared, she sent a text to Gary. "Please call."

By the time he did, she was in a panic. She poured out how rough she was, even confessed she'd used up all the extra medication her mum had packed for her.

"I am dreading tonight. Jennifer is so false, and her kids are spoilt brats. I wish I could get out of it."

"Tell your dad you're not well."

"No, I can't expect Edward to go to dinner without me."

"Well, leave early."

"I guess that's what I'll have to do. Please don't tell Mum what I told you."

"I won't, as long as you promise to call if things get worse."

Somehow sharing her worries with Gary made her less scared.

She managed a shower, dressed for dinner, made her way downstairs and sat quietly saving her energy for the evening.

Edward bounded in, full of excitement, full of details of his fantastic day, the speed of the run and how he couldn't wait for another go in the morning. Their Dad was still missing.

"What do we do if he doesn't turn up?"

"Oh, he will. He promised Jennifer," Edward said, his tone implying his father wouldn't dare fail to fulfil a promise made to Jennifer.

With ten minutes to go her father hurried in, dumped his bags, dashed off to change then ushered them out as if they were the ones who caused the delay.

The change of air from the freezing temperature outside to the heat of the crowded restaurant nearly set Hannah's cough off again. She tucked herself into a quiet corner and got her breath back.

Edward seemed a bit distracted. Jennifer offered him some wine, Hannah was impressed when he refused and asked for a soft drink instead. Everyone else behaved as if they intended getting as drunk as possible including the twelve year old twins. There was a group from Edward's ski group at the next table. Among them was a dark eyed girl, who kept looking at Edward. No wonder he was distracted. At least now she didn't have to make much effort, he wouldn't notice if she stayed quiet. She faked a smile whenever anyone remembered to glance in her direction. Being ignored suited her fine as talking made her cough. If she felt it was going to happen she'd slip away to the ladies until it passed.

At last the food came. She ate what she could, told her dad she had a headache and wanted to go home. He made a half hearted suggestion she wait until midnight. She said she couldn't. Her dad shrugged but Edward insisted on going with her.

Her struggle to breathe became too hard to hide. She was glad Edward was with her, though she hated that she had wrecked his evening. They walked slowly, and when they reached the apartment Edward insisted on doing a physio session. She knew it would help even though she craved sleep. He sensed the need to put force into his pummelling, and gave her the best work out she'd had since leaving home.

On Christmas morning he woke her up and had another go at the physio. She didn't argue. She needed all the help she could get. They had some breakfast together and she put on a show of being fine, knowing he'd insist on staying and miss out on skiing to stay with her if she didn't. She didn't pretend she wanted to go out, and persuaded him to leave present opening until later when their father might be around.

He hadn't come back. Hannah assumed he'd spent the night with Jennifer. He came back for his ski clothes just as she was about to push Edward out the door. Dad mumbled something about falling asleep on Jennifer's sofa. He insisted they all leave together, saying they had to make the most of the good conditions as the weather was due to change.

Hannah had no desire to even stick her nose out the

door, but found herself donning her ski clothes and following them out. She had a plan. She'd wait until they were near the front of the queue for the ski lift to announce she'd forgotten her pass. Her dad would never have the patience to wait. She'd wave him and Edward off and go back into the warmth, curl up and read her book.

Her father was cross and as predicted not prepared to wait. Edward offered to go back instead. She insisted it was her mistake and refused to accept his offer, pushing them forward towards the ski lift, waiting for it to whisk them off up the mountain.

She leant against a wall to catch her breath. A brisk walk would normally help ease the congestion on her lungs, if only she had the energy to increase her pace. Hiking back up the hill to the apartment took every ounce of strength she possessed. It was over half an hour before she let herself back in.

Tiny snowflakes were beginning to swirl around the building. The blue sky had vanished, replaced by massive purple black clouds. Hannah was relieved to be safe and out of the cold.

The apartment, in an enormous wooden chalet style building, had huge windows facing the mountain. Dancing powdery flakes slowly coated the rail of the balcony. The dark sky made it feel like evening time not the middle of the morning. The outline of the mountain disappeared as cloud descended.

She switched on the fire, made herself a drink of hot chocolate, curled up on the sofa and phoned home.

"Happy Christmas, Mum." She desperately needed to hear a comforting voice.

"Happy Christmas," her mum answered. "We all miss you so much. Are you having a lovely time?"

She couldn't tell the truth, or respond to the comment about being missed, or she'd start to cry, and upset her mum. "Yes, had a special dinner last night, with another family in the same apartment block." She didn't add that the family consisted of a gushy woman called Jennifer, and obnoxious twelve year old twins whose father had run off years ago.

"What are you doing today?" Again the truth wouldn't do. Her mum wouldn't want to hear she was miserable and alone.

"Dad and Edward have gone for a morning ski, but I decided not to go. It's started to snow, and my legs are aching because I did too much yesterday. So I stayed home to read my book, and listen to my new CD."

"How's your breathing?"

"Fine." This call was a bad move. She hated lying. "Tell me what you and May and everyone else are up to."

"May stuffed the turkey. Joe peeled the potatoes and Pete and Abby have decorated the table." It all made her feel homesick and jealous, because they were having the Christmas she wanted.

"What about Adam and Gary?"

"Adam's been away for a week, and Gary's gone off on some mysterious mission. No one knows when he's coming back, though he did say something to Joe about it being more important to be here when we celebrate on your return. I do miss you."

"Me too, but I'll be home next week. Save me some mince pies."

"Of course we will, in fact I'll ask May to make an extra batch for your homecoming. Abby loves helping her."

Hannah felt envious and then guilty. Her mum was right to have rescued the children from sleeping rough. She hoped they appreciated their good luck. May would take good care of them. It made her wish May could be with her right now looking after her.

A coughing fit was about to come on, and she didn't want her mother to worry, so she said, "Give May my love. I'll call you later when Edward gets back. Bye."

"I'll look forward to that. Bye."

Hannah disconnected, a racking cough took hold, leaving her too weak to move. She stretched out on the sofa and must have dropped off, because she woke to find it almost dark outside even though it should still be daytime. She was stiff and hot, had a raging headache and needed to find her medication. She swallowed all the pills she thought might help. She hadn't the strength to do any exercises on her own. She'd have to wait for Edward's help.

She wrote him a text. "Where are you?"

She checked to see how much snow had fallen. The balcony ledge had a six inch layer on it and more swirled around, obliterating everything that was normally in view. She hoped Edward and her dad had made it off the mountain. They should have been back by now as it was so dark outside.

An hour later she got a text from Edward. "Sorry, caught in blizzard, sheltering near the top, no chance of getting down today. Don't worry lots of food and drink. Tell Mum and Dad. Battery getting low."

Great. The one person she could trust was out of reach.

She put off phoning her dad, because she couldn't bear the thought of Jennifer fussing over her.

An hour later when her father still hadn't returned, loneliness set in. She couldn't call her mother. She couldn't call May, because her mother would be there. She couldn't call Rosie, because she had enough problems of her own to deal with. That left Gary.

She keyed in a brief message, which she reread several times before hitting the send key. "Need to speak to you."

Ten minutes later he called her.

"Problems?" he asked. Hannah burst into tears at the sound of a friendly voice.

"Hey, I meant to cheer you up, not make you cry."

"Sorry, I guess I've just had such a horrible day."

"I phoned your mum earlier and she said you were having a great time. What went wrong?"

She poured out the whole story, right down to the fact she'd run out of antibiotics, and then made him swear not to tell her mother.

"Okay, call if things get worse. I'll keep my phone on hand."

"Thanks. Please tell mum Edward's stuck on the mountain. He won't phone tonight as promised."

"I will, as soon as I've spoken to someone at that medical centre your Mum found. I'll try to get them to send someone over."

"No."

"Sorry, I'm going to anyway."

"But talking to you has calmed me down. I'm better already."

"Keep up that argument and I'll have to tell your mother."

"Okay, you win."

"I'll call you back as soon as I can."

Her phone rang again.

"Hope you don't mind," her father said, "Jennifer and I have been invited out for dinner, go ahead and eat." His slurred speech made Hannah shiver, reminding her of the terrible evening when he'd lashed out at her mother.

"Edward's stuck up the mountain," she answered, "and I'm heading for bed."

"Fine, guess I'll see you in the morning." The line went dead.

Hannah closed her eyes and waited for Gary's call. She needed something good to happen to stop this being her worst Christmas ever.

Chapter 21

The threatened storm was getting closer and the forecasts more alarming by the hour. Clare, Joe and May and the children had tidied up and secured everything they could think of to reduce the risk of damage.

May put the turkey in the oven earlier than usual, saying it might be a good plan to have Christmas dinner early. Clare could tell she was trying hard to hide her disappointment at Gary's unexpected vanishing act, though both of them were certain he wouldn't have gone off without good reason. The menu was pared down by mutual consent. Today there would be no sprouts, no parsnips, and no fancy stuffing for the turkey. The changed menu was fine with Clare. She wasn't really in the mood to celebrate without Edward and Hannah being there. But she'd do her best to enjoy the event.

The simple feast was delicious, and Pete and Abby had thrown themselves into the festive spirit, picked holly and ivy to decorate the table and drawn a picture each for herself, May and Joe. Clare had bought them some new clothes, and Joe had whittled a little bird for Abby, and had a penknife for Pete. May gave them books. They both seemed surprised to get gifts. Clare didn't think they'd had many presents in the past.

While they ate, the blustery wind picked up. The lights flickered. Clare wasn't sure they would stay alight for long.

Joe suggested he stay over on May's couch to be on hand if any problems arose and because Pete and Abby were so anxious about the storm. His offer was accepted much to Clare's relief. Joe staying left her free to have a few hours alone at home as long as she went quickly before the wind got worse.

"I'll head off now." She zipped up her waterproof jacket, peered out the window at the darkening sky.

"Remember to switch the Aga to manual if the power goes off." May said.

"Thanks for the reminder. Call if you need me."

Head down she battled her way through May's garden, across the field, hating that the gale threatened her newfound haven. Sodden leaves blasted her. The temperature plummeted as the first band of rain lashed against her uncovered hands, numbing them.

She selected a key from the bunch, but in the process dropped the torch. She groped in the dark until she found it. The casing was broken she would have to depend on her sense of touch. She felt for the lock, got the key in and turned the key and pushed. A blast of wind hit and she stumbled inside and it took every ounce of strength to shut the door and slam the bolt home. No way did she trust the lock to withstand such force. She flicked the light switch. Nothing happened.

"Great," she muttered, "just what I need."

Where would she find candles and matches? The only place she'd used matches was in the study when she'd lit a fire earlier in the week. The candlestick Harry left behind would be on the dining room table. It was much darker than expected. She edged her way towards the passage door, tripping over a bag of empty jars and bottles waiting to go out with the rubbish. She lined herself up. Four paces should get her to the dining room door. She inched forward, hands outstretched. One, two, three. She waved her arms to the left and right, nothing. In front, the heavy oak door, the handle. Three paces more. She knocked her knee on the corner of a chair. She reached out for the candlestick. Success. Now to the study and matches.

It took her ages to work her way out of the dining room, along the passage, into the study, fingering her way round the wall to the fireplace, praying that no one had moved the matches. She put the candlestick down on the shelf, and slid her hands over the smooth stone and found the box. Even the simple task of getting a match out without spilling the rest was a challenge. She managed and struck the rough surface on the side. The flare dazzled after so long in darkness. Once all three candles were lit she knelt down and set the ready laid fire alight. She stayed there mesmerized as the twists of paper burnt setting the kindling alight, waiting for the crackle of burning wood to echo round the room. The orange flames took hold, licking the logs and giving out enough heat to thaw her freezing hands. Smoke curled around, reluctant to go up the cold chimney, until a sudden fierce gust of wind created a draught which sucked the smoke away and fanned the flames to a white-hot glow. Clare stayed transfixed by the dancing colours.

A loud tearing crack and a ground shaking thud outside made her jump. Which tree, she wondered. She hated to think of the damage raging in her precious garden before she'd had a chance to explore.

Listening to an unfamiliar set of house sounds was odd, especially as she hadn't yet identified the creaks and groans the building made in normal conditions. A storm added new ones, including a weird rattling, as if slates were lifting and resettling. A door banged upstairs. A branch tapped against a window. Which door, which window, what plant? Would she live here long enough to find out?

The day dreaming must stop, she had things to do. First

157

off, find the switch on the Aga which disabled the electric thermostat and left the burner alight so that she could cook and have hot water while the power was out. Then find more candles. She put the guard in front of the fire in case the wind made it flare dangerously.

Back in the kitchen she put the kettle on and leant against the Aga towel rail, enjoying the heat that came from the comforting appliance. The candlelight dispelled the gloom.

She had eaten enough Christmas dinner to last her for a while. The dim light ruled out reading. A soak in a hot bath was her most tempting option. With the candlestick in one hand and a hot mug of tea in the other she headed upstairs.

A leisurely soak in a lavender scented bath was a treat she rarely had time to indulge in. The flickering candles cast dancing shadows on the ceiling. Clare lay in the bath, safe from the storm, cut off from the world and her worries. She immersed her head under the water, when she came up for air she thought she heard someone call her name. Ridiculous. She slid down once more letting the water cover her face. She came back up and heard the same sound again. The storm was tricking her imagination. No one would be out in this weather. She submerged herself again this time as she came up for air, the door burst open.

Adam stumbled through the door. "Clare, are you all right?"

She wiped the water off her face, and stared in his direction blinded by the powerful torch. All she could think about was her nakedness.

"Fine," she answered, trying to wrap her arms around her chest. "Well, fine for someone who's had the living daylights scared out of them. Why are you here? How did you get in?" She remembered sliding the bolts home.

"May asked me to come. She and Joe heard a tree fall and were afraid it had hit the house. I couldn't open the kitchen door, so I used my front door key."

"I didn't know you'd kept one," she answered, regretting the comment as she spoke. She didn't want him to think she minded him having a key to his property.

"Sorry, I never intended to use it, but I couldn't see any lights on anywhere. I hammered on the door. You didn't answer. I panicked."

"I'm fine, apart from getting cold." She stood up turned her back and reached for the bath towel to restore some modesty. She expected him to back out of the door to give her privacy, but he stood where he was seemingly unaware of her predicament.

"Is something wrong?" She twisted a small towel round her head, her mouth going dry.

"Hannah," he said, turning her dread into reality.

"Hannah? Oh my God, what's happened?"

"I am not too sure. She had trouble with her breathing, Gary arranged for her to go to the hospital. They're pumping antibiotics into her, and he says her condition is improving already."

"How does Gary know? Why didn't anyone call me?"

"The lines are down. Mine's the only one working. Gary asked me to come and tell you."

"I need to get to the airport, get the first flight out." She frantically rummaged through a pile of clothes in search of clean jeans and a top so she could get on her way. "Can you take me?"

"No. Gary was adamant that you mustn't. He's with her.

"What's he doing there?"

"Seems he sensed things weren't right on Christmas Eve, so decided to catch a flight. He was worried the weather might shut down the airports. Hannah made him promise not to tell you she was sick."

She slumped on the edge of the bed, hurt, helpless and angry. Hurt that Hannah hadn't talked to her. Helpless because of the distance involved and angry with herself for letting Hannah go without having that x-ray done. She knew

159

Hannah was pretending she was fine.

Everything boiled down to finding a balance between letting Hannah take control of her health and becoming a controlling ogre. Hannah's lungs had been clogged for weeks, but she would not admit there was a problem. Tears of frustration welled up. The long term damage of a lung infection was too serious to take chances. Surely Hannah understood that much.

Adam put his arm around her and drew her close.

"Gary says she's sorry she messed up."

Clare reached for a tissue.

"What did Mike have to say? How could he let her get into such a state? Why didn't he call?"

"I don't know. Gary didn't mention him."

"What about Edward? Why didn't he call? He promised he would."

"Edward got caught in a blizzard and is stranded in a shelter higher up the mountain waiting to be airlifted out. An avalanche has blocked the route between the two resorts. He can't get back, or charge his mobile. He had just enough charge left to keep in touch by text with Hannah. He said he sent a text to his dad, but hasn't had a reply. Hannah tried him too, but he hasn't picked up, so they are waiting for him to respond to their messages."

"Can we call Gary?"

"No. He's gone to the apartment to catch up on some sleep. He promised to call as soon as he had fresh news. Don't worry. I'll stay here until he calls."

"Won't Belinda be expecting you?"

Did she mention Belinda's name to test his reaction, or did it just slip out? She expected Adam to take his arm away, but he held on. A sign he didn't care about Belinda? No, he saw her as a messed up creature in need of comfort and didn't dare let go in case she did something idiotic. Whichever, she was glad he still held her. His failure to answer got her wondering if the relationship with Belinda

160

was less solid now than on the night they'd all met again. The thought made her less comfortable about his presence in the bedroom.

"I lit the fire downstairs. Fancy a cup of soup?" she suggested, reaching out for her pyjamas and dressing gown on the chair by her bed.

Adam pulled away. "Good idea." He shone his torch downwards while she found her slippers. Then he turned his attention to the array of candles in the bathroom while she dressed. She gave her hair a vigorous rub with the towel, ran a comb through it, and let him guide her downstairs again. While she made the soup, he found the bowls and spoons and buttered some bread. Then he carried the tray, letting her light the way to the cosy fire. She curled up at one end of the settee. He wedged himself at the other end. The soup and the heat of the fire worked their magic, helping her to relax.

"It's strange learning the noises in a new house. Guess which door's rattling?" she challenged.

"Your room."

"How did you know?"

"Easy, I made sure all the others were shut."

"Cheat," she said.

The violence of the wind went up a notch. Another crash shook the house. This one louder than the earlier one, with echoing crunches as smaller branches cracked and snapped. It hurt to think trees that had been standing for years could be flattened in seconds. Neither of them said anything. Later something rattled and hit the fence.

"What was that?"

"A dustbin lid?" he suggested.

"Maybe." She put down her empty cup. "I hate sitting here in the warmth, when I should be trying to get to Hannah."

"Well you wouldn't get far. There was one tree blocking the driveway, which is why I had to park at May's. I suspect by now there are trees across the main road. Nothing will be

161

cleared before morning, so even if you wanted to, you wouldn't get far."

"Do you think May and the children are all right?"

"Oh yes, Joe will make sure of that. He's a real find. I hope he sticks around."

"Me too."

"Do I get a reward for fighting my way through the storm to get to you?" Adam asked looking her in the eyes. Before she had time to think of a reply, he planted a soft kiss on her lips.

His kiss was over almost before she registered what he was doing. He pulled back for a moment then kissed her again. This time she responded. It felt so good, so natural, and her arms went up and round his shoulders, clinging tighter and his kiss deepened and they lay side by side on the settee. When their lips parted, he put a finger to silence her. No need, she was lost for words. She lay still not wanting to lose the comfort of the warmth of his body alongside hers.

The fire died down, and the room got colder. Clare shivered. Her movement alerted Adam.

"You need to get into bed. It will be warmer there than anywhere else," he said, "I've used up the last of the logs."

"Will you stay?"

"Can't go anywhere in this."

"I mean stay with me. I don't want to be alone."

He kissed her tenderly on her forehead. "Yes, as a friend."

It was all she needed for now. They went back upstairs to the bedroom. Adam tugged off his boots, emptied his pockets onto the bedside table and slid under the covers next to her. She didn't mind him staying fully dressed. His presence in the vast double bed he had provided was enough. She curled up, secure in his arms.

Chapter 22

When Gary's call woke them, the blue light of the screen shone on Adam's face, allowing her to catch his concern. Clare held her breath as she listened to the faint sound of Gary's voice.

"The doctor in charge is happy with Hannah's progress. The oxygen and intravenous antibiotics are working, but it's still too early to tell if they've cracked the lung infection."

"Have you seen her?" Adam asked.

"Yes, she's sleeping. She looks all right. They don't think she's done too much damage to her lungs. Everyone speaks perfect English, so no problem with communication."

Adam passed his phone to Clare. For a second she wondered if Gary would make anything of her being by Adam's side at six in the morning.

"Gary, knowing you're with her means so much to me. Any news from Edward or Mike?"

"Edward's fine, he expects to get here soon, nothing yet from Mike. He's probably been stranded somewhere. This has been the worst blizzard for years, even the locals don't ever remember it so bad."

She felt herself choking with tears. "Call as soon as you

can speak to her. Give her all our love." She handed the phone back to Adam.

Clare heard Gary ask, "How bad was your storm?"

"Rough. The power's out and it's still too dark to check the damage. Fill you in later." He pressed the button and the blue light faded.

"Guess we ought to get up," he said, pulling himself up to a sitting position. "Damn I forgot to reset the Aga to keep it going. Better go and scrounge a cup of tea off May."

"No need. May reminded me and showed me how to switch over from electric to manual."

Adam used the torch to give enough light to dress.

Clare put on jeans, several layers of warm jumpers and extra thick socks, ready for clearing up branches and whatever else the wind had destroyed. She stuck close to Adam and his torch until he relit a couple of candles in the kitchen.

"Shall I light the study fire?" he asked.

"Don't bother. I doubt we'll have time to sit down today." She filled the tea pot. "Checking on May is far more important."

"True."

Clare sliced some bread, toasted it on the hot plate of the Aga, passed a slice to Adam, and pushed the butter and honey in his direction. "You feeding me up in the hope I'll hang around all day clearing up the mess?" he joked.

"Good guess."

"I can read you too well."

Adam didn't seem to have forgotten one thing about the past. This house, a classic example, the colours, the way he arranged things. It frightened her that they could be so in tune with each other after a gap of nineteen years. His kiss confused her even more. She convinced herself it didn't mean anything. He was sorry for her. He wasn't free. He was engaged to Belinda of all people, and much as she wished they'd break up, Clare would never be happy if she caused a

164

rift between them. She still hadn't worked out how he had become involved with Belinda. Maybe the fact they had known each other since school was part of the attraction.

"Does that worry you?" he asked.

Had he mind read her last thoughts? No. Clare shook her head and skirted the issue. "Sorry, just thinking about Hannah and Edward. Being a mother is hard."

"Well, I think you're a brilliant mother, stop beating yourself up."

Clare cleared away their plates. The sky was a shade lighter allowing the outline of trees to be seen. She pulled a coat from the row hanging by the door, slid her arms into the sleeves. "We can't put this off much longer. Let's go."

Adam blew out the candles, grabbed his coat, and followed her out.

She stood on the step letting her eyes adjust to the grey dawn light. Dark blobs of tree branches littered the pea gravel. The dustbins had wedged themselves into the hedge the other side, their lids nowhere in sight. Slates from the outbuilding had smashed onto the path. Guttering hung at an odd angle. Adam took her hand and led her round the house. The roof of the main house had survived unscathed. The old barn had taken a real hammering, more than half the roof was missing.

"Good thing we didn't use that one for storage," Adam said, "I was waiting for you to suggest a use before starting the renovations."

Clare kept quiet. She'd never considered these buildings as part of her rent agreement, and wasn't sure she needed them either.

The sky was getting brighter. They didn't need to go far to see that at least three huge beech trees had fallen across the drive.

"Should provide enough logs for a few years," she commented.

"And your car is trapped here until they're cleared."

165

"Good thing I restocked the larder," she said to cheer him up.

They made their way to May's. Her gate was off its hinges and a small tree lay across the path. They clambered over the trunk to get to her door. The house was in darkness. Adam signalled her to follow as he skirted round May's house towards the greenhouses. Two appeared to be standing, the third had collapsed. A large branch had smashed into one end and the wind had popped the glass out of the frame, scattered it over everything. The hundreds of pots Gary tended so carefully with cuttings for the show garden had been battered by tons of broken glass. Clare's dream had turned into a nightmare. Two of the smaller old greenhouses had folded in on themselves. How could the nursery survive such a catastrophic loss? They'd never get this cleaned up and be trading in time for the spring planting season.

Adam put his arm round her. "Don't worry, easily fixed."

She was too shocked to disillusion him. They walked as far as they could round the back of the greenhouses to check the new building under construction. No trees had come down in that area and everything seemed in place.

By the time they circled back to May's house, a glow of candlelight shone through the window. Clare knocked on the door. Joe let them in.

"The rest are still sleeping. The noise kept the kids awake, so we stayed up playing cards until the worst of the wind died down," he informed them. "Some wild night, I was mighty glad of a sound roof over my head." He picked up the kettle, waved it in their direction. Clare nodded.

"Anything still standing?"

Adam told him about the obvious damage. "I'm sure there's more we didn't spot. At least no one got hurt, which is all that matters."

"Won't put you out of business?" he asked.

"I hope not, but it'll take a monumental effort to clean up the mess. Cost isn't the problem, finding manpower will be the hard part."

"Count me in," Joe answered without any hesitation then added, "Any news of your daughter?"

Clare caught genuine concern in his voice.

"She's getting the medication she needed. They think she'll be fine. Thanks for asking and for your offer of help. I'd like to take you up on that.

"My pleasure," Joe answered, and Clare knew he meant it.

"Time is an issue," she said. "We need to be sorted out before Easter or we'll lose our regular customers and face a huge struggle to win them back."

"What about the show garden? May told us about it last night. She's worried this will set you back."

"I may have to drop out. Most of the plants for the show were in the greenhouse that collapsed. Even if we can salvage them, we won't have the space to keep them safe from frosts."

"Don't you dare give up hope," Adam said firmly. "We can overcome all these problems."

Clare wanted to laugh at his optimism. But he was serious, so serious she believed he might just succeed in making the miracle happen. They'd need a miracle to sort out this mess.

Clare drank the tea quickly. She wanted another chance to reassess the enormity of the task ahead and figure out a strategy for the process.

Adam followed her out. "Let's walk down to check if Gary's cottage has survived."

"Good idea," she agreed. They opened the gate and went down the road, soon reaching an area coated with leaves and mud. "The ditch ahead must be blocked. Last time that happened, a willow had fallen across the road," she said. "Look up there. That tree has cut us off. Nothing can get in

167

or out."

"Has Gary got a chainsaw?" Adam asked.

"Yes, but nothing that will cope with something that size. And I'm not sure I'd let you try. They're dangerous things."

Adam smiled, making her feel a complete idiot. He probably knew more about chainsaws than she ever would.

"Don't fret, I wasn't thinking of tackling anything quite so daunting," he answered, "I was thinking more in terms of whether Joe had learnt to use one in the army."

"We must be careful not to let the children anywhere near the broken glass."

"Good point. By the way, what are you going to do about them? Shouldn't the authorities know they're living with May?"

"We decided not to rush into anything. We want them to trust us enough to tell us who their parents are, which could solve a lot of problems. I didn't succeed before Christmas, but hope to get an answer soon. May's promised she'll inform the right people after the holidays, when the offices reopen. She was afraid that if she approached the authorities during the Christmas holidays, she'd get some idiot going by the book, who'd insist on placing them in a soulless foster home. She wasn't prepared to take the risk. Her friend, who works in the fostering department, is away until the beginning of January. May's waiting to ask for her help."

"Is she up to it?"

"What?"

"Looking after two teenagers?"

"Of course she is, especially with me and Gary as back-up."

"And you think the authorities will accept that?"

Clare got cross. "Listen, I'm having a bad enough day without you being the voice of doom."

Adam apologised. "Sorry, from now on, let's discuss solutions not problems."

168

"Thank you. I think the first challenge will be to organize skips for the broken glass. We can't do much until that's cleaned up."

"Agreed, which makes clearing the road a priority." Adam stooped to pick up a stray plant pot, one of hundreds decorating the hedge. "Then get someone to check out the standing structures, preferably before anyone goes into them. The wind could have damaged the frames." He picked up another pot, which he slid inside the first. "Maybe the children can go on a pot hunt after breakfast."

"Good idea. You're right, not to let anyone near the greenhouses."

"The builders left a few hard hats in the store at your place. I'll go and fetch them."

Clare watched him go, and went back to see if May and the children had woken up. May came and gave her a big hug. "You must be out of your mind with worry over Hannah."

"Gary says the doctors think their treatment will kick in soon. She was sleeping so I didn't get to speak to her. He's going to ring later."

"Thank God he acted so fast and got over there before the storm hit. Is there anything still left standing?"

Clare held her hand and led May back inside. The children were sitting at the table eating cereals.

Clare ran through what they'd found. "What's left standing might not be safe so we don't want anyone to go near them." At the mention of danger, both children stopped eating and stared at her. She took a deep breath, time to tell them the truth.

She looked from one to the other then said, "I particularly don't want either of you taking risks. The ground is littered with glass, long spikes sticking up at dangerous angles. They're hard to spot but could slice through to the bone if anyone stepped in the wrong place."

May frowned, possibly thinking she was laying on the

scare tactics too harshly. Abby shivered, Pete bit his lip.

"I'm telling you this, not just because I don't want you to get hurt but because there are other things to consider."

Now they had puzzled expressions. Good, she had their full attention. "You like it here, don't you?" They nodded enthusiastically. "May hasn't told anyone you're here. If you got injured, she'd be in serious trouble. Any chance of your staying would disappear." Now they looked frightened.

"I know we talked about you working and that you want to help but please only do what we ask you to do, in areas we say are safe."

Abby didn't hesitate with her response. "Promise."

"What about you, Pete?"

He nodded his head. "Fine."

"One other thing." Clare had to make the most of the moment. "Nobody has talked about your family. My daughter is stuck in a hospital in France and I can't get to her. Luckily, Gary went over there to be with her, but knowing she's ill and not being there with her is hard. I'm not saying you have to go home, but please agree to let your mother know you're safe."

Abby went pale.

"You don't have to do it today. All the phones are down. You can send a message home without saying where you are. Just think how difficult it is for her wondering all the time if you are dead or alive."

Joe chipped in, "I agree."

"It would make me happy too," May added, touching Pete and Abby on their shoulders, before diverting their attention by asking, "Is that a chainsaw buzzing?"

Joe went to the door and listened. "Sounds like one to me."

"I guess that means hoards of hungry people," May said with a big smile. "Pete and Abby can you two help me make a big pot of vegetable soup for later?"

The two children, delighted the discussion about

contacting their mother had ended, were ready to take on any task offered.

"Abby, can you keep an eye on Shep for me? Don't let her out unless she is on a lead. It's too dangerous for her." Joe asked.

His request brought back Abby's delightful smile.

Chapter 23

"Is Mum mad with me?" Hannah asked as she fiddled with the oxygen tube lying across her lap.

Gary squeezed her hand. "No. If anything, she's mad with herself for letting you go away, knowing something was wrong and admitted it long before you sent your text. She was convinced you'd pretended to be okay in case she cancelled the holiday."

"She's right. I didn't want to let Edward down."

"For God's sake don't tell him. He's stressed enough about not being around when you most needed him."

"Where is he?"

"He went to the apartment to sleep, also to see if there was a message from your father. Good thing he did, it seems your father got stranded with Jennifer and some friends of hers, they are staying at another resort for now. He fixed for the cafe to run a tab for you which he'll settle when he gets back."

"That's it?"

"That's what Edward told me."

"So he doesn't know I've been ill."

"I don't think so."

"God, I'm dreading him finding out. He'll either pretend I'm fine, and wonder what all the fuss is about or he'll go ballistic!"

"Rubbish, he's going to be gutted to find you here."

Hannah loved Gary's positive outlook, but he didn't know her dad. He couldn't begin to guess his reaction. It might range from anger to accusations that she was trying to wreck their holiday and calling her ungrateful and inconsiderate. The least she could expect was for him to rant about her mother letting her travel if she wasn't fit.

A nurse brought in a tray with two cups of hot chocolate and a plate of biscuits. "I thought you'd enjoy this," she said as she put the tray down. "Here are your pills, Hannah. Take them now. The physiotherapist will be ready for you in an hour."

"Thanks."

The clinic was like a classy hotel, room service, carpeted floors, and so much kindness it made her want to cry. They also had an amazing physiotherapist, who had taught Gary some new movements to shift gunk from her lungs. Hannah was pleased because, before this episode, Gary had offered to learn about her exercises so she'd be able to go plant hunting with him. Now he had.

"What news of the storm damage?"

"One of the big greenhouses has been destroyed, and two of the old ones. They're waiting to find out if the rest are safe."

"Wow!"

"There's glass all over the site. Salvaging the plants is going to be tedious work. Best news is that Joe's staying on."

"And May?"

"She's in her element, feeding all the helpers."

"She'll enjoy that."

"Sounds as if Abby and Pete are helping with serving and clearing away."

"Bet you wish you were able to help too, instead of

sitting here with me."

"Cheering you up is helping and your Mum's very glad someone's here for you," he said touching her hand. "Also, learning to help with your physio is going to be useful."

"I didn't mean to sound ungrateful."

"You didn't."

After the exercises and pummelling all Hannah wanted to do was sleep. Gary walked back to her room with her. Her father was waiting for her.

"What happened, you were fine when I last saw you?" He paced up and down the room. "Where the hell have you been? They wouldn't let me see you."

Hannah tried to answer, but he kept on and on about how uncooperative the staff had been.

Gary quietly helped Hannah onto her bed, winked at her, and was about to move away. Hannah grabbed his sleeve and shook her head. She wanted him to stay. Her father spotted the gesture and registered Gary wasn't a member of staff.

"What the hell is he doing here?"

Hannah stared at her father. How dare he question Gary's presence? She might be ill, but she wasn't going to let him dictate who sat at her bedside.

"I asked him to come," she answered firmly. Her father glared and opened his mouth as if he was about to snap back at her. Instead he shoved his hands in his pockets and faced the window. Hannah smiled at Gary and pointed to the chair in the corner.

Her father spun round. "How long are they planning to keep you here?"

"I should be able to fly home on Friday as planned. Gary's booked on the same flight."

He looked Gary up and down and said. "Good."

Hannah was baffled. Not just by the change of tone. A minute ago he appeared angry that Gary dared to be in her room, now he seemed pleased.

"That solves one problem."

174

Did he expect her to figure out what problem had been miraculously solved?

Then he nodded thoughtfully. "Yes, that's good. There's a big silver sale in Geneva on Wednesday. I need to be there first thing tomorrow for the viewing. It's a relief to know that there'll be someone to help with your luggage on the journey home. He can stay in the apartment."

Hannah could feel her jaw drop open. Several things crossed her mind. The first was gratitude Edward was not in the room. The second was anger. Anger that she had put her own health at risk thinking there was a chance he and Edward might become closer. But he was choosing to leave them to buy silver. The image of her mother's reaction when Belinda had recently tried to hand her a piece of silver flooded back. At the time she had thought the reaction odd, now it made perfect sense. His silver collecting had caused trouble at home before, but never in a way that left Hannah feeling the direct impact. It hurt. She swallowed, blinked back tears and said. "I'm sure Gary will be pleased to help. I'm very tired. I need to rest."

"Fine," he answered, spun round and was out the door before she had a chance to say more.

Gary came over to the bed, gently touched her arm and said softly. "Don't worry. I'm sticking around. Rest, I'll only be down the corridor. Get someone to call me when you wake up."

Chapter 24

Clare struggled not to laugh when Belinda, who had put a lot of thought into her outfit, picked her way down the drive towards May's house. She wore denim jeans, clothing so alien to Belinda, Clare knew they'd sport an exotic designer label and have cost at least ten times the price Clare would ever pay. Belinda completed her ensemble with a spotless, ivory sheepskin coat and a pair of high heeled boots made of the softest looking leather Clare had ever seen.

"Welcome," Clare called out, wishing Belinda had put off her visit for a bit longer. The tree across the road had taken two days to clear, so she hadn't seen her since the week before Christmas because Belinda had been too busy with her gift shop to venture over to visit them.

"I thought I'd bring some emergency supplies," Belinda shouted, waving a small bag in the air and avoiding stepping into the muddy area where she and Adam had been clearing glass.

"I brought you pâté and a goat's cheese and some quail eggs."

Clare heard Adam chuckle behind her, she didn't dare look at him in case she got the giggles. She was already trying to imagine the reaction the tasty offerings would spark. Still, a kind thought deserved gratitude.

"Thanks," she called back. "You'd best go straight in. May's inside. We'll join you in a minute, just got to finish this line of plants and shift this barrow load of glass."

As soon as Belinda disappeared through the door, Adam burst out laughing. "Can you picture Joe's reaction to quail eggs?"

"Never mind that! How will Belinda react to Joe's tattoos?" As she said it, she felt mean, laughing at her friend rather than with her. "You have told her about him?"

"You mean describe him? No I don't think I did. You're right, it'll be fun to watch her reaction, we'd better hurry. Are you ready for me to take this barrow now?"

Clare emptied the last dustpan full of glass splinters on the top. She was ready for a break. The tedious search for fragments of glass was backbreaking work. They were working to a systematic plan, lifting every plant, checking for broken glass, then relocating it to an already cleaned area. Every leaf, twig and scrap of debris had to be shaken off each pot, so that not one bit of broken glass was overlooked.

Joe had volunteered to clear the tree blocking her drive. He'd donned the necessary protective clothing and set to work with the chainsaw, leaving her and Adam to do the lighter work. It was criminal that a man with so many skills could end up on the streets. She hoped that he'd be persuaded to stay at Dovedales on a permanent basis after the crisis was over. He was so protective of Pete and Abby and still hadn't moved back to Gary's house, preferring to sleep on a camp bed, he'd fixed up in the corner of the office. He used the excuse that he needed to be there to keep the fires going, and to make sure Pete and Abby kept out of the danger zone. He was happiest when he had someone to care for. All his usual candidates for care were enjoying a break from the cold weather in a temporary hostel that had opened for the Christmas period.

Adam wheeled the barrow away to tip it into an old bath that had become their makeshift skip until a proper one was delivered. Clare moved the tools to the next area they would tackle. She took off her gloves and made her way to May's, looking forward to a steaming bowl of vegetable soup and some home baked hot crusty bread. The lack of electricity didn't seem to bother May, who churned out nutritious meals at a great rate even though no one had been to the shops. She used vegetables from the garden and food salvaged from the rapidly thawing freezer.

A waft of oven fresh bread filled the porch. Clare hung her muddy coat up on the row of pegs, noting the absence of the ivory sheep skin. Sensible really, it'd be a shame to risk getting a mark on it. She removed her boots. Adam followed her in. She slipped on fleecy clogs to keep her feet warm and waited while Adam changed his footwear. She'd never known him take so long. Didn't he want to go in? Was he avoiding Belinda? God she must stop. She was beginning to imagine the most ridiculous things.

She pushed the door open and stepped inside. Belinda was standing, coat still on, awkwardly in the corner. May's easy way with everyone made Belinda's awkwardness uncomfortable to watch.

May had her back to the room, stirring her pot of soup. Belinda's dainty offerings sat neatly on the table, next to the crusty loaf May had baked for their lunch.

Clare, having decided to avoid getting caught up in whatever was making Belinda so tense, made a dive for her usual seat.

As she pulled out the chair, she asked. "Are you joining us for lunch?"

Adam sat down too, and looked over to Belinda, waiting for her to respond.

Belinda shook her head. "Thanks, but I already explained to May I must rush. Did Hannah and Edward enjoy their holiday?"

178

"They're not back yet."

"Oh, when Mike said to meet him in Geneva, I assumed they'd already be home."

Clare was confused. Mike being in Geneva while Hannah was in hospital in France didn't make sense. His being in contact with Belinda didn't either.

"Did he phone you?" Clare asked, wondering if Belinda would assume she was acting the part of the jealous wife.

"He's found an amazing company selling just the sort of things I wanted. He's such a sweet-heart. He's arranged to introduce me to the owner, so I'm flying to Geneva this afternoon. I didn't realize the children would be with him."

Clare saw Adam looked confused too. But before either of them could query Belinda's plans, Joe walked through the door. Clare, having joked with Adam about how Belinda would react to their new helper, found herself distracted by her reaction. Classic. Belinda's mouth dropped open, no sound escaped, her eyes widened and she wrapped her arms tight across her chest.

Joe reacted as he would with any other stranger in their midst, nodded in her direction and mumbled, "Hello." He plonked himself down at the table. He reached out and picked up the big loaf of bread, cut a chunk off and passed it on.

May was filling bowls with soup which Pete brought to the table and placed in front of Adam and Joe. Abby brought a bowl for Clare and one for May, before coming back with their own bowls.

Adam ripped off a chunk of bread, and handed the loaf down the table to Clare, who passed it on to the children.

"Belinda, are you sure you won't join us?" Then almost as an afterthought added, "Sorry, I don't think you've been introduced to Joe. He's been giving us a hand. And this is Pete and his sister Abby."

Belinda muttered, "Hi."

Clare, still reeling from the shock of knowing Mike

might be in Geneva rather than with the children, sensed Belinda longed to talk to Adam alone, but he was far too busy tucking into his food, dunking his bread into the soup, concentrating on each mouthful, to spot her pleading looks.

"I'll ring you when I arrive." Belinda said.

Adam looked up at her, "How long will you be gone?"

"Not sure, two, maybe three days," she replied.

"I'll probably spend most of my time here, there's so much to do."

Belinda's rather forced smile was a sure sign she was unhappy. Her eyes darted towards Joe. She seems unable to cope with the fact that Adam could share a table with a tattooed man with dreadlocks.

Apart from the confusion about Mike being in Geneva, all Clare could think about was how Belinda would describe the assembled entourage to Mike. She was certain the description would not be complimentary. Still, why should she worry what Mike thought? He'd lost the right to interfere with her life, or comment on her friends.

Belinda still hovered by the stairs. "I'll be off now," she said.

Clare wondered if Adam would get up and follow her out. He stayed put, blowing a kiss across the table. "I hope you find some nice things. Do you have a contact number for Mike?"

"Yes," she dug into her little leather bag and pulled out her phone, fiddled with it for a minute. "Anyone got a pen?"

May passed over a jotter and a pen and Clare wrote down the number as Belinda read it out.

"Thanks for coming and for the contribution to lunch," Clare added, willing Belinda to make a move soon before Joe commented on her offerings and everyone got the giggles.

"My pleasure," Belinda answered, and stepped towards the door. "Speak to you soon."

May waited until the door had closed before she spoke. "Tell me I'm not hearing things. She did say Geneva, didn't she?"

Clare nodded, and turned to Adam. "You knew?"

"Not that he'd gone to Geneva, only that he wasn't around."

"Can you text Gary? Get him to call when he's alone. I need to discover what's going on."

Adam pulled out his mobile, keyed in the message and put the phone on the table. Then with a big grin pushed his soup bowl to one side and said, "Now for the main course." He took the bowl containing the tiny speckled quail eggs and offered them round.

Joe gamely took one, shelled it faster than expected and popped it into his mouth. "Trying to make me fat?" he asked.

Pete and Abby looked at the offering with suspicion. They'd probably never heard of a quail, let alone eaten a quail egg. Clare reassured them. "They taste like ordinary eggs, only the size is different."

Pete reached out bravely. Abby as always followed his lead. They nibbled the ends of their eggs to test them, and in no time at all had eaten them up.

The goat's cheese and the mushroom pate were a step too far for Joe and the children. One new tasting experience was enough for one day.

As Joe was putting on his boots, he turned to Clare. "You mentioned the other night you wanted a gnarled old willow for your show garden. I think I've found one."

"Where?"

"At the bottom of the field, between your place and the pond, a neighbouring tree knocked it over exposing the roots, which will make salvage much easier. I'll need a quick decision before it gets sawn up with the rest."

Clare wanted to go, but didn't want to miss Gary's call. Adam must have sensed her hesitation, because he solved the dilemma. "Go with Joe. Don't worry, I'll ask Gary about Mike," he told her. "He might be more open to me than you. Remember no one mentioned Mike when you spoke to them earlier today."

The omission scared her. If no one was prepared to tell her about Mike, what else were they hiding? Adam was probably right about Gary talking more freely to him if she wasn't around.

"Find out how long Mike was away, and when he came back and if he left them a contact number. Please get the truth about Hannah. I can't handle a cover up."

"Gary wouldn't lie about that," May piped in. "He knows me too well to think I'd forgive him."

"I agree, May, but he'll have split loyalties if Hannah swore him to secrecy." Adam added.

"Hannah's a devious minx when she puts her mind to something," Clare answered.

"So are you going to come and give us your verdict on this tree?" Joe said as he pulled his coat on.

"Yes. Can Pete and Abby come too?" Clare looked across at the pair. They needed fresh air.

"Yes, as long as they steer clear of the pond," Joe answered.

"What about you, May? Fancy a walk?"

"No, love, I think I'll put my feet up for half an hour."

An unexpected response, May never normally put her feet up. Coping without power and a houseful to cater for was clearly wearing her down.

Adam said, "I'll do the dishes while I'm waiting for the phone."

The children didn't need encouragement. They grabbed their coats, put on their boots, eager to follow Joe out the door.

Chapter 25

The sun sat low in the sky. Pete and Abby were behaving like children, kicking leaves and chasing each other. The serious, frightened bravado Pete displayed when Clare brought them to May's was slowly easing, and Abby no longer cowered when meeting new people. The fact that they were too young to fill the post on offer didn't matter, that they were safe and well did.

Clare couldn't decide which of the tangled trees Joe wanted to save. She clambered over slippery branches and was about to give up when she spotted it.

The knobbly trunk and splayed roots matched the illustration exactly. The only fault was the size. The girth, the height and the bulk would dwarf everything else. Her planting plan would need to be scaled up to compensate. She shook her head. A mad woman's foolish dreams. Shifting, transporting and positioning something this large was well beyond budget.

In some ways she wished Joe had never found it. The gnarled trunk had woven a magic spell on everyone who had seen it, leaving them to face disappointment that it couldn't be used.

"You're right, Joe. It's beautiful. But it's far too big to

move." Clare said.

"Rubbish." Joe answered as he scrambled over the trunk and wrapped his arms around it. "A sling round here and another three foot lower will do the trick. With careful root pruning and a hole with decent soil in it, by Easter, it'll be in leaf again."

Clare hated to dampen his enthusiasm. "It's still too big to fit the plan.

"Tell you what," Joe said. "I'll clear the stuff all around here. Let Gary and Adam see it before you make a final decision."

"It's just like the one in the picture you showed us," Abby said. Joe smiled, pleased to have back-up.

Abby was right, but looking like the tree in the picture didn't make this one any easier to transport.

"Clear whatever you think necessary." She said, knowing she would never be forgiven for not giving Joe the chance to continue.

He smiled. "Great, I'll get on with it."

She turned to the children. "Let's go. May needs more carrots and potatoes for supper."

Clare helped the children to collect the vegetables. She wanted to talk to Adam, so asked the children to start at the furthest end of May's garden, picking up the plant pots scattered by the storm. "Sort them and stack them upside down against the hedge. If you find any broken glass don't touch it." She had already had a good look round this area, and hadn't spotted any dangerous debris for the youngsters to avoid.

She was anxious to check that May had gone to put her feet up. If she hadn't, Clare would have to convince her she must, if only to stay fit enough to care for Pete and Abby.

On entering the kitchen Clare heard Adam talking on the phone. "If something goes wrong, no one can contact him?"

Clare froze in the doorway, unwilling to interrupt.

"Not even the Doctor?" he asked. "Are you sure? Please

184

check." After a long pause he continued, "But progress is good. You haven't been lying because Hannah wants to please her mum?"

He listened intently for what seemed ages then he said. "Good. How's Edward coping?"

The floor creaked. Adam turned, nodded to her, and continued. "You're staying in the apartment?"

He gave the thumbs up signal.

"You're certain she'll be fit to fly on Friday. Good. I'll pass the news on. Bye." He pressed the disconnect button and took a deep breath.

"Hannah's doing well. Edward's fine. Mike showed up at the hospital, ranted on about how unhelpful everyone was, stayed long enough to learn Hannah would be fit to fly and that Gary had a ticket for the same flight, at which point he handed responsibility for getting Hannah home to Gary. It seems there's an important silver sale he has to attend.

"A silver sale!" Clare took a deep breath to try to calm herself.

"He took all his stuff from the apartment," Adam continued, "seems he didn't wait to speak to Edward, or even leave a note for him. Edward only found out when Gary told him."

Clare's anger left her momentarily speechless. She'd wanted to believe Mike had changed, abandoning his daughter in hospital proved he hadn't.

"I should never have let them go," she muttered.

Adam touched her shoulder. "You can't blame yourself for his failings."

"No, but he'll pay." As the words came out she shivered, hating sinking to this level. Revenge wasn't her thing, but she'd never defend his actions again.

"Do you think I should get a flight over?"

"No. You're needed here more than ever."

Clare shot to the window to check on Pete and Abby. They had turned the task set into a race. "They don't need

185

me."

"May does," Adam said, almost in a whisper as he pointed up the stairs. "She had a funny turn. She pretended to be fine but let me help her up the stairs, which I'm guessing has to be a bad sign from such an independent individual."

"You're right, that's worrying. She never asks for anything. I'll nip up and check on her."

Clare tip-toed upstairs, May's bedroom door was ajar, allowing her to peer in. May lay on the bed, propped up against a mound of pillows, eyes closed, hands folded on her lap, with a big squashy quilt over her legs. She looked peaceful, her breathing steady enough for Clare to relax.

Adam looked up when she got back to the kitchen.

"Sleeping peacefully," she reported. "Do you think I should move the children over to Manor Croft?"

"No. It could make matters worse if you treat her like an invalid. Anyway having them here means more people can keep watch over her. Joe will help. Once Hannah is back you'll be wrapped up in her recovery."

"You have everything figured out." Clare slumped onto one of the kitchen chairs. "What else can go wrong?"

"Nothing. You've had your quota for the month. Your problems will slowly get resolved."

Clare couldn't completely accept his optimism.

"With the storm and everything, I want to scale down our plans." It was not a declaration of defeat, more of intent. 'Do one thing well rather than two things badly', had always been her motto, and now was the appropriate time to act.

Adam frowned. "How?"

"Drop the show garden, see if I can postpone to next year."

"No. You can't let your children down. Not now. Not after what Mike has done. They need this challenge as much as you do." Adam answered firmly. "May too, think how she will feel if she thinks her health is to blame for you backing out."

His argument made sense. But so did wanting to create enough time to be able to care for the people she loved without killing herself in the process. No one was taking that into consideration.

"Everyone wants you to succeed." He sat down next to her and took her hand in his. "Trust me, the show garden is important."

She longed to pull away, his touch was adding to her confusion. She must not let his presence distract her.

"Tell me about Joe's tree," he asked breaking the spell of his touch. "Is it any good?"

"Almost perfect, identical to the tree in the picture that inspired me, except it's far too big, and too expensive to move. As for how anyone would keep such a top heavy plant alive and upright is beyond me."

"So what's he doing?"

"Clearing more of the trees nearby, to allow closer inspection, if we decide not to use it, it'll be chopped up like the rest."

"I'll go and give my opinion. Not much to do here until the skips arrive. They should be here in the morning."

Clare was relieved. Their normal staff should be back then. For the first week none had been able to get in because of fallen trees. After that Clare had felt there was little they could do until the building inspectors had passed the buildings as safe.

"You stay here, take a break. I'll get the kids to show me."

After he'd gone, Clare realized she'd hardly had a moment alone since they'd collected Joe, Pete and Abby. The two weeks with an empty house while the children were in France had not been as quiet as she'd expected. The storm forced Adam to stay at Manor Croft. Not in her bed though. He'd only shared her bed on the first night. She wasn't sure if she was disappointed or relieved. Coping with extra

187

emotional stuff was more than she could handle, never mind stretching her renewed friendship with Belinda.

She started preparing things for supper to get the benefit of the remaining daylight. She scrubbed six large potatoes, spiked them ready for the oven. Grated a bowlful of cheese and opened two cans of baked beans which she transferred to a pan ready for heating, finally she speared the sausages ready to go into the frying pan. Anyone expecting a gourmet dinner would be disappointed. A hot nutritious meal was all she could offer. Next, she chopped a load of vegetables for lunch the next day to ensure May had a quiet day for a change, though Clare was sure she'd find tasks to occupy any spare time.

She heard footsteps upstairs, followed by an extraordinary noise. She hurried to investigate.

May was standing on the landing under the loft hatch, pulling down the loft ladder which needed a drop of oil.

"What on earth are you doing?" Clare asked, horrified by the thought of May trying to climb the rickety steps.

"Oh, good, I need you to get something for me. There's a purple painted chest up on the left. Inside you'll find a green fabric covered box, about the size of a shoe box."

Refusing would be foolish, May would go herself. "Okay, but I'll only go if you sit down. You look exhausted. I'll get a torch, so I can see what I'm doing."

May was sitting on the edge of her bed when Clare returned to climb the steps into the dark abyss above. She shone the torch around, amazed by the size of the space. Cobwebs hung over everything. Wooden chests, cardboard boxes, hat boxes, suitcases and tin trunks lined the edges with only a tiny space left for her to stand. On the left, as described, was the purple wooden chest, instantly recognized as her toy box, which she hadn't seen for years. She fingered the lid. The three drawing pins stuck under the rim, used for pinning up her paintings all those years ago, were still in place. What was this doing in May's house? Then she remembered her mother asking May to store some of their things. Obviously she didn't bother to reclaim this.

She moved three small round hat boxes off the lid so she could open the chest. The green shoe box was where May said it would be. Clare eased it out of the tight space, closed the chest, replaced the hat boxes and reversed down the ladder, torch in one hand and the box under her arm.

She put the box and torch down on the floor so she could brush the cobwebs off her sleeve. Then using the pole provided, pushed the folding ladder back up into the roof space and pulled the trap door back into place. With that done, she took the box into May, wondering what treasure it might contain.

May rubbed her forehead, making Clare ask, "What's wrong?"

"Migraine. I haven't had one for years. Can you deal with supper for the children and Joe?"

Trust May to be worried about others when she was so clearly in agony herself. If their roles were reversed Clare doubted she'd be so concerned for others.

"Don't worry about them. Supper's sorted and I've made a huge pot of vegetable curry for lunch tomorrow. I won't let them starve." The news produced the hint of a smile. "How can I help, a cup of tea, something to eat?"

"Tea please, and my pills. They're in a blue box. I can't remember the name. They're on the shelf above the sink."

Clare went to fetch them and made tea the way May liked it, put biscuits on the tray because the pills ought to be taken with food.

May was back in bed, fingering the contents of the green box. It looked like a box of letters, but May furtively closed the lid, and kept one hand on the lid in a rather protective way.

"Should I call Dr. Webb?"

"No. I'll be fine once these kick in. Thanks for the biscuits." She let Clare pour the tea for her, popped a pill out of the foil, swallowed it and ate one of the biscuits.

Clare left her to rest. "I'll come back up later before I go home in case you need anything else."

May gripped her hand, "I wish you'd been my daughter."

Clare kissed her forehead. "Me too," She went to move the green box off the bed. May's hand flashed out to stop her.

"Leave that," she snapped. There was a hint of panic in her voice

Clare pulled back, surprised.

Should she say something? No. The box and its contents were May's concern, not hers.

"You rest." She had always been close to May, and never seen her like this.

The kitchen was in darkness when she descended. She lit a couple of candles, stoked the fire. Candlelight suppers had lost their charm. Clare longed for the normality of electricity, the comfort of a fridge light, not to mention the delights of electric toasters, electric blankets and all the other gadgets she took for granted. She popped the potatoes in the oven. Sure everyone would be happy with an early supper and an early night. She wondered if Adam would stay at her place again. Belinda flying off to see Mike had been unexpected news, taking them all by surprise. Perhaps, she was more upset than Adam, because Mike wasn't being the dutiful parent in France with the children.

Joe, Adam, Pete and Abby trouped in bringing the damp evening air with them. "Shut the door," she called out to them. "Keep the noise down. May is resting."

"Is she all right?" Joe asked.

"She has a migraine, reckons she'll be fine tomorrow. I wish there was more we could do to stop her overdoing things."

"Not easy." Joe answered, "Do you think we haven't tried already?"

"No criticism from me," Clare answered quickly. "I

190

know what you're up against. Now the road is clear we ought to buy bread and cakes and stuff so she needn't do quite so much baking."

"Good plan," Adam said. "While we're on the subject of food, what's on the menu tonight?" He rubbed his stomach. "I'm starving and they are too." The children nodded in agreement.

"Have some fruit cake now. Later we'll have baked potatoes, sausages and beans."

Good menu, beaming smiles all round.

Joe took the cake out of its tin, cut great big slices and handed them round. "We've worked out how to lift the tree."

He had to be joking. She was convinced the tree was beyond help, let alone rescue for use in her garden. She listened while the four of them described their plan between mouthfuls of cake, not daring to share her doubts.

The evening sped by, everyone seemed relaxed and supper vanished fast including the apple pie May had made earlier. Afterwards, she made May fresh tea, with toast and honey, and sat with her while she ate and took her pills.

As Clare was leaving, May reached out to stop her. "I discovered this a few years ago." She put her hand on the green box. "I should have given it to you before. Sorry, a bad decision... now may not be the right time either... forgive me anyway."

Clare heard a foot step by the door. Adam had come up.

May became flustered and whispered, "Open it in private." She focussed on Adam. "I hope you're keeping everyone in order. Please say goodnight to the children from me. Perhaps you could carry the tray down for Clare."

Clare could tell he thought, 'neat dismissal', because he nodded and left. She took the box and followed, pulling the door shut behind her. She couldn't resist taking a quick peek. The box was full of unopened letters, some stamped, some not. All the stamped and postmarked letters were addressed to her, the rest were addressed to Adam.

Her first instinct was to rush back in and ask May questions. Why did she have them? Where did she get them? But she knew it was a waste of time. May had no answers. Her mother was the one to blame. May didn't have it in her nature to be so cruel. Just keeping the secret would have bothered her conscience, especially after Adam returned. Poor May. No wonder she wanted to hand them over. What difference would it make? Impossible to pretend they wouldn't make a difference. First she had to read them.

Adam peered round the bend in the staircase. "Are you all right?"

"Fine," she answered. How would he react to what she held? One thing for sure, her mother would be off his Christmas card list.

Pete was the first to ask, "What's in the box."

"Some old papers," she hoped her tone would make the contents appear to be of no consequence.

Abby yawned.

"I'm exhausted too. Time to go home," Clare said and headed straight to the door. "Good night."

Adam reached for his coat to walk with her. She didn't like to ask if he was staying or heading to his car. Earlier in the day, before he knew Belinda was flying to Geneva, he'd said he'd stay.

He carried the torch, and she carried the box, the contents of which had thrown her into utter confusion.

She now had cause to regret not having the one conversation that might have cleared her misconceptions. If she'd had the guts to ask why he'd ended their relationship, the power of the box would be minimal. The break up still hurt. She thought him uncaring. Perhaps he felt the same way, but his engagement to Belinda prevented her from seeking answers.

What difference would these letters make? Would her words seem childish? Would she want him to read them? What was the point? They had both moved on. Why open

192

old wounds?

She stuck the box under her arm while she struggled to detach the key from her coat lining. The box slid out of her grasp, scattering the contents on the step. Adam immediately bent down and grabbed handfuls of letters and started stuffing them back. She managed to get the door open and turned to take the box from him, hoping he hadn't had time to register what he was holding.

Too late, he was studying the address on one of the letters. It was a stamped one. A letter he'd sent to her. He carried the open box to the table and put it down, picked out another envelope. This one addressed to him. He hesitated for a minute, then without turning to check her reaction, put it carefully next to the other one and continued sorting the rest, checking each one as he did so.

Clare didn't know what to do or say. She peeled off her coat, and hung it up, moved across the kitchen, lit a few candles in jam jars around the room and went to the Aga to put the kettle on.

Adam, having sorted all the letters, put them neatly back in the box, slid it to the middle of the table with the lid off.

"Is there an explanation?" he asked quietly, as he sat down.

"I wish..." She tried to fill the teapot. Her hands were shaking so much she almost dropped the kettle. She kept her back to him, unable to watch his face, afraid of his reaction. "May made me get that box out of her attic this afternoon. She gave it to me just before supper. I had no idea what was in it."

Adam said nothing. When she turned he was running his finger over the unopened envelopes, disbelief etched on his face. She put the tea pot down. Found two mugs and milk and was about to go in search of biscuits.

"No biscuits. It's time we talked."

Clare nodded and sat opposite him, the box between them.

193

"What happened?"

"Mother," she said, unwilling to brand her step-father with such interference with her life.

Her mother was the only person in a position to ensure the non-delivery of so many letters, with the opportunity and desire to keep them apart. Social snobbery had stopped her ever giving Adam a chance. But that was no excuse to actively intervene.

"What happened?" he asked.

"Do you remember I went to Portugal on holiday with my mother after she remarried?"

"Yes, when you came back and I phoned you, your mother told me you didn't want to speak to me. I didn't believe her and tried again. Then she said you'd met someone. And you didn't want to see me again."

"She lied."

"She even described the wonderful man who'd swept you off your feet."

"The only feet I was swept off were my own. I slipped on some stairs, smashed bones in both my feet and ended up in a wheelchair for six weeks.

"I wrote and asked you to meet me. I turned up at our usual spot in the park. You didn't. The third time you failed to show. I wondered what was going on. My mother kept reassuring me you would have a good reason for not being there. I had to rely on her to take me to the park three more times. Then she told me you'd called her and said you were leaving town and to tell me not to bother writing."

Adam clenched his fist, and muttered, "Bitch." He realized she had heard his mutterings. "Sorry, I know she's your mother, but..."

"Bitch is right. A manipulating one at that... I learnt that a long time ago, this is confirmation."

"Why?" he asked. "What did I do to upset her?"

Clare shrugged. Her mother had always been a mystery. She spent her life climbing some imaginary social ladder. Her

194

quest had driven her father to the point where he'd died from a massive heart attack. Her remarriage had destroyed an already fragile relationship with her mother.

Now she understood her mother's unusually subdued behaviour at Hannah's birthday lunch. It all made sense. Seeing Adam there, she'd have been terrified the depth of her meddling would be uncovered.

Clare poured the tea, her hands no longer shaking. She wished that someone would come to the door. She was desperate for a distraction. She wanted to hide the letters. God, right now to have Belinda turn up would be a blessing.

Adam took his mug of tea, stirred in some sugar and drank it, all the time peering over the cup at her, as if trying to read her mind. Occasionally his eyes rested on the box of letters.

Did he want to whisk away the letters he wrote so long ago? Or was he wondering what intimate thoughts she'd committed to paper? Would her outpouring seem childish twenty years later? She must have been desperate to have written so many letters without waiting for a reply. But he'd written nearly as many himself. Would he want her to read those?

The silence between them in the kitchen was intense. The ticking clock, the splutter of a candle, the clicking of a cobweb-trapped leaf tapping the window in the wind all seemed a million times louder than normal. She was glad of the distraction.

Eventually Adam pushed the box to one side, reached over and took hold of her hands. "I don't care what she told you. I loved you then, and I love you now. Nothing's changed."

She nearly choked. How could he say nothing had changed? Everything had changed. Telling him she still loved him wouldn't make everything perfect, it wouldn't make Belinda vanish.

The longer she took to reply the more his shoulders

slumped. She hated that she couldn't bring herself to tell him she'd never stopped loving him either. Sharing him was not an option. A tear escaped and rolled down her cheek. She wanted to wipe it away, but he didn't let go of her hands. He must know she wouldn't two-time her friend. If he didn't, he wasn't the man for her.

"Everything I wrote then is true today." He drew one of his hands away from hers, stood up, stretched over the table and wiped the tear off her cheek. "This has come out too fast. Too many complications, Belinda for one, right?"

There was still hope. Thank God he seemed to understand. He had to make that decision. She reached for her mug of tea. It was cold. They had been sitting with the letters between them for over an hour.

"I think it would be better if I didn't stay tonight," Adam said. "You need some sleep."

He moved away from the table, put some fresh candles in jars and lit them. He put the torch down beside her. Half of her wished he would hurry up and go. The other half longed for him to take her in his arms and hold her. Ever since he had come back into her life she had been making herself believe that there was no hope of their getting together, but now she was terrified.

Was she ready for a full on relationship with anyone? Mike had suffocated her, and for the first time in years she was free to make her own decisions, her own mistakes. Having found freedom she wasn't sure she was ready to give it up. Not for anyone.

She watched as he moved around the kitchen. He was so at home here, but then it was partly his creation and he owned the place. Was that a problem? Maybe. He had started controlling her life. Taking over everything, from where she lived, to the expansion of the nursery, and today, he had even begun to interfere with her show garden, getting all excited about the prospect of rescuing the tree, deeming the cost incidental. At this rate she'd find herself with less control of

196

her life than when she lived with Mike.

"Don't leave Belinda because of me." The words were out. She could not reclaim them. But she had no regrets.

Adam spun round, his eyes wide in disbelief at what she had just said. He would know this was not an invitation to have an affair. He chewed his bottom lip, took a deep breath, and walked towards her.

He placed a tender kiss on her head, and whispered. "Don't let your mother win." He didn't hang around for a response, within seconds he had opened the back door and stepped out into the night.

Clare hadn't the energy to move. Tears flowed unchecked. Had she made the biggest mistake of her life? Would he understand? She still loved him, but getting locked into another relationship could destroy her. But that was madness. Avoiding one might destroy her too.

Chapter 26

As Hannah came through the arrivals gate her mother enveloped her in a hug.

"Don't ever scare me like that again," she said.

Hannah hugged her back. "I won't, I promise."

Her mum released her, checked her up and down. "Good." She turned her attention to Edward. Hannah was glad, he needed a hug too.

Hannah was still waiting for the lecture. Instead her mum turned to thank Gary and got involved in sorting out the bags.

"Let's get you home."

Hannah took a deep breath and asked, "Can we go via the hospital?"

"I thought you said your new medication was working?"

"It is. I'm fine, but Rosie's mum called. She's asking for me."

"Do they know you've had an infection?"

"Yes. They said it didn't matter." Her mother nodded. She understood. Not mattering meant nothing was going to help Rosie.

Then the protective maternal instinct kicked in.

"You will wear a mask. I couldn't bear for you to go down with something else."

"Don't worry. I've learnt my lesson."

During the walk to the car she outlined what to expect when they got home. She didn't mention their father.

"Why don't I drop Gary and Edward off at the nursery before I take you to the hospital.? I'm assuming neither of you will want to come."

"I'd rather help with the clear up," Edward answered.

Hannah was glad he hadn't pretended he'd like to visit Rosie. Edward hated hospitals and he didn't know Rosie well enough to cope with the fact she could be close to death.

"I think I should get back to work too," Gary said.

Once they were alone in the car, Hannah expected her mum to say something about the risk she had taken with her health. But again she said nothing. It was odd, so odd Hannah thought maybe she ought to say something herself, and would have except they had reached the hospital before she decided what to say.

They knew where to go, and quickly found Rosie's parents waiting in the corridor. Hannah had never seen anyone look so exhausted before. It was hard to believe how much they had aged in the few weeks since her party. Hannah shuddered. Would her mother suffer like this? The week in the hospital away from home had taught her a valuable lesson. She had come to understand and appreciate the effort her mother invested in her welfare and vowed never to be such an idiot again.

Hannah took extra care when she gelled her hands. She asked a nurse for a gown and mask before approaching Rosie's parents. It was touching to feel their genuine reaction to her coming.

"She'll be thrilled you're here. The doctors will be out in a moment. After that you can go in," Rosie's dad said.

A few minutes later the doctors emerged. Hannah remembered them from previous visits to the hospital. She registered the lack of hope on their faces.

Dr James greeted her, "Go on in, but don't stay long."

Rosie's parents seemed grateful to know someone would be with Rosie giving them a chance to talk to the doctors.

"Would you like me to come in with you?"

Hannah shook her head. "No, Mum, I'd rather go alone." She pushed open the door and went in.

Rosie seemed smaller and she had lost all her colour. Even her normally fair curly hair had gone dull and limp. Wires and tubes dangled round the bed. Both her eyes were closed, her finger encased in a big plastic clip. A drip was attached to her arm and an oxygen tube was taped to her face to keep it under her nostrils.

Hannah glanced at the other beds. The occupants appeared to be in a far worst state than Rosie, with drainage bags hanging from the side of their beds and computerized monitors beeping in time to the green lights of the pulse graphs. The monotonous swoosh bang of their breathing machines filled the room.

Hannah hated seeing Rosie, who had bravely climbed into the horse-drawn trap so recently, stuck in a place like this. They'd discussed dying several times. This scenario was the one Rosie had dreaded most of all. Hannah approached the bed and touched her hand.

Rosie opened her eyes, blinked as she focussed. "Glad you're here," she gasped. "I need help."

"I'll call someone."

"No. Not that sort of help." Rosie grabbed her hand. "Persuade them to get me out of here. I've had enough. Please make them understand what I want."

Hannah squeezed her hand. She wasn't sure Rosie's parents were ready. "I'll try."

"Thanks." Rosie's grip eased and she closed her eyes.

Hannah stayed by her bed recalling their previous conversations, trying to work out how to approach Rosie's parents. After a while Rosie's hand went limp, she'd gone back to sleep. The machines in the room carried on their monotonous chorus.

Hannah slid her hand out from under Rosie's, trying to make sure she didn't wake her. Her mother met her at the door and pulled her into her arms.

"You okay?" she whispered.

Hannah managed a nod. "I will be. I need to talk to Rosie's parents. Where are they? I thought they'd be here."

"I convinced them to go and get something to eat."

"Can we wait for them to come back?"

Her mum made her sit down. "Of course, they shouldn't be long. We can wait here." She sat next to her, not pressuring her to talk.

Hannah worried she wouldn't be able to make them understand.

A few minutes later they were standing in front of her, their faces wearing their sadness, anxiously waiting for her to speak.

"She wants you to take her home. She doesn't want to die in hospital."

"She said that?" Rosie's dad queried in a voice which implied she was making it up.

"Not exactly, we've discussed dying before. The thing she dreads most is dying in hospital." Then, realizing she had given the wrong impression, qualified the explanation. "Sorry, badly worded. She is not afraid of dying, just afraid of dying in a room surrounded by machines."

Rosie's mum gave her a hug. Her eyes were full of tears. She took her husband's hand and they walked away as if her words had hurt too much to bear.

Her mother's grip tightened round her shoulder. She whispered, "Well done. Please don't ever be afraid of talking to me about your fears. I need to know them too."

Hannah hugged her back and nodded. "Okay."

"Are you scared?"

"A little, but like Rosie the worst part is the thought of

being surrounded by machines. Mum," she pulled her tighter, "I'm going to take extra care. I won't lie to you again."

Her mum kissed her on the head. "Good, I'll hold you to that."

Rosie's mum came back. She seemed much calmer than earlier.

"Thank you," she said, "what you said has helped a lot. We needed a reminder. We're going to try to get her home. Her dad's asking the doctor now. If we manage to get her home, will you come and visit?"

"Of course, I will."

On the way off the ward they had a chance to talk to Dr. James about Hannah's time in France and the things they'd taught her. He read the notes she had with her, listened to her chest, and reassured her mother she was doing well. Which was good, her mum needed reassurance.

"Keep up the exercises, they seem to be working. Make sure you tell the team here what you learned, it might be useful for someone else."

"You must show me too," her mum said.

"Gary will be able to explain better than I can. He got very involved with the diagrams and statistics and made a ton of notes. I have to admit I didn't pay too much attention at first, it took a while before I realized Gary was actually doing the tapping. After the initial shock, I liked having him pummelling me. He persuaded Edward to learn how to do it properly as well."

Hannah wondered how her mother felt learning that other people had taken her place and could do things she knew nothing about.

"Well there's plenty of time for all that. You look exhausted. Let's go."

The storm damage was far worse than Hannah had expected. She lost count of the fallen trees that littered the countryside.

"I'm hoping the power will come back on today and the

phone by the end of next week."

"Is that why you called on Adam's phone?" Hannah asked. Both she and Edward had thought it odd. He always seemed to be with her when she called them. Adam obviously fancied their Mum big time. Shame he was engaged to Belinda, because he was just the sort of man their mum needed.

"Yes, he has a charger in his car." Her mum blushed as she added, "I'd have struggled without his help."

Chapter 27

"Do you want to go straight home?" Clare asked as she changed gear. She wasn't sure how badly the visit to Rosie would hit Hannah, but was determined not to let it undermine her decision to let Hannah take responsibility for her wellbeing. It was going to be hard to keep it up, especially if Hannah made bad choices.

"No. You said May had baked mince pies for me. And I want to meet Pete and Abby and Joe after all Gary told me about them."

"I didn't want to make a big thing of it but May hasn't been well. Nothing too serious, just remember she needs to rest as much as possible and don't let on that we're worried about her."

"Will she be okay?"

"Yes, if we can keep her from getting stressed."

"Anything I can do?"

Clare loved that Hannah's first reaction was to throw out an offer of help.

"Actually, there is something. May's worried because she hasn't told social services about Pete and Abby. She thinks, especially if she's unwell, the authorities might not believe she's capable of looking after them. If the kids agree to contact their mother, she might give her permission for them to stay, so May won't have to involve outsiders"

"I'll try."

"Thanks."

"One other thing, the belated Christmas party we promised, would you mind terribly if we postpone? The storm and May not being too well has put everyone under a lot of pressure. We can reschedule once the nursery is open and the show garden plans are back to normal."

"Of course, I don't mind. We could have a reopening celebration instead.

"Good idea."

"Mum, you won't expect us to go back and stay with Dad, will you?"

Much as she would love to stop them ever seeing him again after his behaviour in France, she feared repercussions if she did.

"No. I'll accept whatever you decide."

"Edward swears he'll never go back."

"Let's not worry about that today."

Hannah got an excited welcome from Limbu. Once she had calmed him down she hugged May and within minutes was chatting to Pete and Abby and was introduced to Shep. It was wonderful to watch the way Abby behaved as if she had known Hannah for years.

Clare noticed Gary's protective gaze. His dash to Hannah's bedside showed their relationship was close. How the event would change things remained unclear. When her own mother had delivered her unwelcome advice concerning Gary after the birthday party Clare had dismissed her concerns. She trusted Gary not to take advantage of Hannah. What she thought then still applied, whatever happened, it was not her place to interfere.

Clare sat with May enjoying the closeness of family. May had made sure there was enough food for everyone so Clare

205

wouldn't have to rush home to cook.

After they'd eaten May tapped her arm, nodded towards Edward and said quietly, "Spend some time with him."

Across the table, Edward was crumbling a mince pie pastry into a powder. Alien behaviour, as he'd usually demolish a mince pie in two mouthfuls. May's astute observation prompted Clare into action.

Hannah was happily playing monopoly with Pete and Abby. Edward, never keen to play, had declined join in. Clare saw her chance to have a proper conversation with him for a change. She had wanted to talk to him before the ski trip, but the opportunity never turned up.

"Edward, let's leave them to play and go home. I've found lots of information for your family history project."

Edward hesitated before answering. "Okay."

"Gary can you walk Hannah back when the game is over?" she asked.

He nodded, and after a quick farewell, they headed off.

As soon as they got inside, Clare dug the envelope from the records office out of the drawer and placed it on the table. Edward opened his rucksack and took out a folder which he put down beside it.

"You took your project with you on holiday?" Clare asked.

"Yes, I hoped to get some answers from Dad, but he never stuck around long enough for us to talk."

"Maybe there's a clue in here." She tapped the envelope which contained the replacement documents. She'd had a quick look through them, wondering if they would help Edward with his project.

He flipped through the contents. "These are copies of the ones I found in the kitchen drawer ages ago." He sounded disappointed.

"I wish you'd said something. I thought your dad had taken them, so I sent off for duplicates. Weren't they useful?"

"Not really, except that it helped link to some stuff I'd

found on the web. Uncle Norman's daughter, the one who lives in Australia, has done a family tree. At first, I wasn't sure if I'd found the right family because some entries didn't fit."

"Such as?"

"Dad having an older brother... and a twin sister."

"Must be a mistake. He always said he was an only child."

"That's what I thought. Anyway since then I've got copies of their birth certificates."

"Show me."

Edward dug through the pages in his folder and pulled out two sheets of paper.

Clare studied them, wanting to find some entry that would prove Edward wrong. The documents appeared to be correct, which contradicted everything she knew about Mike and her belief that he was an only child. If they existed, what had happened to them? More to the point, why had the family kept this secret?

"I wanted to ask Dad, but I'll ask Gran Hilda and Grandad Denis instead."

Mike's over-reaction when she suggested going to them for family history information was starting to make sense.

"Don't rush into anything. Let's dig for more before we bother them." She wanted to have time to think. "Let me talk to Uncle Norman first, if his daughter made the family tree, the information probably came from him." Norman was older than Mike's father, and might be able to explain the mystery of Mike's siblings. "I owe him a call. I've neglected him since Aunt Elsie died."

Edward nodded, and shoved the folder towards her. "You'd best read through what I've found so far."

Clare's imagination whirled into overdrive. Why had Mike and his parents kept this secret? She distinctly remembered several conversations when her mother-in-law referred to Mike as her only child.

The door burst open. Hannah was back. She invited Gary in, but he shook his head.

He waved to Hannah. "See you tomorrow."

Hannah looked at the papers spread out on the table. "Don't stop, I'm heading straight up to bed. Oh, you'll be pleased to hear, Pete's agreed to let Joe go and look for his mum."

"Wonderful. What a relief. I bet May's happy."

"She is, and Adam stopped by, he said to say he was sorry he missed you. He's taken on a big project in London, so won't be around for a while."

Clare tried not to show her disappointment, though deep down she was rather relieved he'd be away. Her response to his declaration of love made things awkward between them, a strain she was happy to live without.

"Goodnight." Hannah slipped out of the room leaving them to finish going through the papers.

"Do you think," Edward said as he pointed to the entries on the family tree, "that they're the reason Dad didn't want to talk about his family and kept avoiding getting involved?"

"I'm sure it is. Do you remember when you first mentioned the project, how uptight he got?"

"Yeah, he did go funny, went into a right grump."

"It can't have been easy for him having a brother and sister die. Back then people didn't talk about things the way we do. He probably never got help to deal with it, nor did his parents. Perhaps they still aren't dealing with their grief. They might have just pushed it to one side hoping to keep it there."

"Do you think there's a link to Cystic Fibrosis? Perhaps that's why Dad doesn't talk about Hannah's illness?"

"I wish I knew," she answered, not wanting to let him guess how much his question bothered her.

"I've been looking up how the genes carry forward from one generation to the next. Do you think I'll pass the gene on?"

"There are a lot of factors involved and tests to be done, but it rather depends on whether your partner is a carrier. Sorry, I haven't kept up to date with the latest research. I should have realized you'd need to understand how it might affect you."

"I doubt I'd have paid much attention if you had. There's no rush for that info right now, it's not as if I'm ready to have kids."

"Thank heavens for that!"

"Let's carry on with this, after you've spoken to Uncle Norman."

"Suits me, I'll go through your notes and see what gaps need filling."

Edward took a glass of milk, an apple and a banana and headed off to his room. Clare fired up her laptop, and followed the link to Norman's family tree. Virtually every branch had a record of a child that died young. None had any indication of cause of death.

If illness had played a big role in Mike's family history over several generations it seemed odd that the family would keep it secret. Especially not mention the deaths of Mike's siblings. She had to remind herself that, without proof, she must not assume Cystic Fibrosis was to blame.

What hurt most was that she'd been married to Mike for nearly 20 years and never found out about his siblings.

She tried to recall Denis and Hilda's reaction to Hannah's diagnosis. Mike hadn't wanted to tell them. She'd insisted they were told and had eventually taken the task in hand and broken the news to them. They hardly said a word, and certainly didn't mention having to deal with sick children let alone death. They had treated the information the same way as Mike, and ignored it, pretending Hannah was one hundred per cent fit.

Thinking about it, the fact that his mother often referred to Mike as her only child was the truth. He was her only surviving child.

Chapter 28

In the following week everyone seemed cheery and engrossed in their varied projects. The nursery was beginning to look as if it might be fit to open sooner than Clare had expected. Their usual staff had really worked hard to create a sense of normality.

May cornered Clare and asked, "Why has Adam gone off?"

"I only know what Hannah told me, something to do with a new project in London."

"Are you sure that's why he's gone?"

Clare guessed what May was thinking. She shrugged hoping May wouldn't press for information. Her emotions were too raw.

"I thought it might have something to do with those letters. I've been fretting I made a mistake in letting you have them and you think I'm interfering."

"Of course I don't. I needed to know, even if it is too late to undo mother's mischief."

"Will you tell her you know?"

"No, not worth the bother." Clare wasn't sure why she gave that answer. Maybe keeping May happy meant more than having a row with her mother.

In the same way she'd never tell May how Adam reacted to the reappearance of the letters. Or why she'd responded the way she had. It was madness. Every bone in her body screamed out with happiness because he'd said he loved her. What self preservation instinct stopped her from telling him she still loved him too? The complication of Belinda provided an easy excuse. No, it was more than that. The fear of having her life taken over again was what kept her silent. Having escaped one difficult relationship, she had no desire to leap into another.

"Did you ever ask why she kept the letters?" Clare asked, wondering if prolonging the torture was necessary.

"Yes, about two years ago," May explained, "when I found the box in my loft. She didn't explain, but convinced me it was too late to change things and not to meddle. I made it clear I wasn't happy, I think guilt has made her keep her distance ever since."

Clare had often wondered what had created the frosty atmosphere between her aunt and her mother. This solved the mystery.

"Why tell me now?"

"Adam's back and it is so obvious you both still have feelings for each other." Clare wanted to deny it but May continued, "I couldn't let him marry Belinda, without you having a chance to put him right about what your mother did."

A tap on the door ended the conversation. Belinda swept in. Clare hadn't seen her since the day she left for Geneva to meet Mike.

"Hi, everyone," she said with more confidence than usual, glancing round to see who was there. Clare thought her smile faded for a second when she spotted Joe. She turned her attention back to Clare.

"Can we have a word in private?" she asked.

Clare was terrified Belinda wanted to announce Adam

had dumped her. She dismissed the idea. Belinda appeared too happy to be about to divulge anything as dramatic. But Belinda requesting a word in private was out of character. What could she have to say? May's raised eyebrows mirrored Clare's puzzlement.

"I was about to pop back to my place for some papers. Should we walk across?"

Belinda stiffened and shook her head. Clare glanced downwards, caught sight of Belinda's narrow strapped stilettos and revised her suggestion. "Perhaps you'd prefer to drive me over."

Belinda nodded and turned back towards the door. Clare followed, grabbing her coat off the peg in the porch. "Don't wait lunch for me," she called over her shoulder, "I'll have something at home."

Belinda was already clearing catalogues off the passenger seat of her car when Clare opened the door and got in beside her. Belinda thrust the pile of papers into her hands and switched on the engine. She had the car in reverse before Clare had time to get the seat belt fastened. She had never known Belinda do anything so fast in her life. Something serious had happened and Clare wasn't sure she wanted to find out what. When Belinda was ready the story would tumble out. So she sat quietly waiting for the onslaught.

Belinda's silence increased Clare's anxiety. Belinda swung out onto the main road, turned down the lane and then on to the entrance to Manor Croft Farm and pulled up on the crunchy pea gravel.

Clare's natural instinct on entering the house was to put the kettle on. As she lifted the Aga hot plate lid, she wondered if she was going to need something stronger than tea or coffee.

Belinda, no longer in a rush, calmly took her coat off, checked her appearance in a mirror, fluffed up her hair, went to where Adam normally sat and eased herself onto the chair.

"Have I done something to upset you, Clare?"

"Of course not. What makes you think that?"

"You didn't say a word on the way over."

"Well, I've been trying to figure out what you had to say that required privacy."

"Oh, I wanted to talk about Mike. I didn't think you'd want an audience."

Clare nearly spilt boiling water over her hand. Mike, what could Belinda have to say about him? It had to be bad to make Belinda worry about others being present.

"Mike?" Clare said, trying to keep her voice calm. She made a concerted effort to concentrate on the task in hand, carefully filling the teapot, and putting the kettle down without slopping boiling water all over herself.

She brought the pot to the table, went back for mugs and milk, then sat opposite Belinda and waited for a reply.

"He's depressed," Belinda said with a sigh.

He's not alone, Clare thought, but stayed silent.

"He wants to see the children. He says you've forbidden them to go and stay with him."

The accusation shocked her. They had made up their own minds not to return to his house. Admittedly, she had done nothing to persuade them otherwise. Why should she? His irresponsible behaviour had wrecked any trust the children might have had in him. She must control her anger. Belinda was only the messenger.

"Sorry, but it's not my fault. For a start, he hasn't bothered to tell them he's back from Europe. If the children decide not to go back, I will stand by their decision. Personally I don't blame them."

"But he's suicidal" Belinda said, her voice breaking with emotion, as she rummaged in her bag for a tissue.

"Suicidal, you have to be joking."

"I'm not."

"Well I don't believe it," Clare answered, placing a tissue box in front of Belinda.

"How can you take that risk?"

213

"I lived with him for eighteen years," Clare snapped back. "He hasn't the guts to commit suicide, just like he hasn't the guts to come and talk to the children."

"But he said you wouldn't let them speak to him."

"He's lying. They don't want to see him. Why should they? He abandoned them in France to go trinket shopping with you in Geneva."

Belinda sat upright.

Clare decided Belinda was reacting to the term, trinket shopping, rather than to the comment about Mike neglecting his children.

Clare carried on. "Bad enough under normal circumstances, but at the time Hannah was in hospital, barely able to breathe. Not exactly a great example of concerned parenting."

Belinda gasped. "He didn't say anything about her being ill."

"No. And I'll tell you why. He's never come to terms with the fact that she has Cystic Fibrosis. He never will. He's been in denial since the day she was diagnosed." She was tempted to add he couldn't handle knowing he carried the gene that combined with hers had passed the disease on.

"But he wouldn't leave them unless they were safe."

"Belinda, he didn't bother to give them a contact address. If you hadn't told Adam about meeting him in Geneva, we'd never have known they'd been left on their own for three days."

"Hey, don't try to pin the blame on me."

"I'm not, but for heaven's sake don't let him fool you with his lies."

"Did he lie when he told me Adam stayed on here after I left?" There was an icy sharpness in her tone.

"You saw the damage the storm caused. Did you expect him to leave May and me to cope?"

"No, I suppose not," Belinda mumbled.

"But Mike did lie to you. Adam didn't stay on after you

214

left."

Belinda stirred her tea, even though she didn't take sugar, and looked Clare straight in the eye. "So where is he now?"

"I believe he's in London," Clare answered truthfully. Belinda's frown made her add, "He told May he'd be gone for a while. I presumed you were with him."

"No, I can't even get him on the phone," Belinda admitted. "Do you think he's mad with me because I went to Geneva?"

Clare, keen to avoid getting involved, got up and went to the fridge. "I'm sure he isn't." She pulled out a chunk of cheese. "Fancy a cheese and tomato sandwich? I must eat something before I go to fetch Hannah. She's over visiting Rosie."

"The girl at the party in the wheelchair?"

"Yes."

"How is she?"

"The doctors can't do any more for her at the hospital, so they've let her go home." Clare spread butter on the bread in front of her.

"Will she survive?"

Clare shook her head. "It doesn't look good, but she's a remarkable child. She's so cheerful and so pleased to be out of hospital. She sleeps a lot. Hannah likes to be there when she wakes up." Clare made up the sandwiches and passed a plate across to Belinda. "I'm dreading getting the news she's gone. Hannah will be devastated."

"I'm sure she will," Belinda agreed. "But what are you going to do about Mike?"

Clare nearly choked on her sandwich. Why couldn't Belinda listen? Next she'd be asking advice on how to get Adam to fix a date for their wedding. "Nothing," she said firmly. "I thought I'd already made that clear to you."

Belinda didn't seem at all put out by the response. "You know he's worried about Edward. He thinks he's mixing with a bad crowd. He's been seen out drinking."

Clare pushed her sandwich aside. She'd heard enough. "Sorry to rush you, Belinda. I must head off now. Hannah will be waiting for me."

She stood up to make the point. Belinda looked up at her and said, "Ok, I'll tell Mike you're not interested in what the children are up to."

Clare had to react. "Belinda, if you value our friendship you'll not interfere. If Mike's concerned about the children he should speak to me, not send you as a messenger. Tell him that. You can also tell him I am well aware of Edward's activities."

Belinda's eyes opened wide. "Sorry, I didn't mean to upset you."

"I know, but I must go now."

Belinda, who had barely touched her sandwich, stood up and grabbed her coat. As she reached the door, she turned to Clare. "And they weren't trinkets. We found some exquisite silver ornaments for the shop. It was so kind of Mike to arrange for me to meet the supplier."

Clare forced a smile but kept silent. This conversation had to end. Nothing excused Mike for neglecting his duty to his children.

Belinda drove off, and Clare followed soon after, not caring how early she'd be. She turned on the radio, wanting to forget her conversation with Belinda. She considered stopping off at the shops but the urge to be close to Hannah was stronger. Rosie's parents could do with some support.

She shivered, thinking how easily their situation could be hers.

Hannah, was two years older than Rosie, and more fortunate. Clare knew a lot of that was down to her insistence on daily physiotherapy sessions and her constant vigilance to ensure Hannah took all the enzymes, supplements and antibiotics needed to allow her to lead a reasonably normal life. People often commented on how slim Hannah was considering her appetite No one understood that Cystic

Fibrosis wasn't restricted to lung problems, nor did they want to hear about the sticky mucous that clogged Hannah's digestive system.

The sun was blindingly low in the sky making driving difficult. Shadows cast by the hedges had stopped the sun drying out the road. Clare drove cautiously down the narrow lane towards the village where Rosie lived, spotted a parking space two doors away from their house, pulled in and checked her watch. Twenty minutes early. She scooped up her bag, got out of the car, locked the door and rang the doorbell.

Rosie's mother greeted her with a hug and a sense of desperation.

"Thanks for letting Hannah visit. It means so much to her. She's had so little opportunity to make friends her own age." The rush of words stemmed from the anguish. Clare listened, not sure whether to interrupt or let her pour it all out. "Yesterday she said how happy she was to be at home. She wanted to thank Hannah for making us understand. Hannah's so sweet... it's hard for her too, seeing her friend like that, knowing... knowing..."

Clare had to stop her. She squeezed her hand. "Hannah wants to come, whatever anyone said and no matter how tough it is."

"Rosie's so weak, she can't hold out much longer." Ellen wiped away an escaped tear. "Can't break down now... let me make you a coffee?"

Clare accepted, mainly as a diversion for Ellen.

"Why don't you stick your head in and tell Hannah you're here while I put the kettle on."

To refuse was impossible. Clare took a deep breath, and walked down the corridor to the downstairs room they had converted into a bedroom for Rosie. She listened for voices but heard none, so quietly slipped into the room. Hannah sat on the edge of the bed, holding her friends tiny almost translucent hand.

217

Both girls looked at her as she entered. She moved over to the bedside and took Rosie's other hand in hers. The two girls had tears in their eyes. Clare sensed a tension she'd never noticed on earlier visits. Words seem inappropriate, so she stayed silent.

After a moment Rosie gasped, "Bye, Hannah. Thanks..." One of Hannah's tears splashed onto the mask she was wearing. Rosie's grip tightened on her friend's hand as she added, "Ask my Mum to come... and please make that call for me."

Hannah wiped her eye with the back of her free hand. She stood up, leaned over, and hugged her friend. Rosie made one more whispered plea. "Don't be sad."

Hannah bravely let go of Rosie, nodded to Clare and walked to the door. Clare bent down and kissed Rosie's forehead and followed Hannah out.

"Rosie needs you." Hannah said simply to Rosie's parents. Ellen and Bill seemed torn between comforting Hannah and going to Rosie's bedside.

Clare put her arm round Hannah. "Go on, we're okay."

After they had gone, Hannah took off the mask, went to wash her hands then took her phone out. Clare wondered who she had to call.

"Dr. James, Rosie says the pain's worse, can you come?" Hannah's voice faltered as she ended the call.

She slid the phone back into her pocket and turned into Clare's outstretched arms.

Nothing would make the situation better. All Clare could do was offer comfort and help Hannah to find the strength to cope.

To leave at this point was impossible. Clare had to respond to Hannah's needs, which most likely would be to stay, at least until after Dr. James arrived. Clare called May, explained the situation, asked May to get Gary to keep an eye out for Edward and to feed him if they were late home.

Hannah sat down at the table. Clare joined her. The cup

of coffee Rosie's mother had made for her had gone cold.

To break the growing silence she said, "Your friendship means a lot to Rosie." She hoped that might be a comfort to Hannah.

"She knows it won't be long," Hannah said.

Clare reached out and held her hand. Silence engulfed them. Gradually unfamiliar noises kicked in, the humming of the fridge, the slosh of the washing machine and then the tapping of rain against the window.

Hannah eventually spoke. "Mum, I've decided to leave school."

Clare knew this was not an impulsive decision. Hannah needed acceptance. Clare felt trapped by the timing as well as the request itself. How could she object? The mother in her wanted to insist Hannah continued with her studies, but first she must discover what had prompted the change of plan.

"Why?" Her response being neither acceptance nor refusal.

"I want to get involved with stable day outings for sick children. I've talked to Sue who thinks it's a brilliant idea." Clare couldn't argue against that. She'd seen the joy Rosie experienced on Hannah's birthday when she got close to a horse, and the joy Hannah got from organizing the event.

Hannah must have thought her silence meant disapproval, because she added, "You saw how much it meant to Rosie?"

"I think it's a wonderful idea, but..."

"Oh, Mum, you always have a 'but'..."

"I know, just being practical. You realize setting up something like that takes time. I also think staying on and doing your exams in June is important."

"What do I need exams for? Sue didn't seem bothered."

Clare hated to burst the bubble of enthusiasm, but honesty was called for. "No one is disputing your skill with horses or people, but if you want other adults to take you seriously you need to pass those exams. No one will trust a sixteen year old school drop-out with their sick child." Hannah's shoulders drooped with disappointment. Clare added, "Otherwise I think it is a great idea, and I'll do all I can to help you."

"Do you really mean that?"

"Yes, and if you can bear waiting, you'll get more support from me than I can offer right now. What with the storm damage and the show garden, I am going to be short of time for the next few months."

Hannah sat looking glum then muttered, "Okay, point made. I'll stay until after the exams."

"Good. Meanwhile you and Sue can make plans, work out the practicalities and look for others willing to help you. You could even build a website, plan your advertising material. Maybe you can turn your marketing and business plan into a project for one of your exams."

Hannah's face lit up. The idea of combining her new project with her schoolwork cheered her up. Then her frown returned. "What will Dad say?"

"Don't worry, I'll tell him," Clare promised. He'd probably lose his temper, but she didn't care. Hannah needed to do this, just as she needed to do her physio every day. "Have you discussed your plan with Gary?"

Clare was adjusting to the closeness between Hannah and Gary. It was silly, but sharing the responsibility for Hannah's physio still felt rather strange. The timing was right to have someone else involved. Being over-possessive was unhealthy and, while the twice daily sessions over the years had bound them together, she had to let go or she might lose the special bond those sessions created.

Dr. James arrived. Clare let him in, and watched him head off towards Rosie's bedside. When she got back to the kitchen, Hannah was in the throes of a violent coughing fit.

"Want some physio while we wait?" Clare suggested.

Hannah nodded and positioned herself at a good angle for Clare to start the rhythmic tapping on her back to shift

220

the mucous. Time seemed unimportant, as Clare steadily pounded the different lobe areas, stopping occasionally while Hannah coughed up the loosened matter. Normally Clare would end the session when she thought Hannah's lungs sounded clear, but there was something soothing about the activity.

Dr. James returning brought the session to a close.

His serious expression showed his concern over Rosie's condition.

"I think you should go," he said. "I've increased Rosie's pain relief. She'll sleep now longer than before."

"Is there anything we can do?" Clare asked as she wrapped her arms round Hannah, knowing from his expression that things were reaching crisis point.

"No. I'll stay as long as they need me," he answered. Clare shuddered, thinking how often he faced situations like this.

"Will you let us know if something happens?" He nodded and held the door open for them as they left.

Chapter 29

When they got back to the nursery, Pete and Abby were looking tense. Joe hadn't come back from his trip to find their mother. May appeared to have run out of ideas to keep the pair occupied and was more than happy to have someone arrive to share the task. Clare hoped that cheering the children up would distract Hannah from the harrowing afternoon she'd spent at Rosie's bedside.

Hannah pulled out a game to play and soon laughter filled the room. Clare helped May prepare an evening meal for them all. Edward was still not back from his rugby practice, which gave Clare time try to once more to talk to Uncle Norman, who was due back from holiday.

She slipped into the office to make the call.

"Hello, Norman," Clare said, "I'm sorry I missed you at Christmas." He had been among the family gathered by parents-in-law to celebrate together in Cornwall. Clare regretted not doing more about keeping in touch in the two years since his wife died.

"Me too. The weather was terrible. Stopped us from walking as much as I'd have liked, but it was lovely to be together with my daughter. She was over from Australia to visit the rest of the family. I hope you enjoyed the ski slopes."

This comment warned her Mike's parents were either ignorant of the break-up, or pretending not to know.

"I didn't go. Mike took the children. They had some bad weather too."

"What a shame."

"I wonder if you can help me," Clare said.

"Be delighted."

"Edward's doing a family history project and found a link to the family tree your daughter put on the internet. A couple of entries puzzled us."

"Such as?"

"Mike having a brother and a sister."

"You didn't know? You really ought to get Mike or his parents to fill you in?"

"Not so easy, Mike and I have separated, communication is strained, and his mother barely talks to me."

"Ah, I see your problem, but I'm not sure I can help. I was serving abroad with the Navy when the children died."

"Do you remember anything about them?"

"The older boy had always been sickly. He'd have been about seven when he died. The shock of losing a second child within two months nearly destroyed the family. She was younger, about three, and I believe she had been quite healthy, so they were totally unprepared for her death."

"Do you know what they died of?"

"No."

"How did Hilda and Denis take it?"

"Very badly. I always regretted that I missed the children's funerals. On my return, my wife warned me not to say anything. Said the family preferred it that way. I was cowardly enough to agree and never broached the subject, and neither did they."

"Do you think they ever came to terms with their loss?"

"No, they just coped as best they could. Luckily they still

had Mike. They had to keep going for his sake. I wish I could tell you more."

"Can I come back to you if I think of anything else?"

"Be a pleasure. I'll look forward to hearing from you. Don't let leaving Mike keep you away."

"I won't, thanks."

After she put the phone down the phrase about the sickly child kept going through her head, making it hard to dismiss the idea that CF caused their deaths. The secrecy was another issue, but could have been part of their coping strategy.

May asked what was bothering her, but Joe returned from his search for Pete and Abby's mother before she had time to explain.

Joe sank into a chair. Everyone gathered round, eager to hear his news.

"Your mum sends her love. She's really missed you."

"You didn't tell her where we are?" Pete asked

"No, I promised you I wouldn't, but she really wants to see you. She begged me to persuade you to fix a meeting. The boyfriend's gone. She threw him out when she read your note. She wishes you had told her rather than run off, but understood your fear that he'd convince her you were liars. Your letters made her cry. But she's not cross with you, just happy you are okay."

"What happens next?" Clare asked.

"I said I'd arrange for her to meet May. That way she can judge for herself that you are getting good care. She understands the authorities will get involved if she doesn't give her permission for you to stay and she doesn't want that under any circumstances."

"Sounds promising," May said.

"I think so. All that matters to her is their wellbeing."

"Will you go and meet her?" Pete asked May.

"Of course I will."

"I fixed to meet again on Saturday. She's called, Dawn.

We can work from there."

Later when the children were distracted, Joe gave May and Clare a more detailed report of Dawn's circumstances. "Didn't take long to see what a rough area it was. The gardens are overgrown or covered in concrete and junk. No sign of kids playing and the only people hanging about looked like drug addicts."

"What did she have to say about the place?" May asked.

"She hates it, but she can't afford to move. Also she was afraid if she did the children would never be able to find her."

"Does she work?"

"Not at the moment. She had a job catering in a nursing home, but that closed six months ago and she hasn't had any luck since."

"Do you think she's genuinely trying?"

"Yes, she's smart and bright like her kids. I know you'll get on. I waited until I knew she was home, stuck a note through her letterbox saying I'd meet her in the café on the corner if she was interested in finding her children.

"I hadn't even ordered a cuppa before she arrived. She was that desperate for news of them. She cried when I handed her their letters and even more when she read them. No faking those tears."

"What did she say about getting the authorities involved?"

"She doesn't want them involved if it can be avoided. Though she said she would have to let the police know they were safe and get them off their records, and also have to get them off the missing children register. She isn't sure of the procedure or if any of them would want to follow up. But she is happy to go along with whatever the children want.

Chapter 30

Hannah struggled to put Rosie out of her mind. Every time the phone rang she expected to hear her friend had slipped away. Visiting wasn't an option as her high dose pain killers meant she was asleep most of the time.

It was impossible to talk about Rosie's failing health without it sounding as if she wanted sympathy which was so far from how she felt. The unexpected stay in hospital in France had brought home how lucky she had been to stay so active for so long. Now she knew how quickly things could go downhill she was determined to avoid letting anything like that happen again.

Health aside, she was more aware of how everything had changed since Christmas.

Her mum acted differently. She'd stopped crowding her and attempting to control her every move. Instead she was actively encouraging her to make decisions. For years she'd wanted this, but now she longed for the comfort of the old regime.

She did wonder if getting Edward and then Gary involved with her physio had left her mum feeling sidelined. True, she wanted her mum off her back, but she never expected it to feel so odd.

The fact that she and Edward no longer had to remember which house they were sleeping in should have made life easier. In a way it did, but the time they'd spent together at their father's house had brought her and Edward closer. Now he was being rather distant. There were no signs that drink was to blame, but when pushed he said he was struggling with one of his school projects. She didn't believe him, and was convinced something more serious was bothering him.

May was doing okay, but not quite her normal bubbly self. The invasion of extra people into her household kept her occupied. Pete and Abby helped, but preparing food for the endless flow of people using the house as a base, while the nursery was being pulled back into shape, meant there was never much of a break for any of them. In addition to the usual staff who worked at the nursery, Joe had asked some of his mates, an odd assortment of ex-soldiers to help out. May naturally took on the task of feeding them too.

Hannah knew that all the extra man power was necessary, but it changed the pace of Dovedales and had even spilt over into their new home. The calm atmosphere she was used to had become charged with continuous activity, everyone rushing from one task to the next without stopping.

Hannah hated the bustle and found herself wishing she could sneak back to her father's house for some peace. But, as she hadn't forgiven him for his reaction to her illness in France, going there was not an option. He didn't even know how she felt. He hadn't attempted to make contact since then.

Gary was the only person in his usual place, in the greenhouse, sorting out what could be saved. She had wanted to spend time with him, but felt she was needed more helping May. It seemed ages since the flight home. She knew their relationship had altered ever so slightly, but was afraid

227

to test how much. His coming to rescue her and his willingness to learn to do her physio had been unexpected, but wonderful. She knew what she wanted from the relationship, but was terrified the slightest hint might scare him off forever.

Hannah used the time to help with the relentless round of prepping vegetables for soups and stews and making cakes and apple tarts for supper.

After they'd eaten, her mother got a phone call from Belinda. It was obvious from the one sided half they overheard that Belinda was in a state.

"I'll come over as soon as I can. Don't do anything until we've talked. See you soon."

Once the call was over, her mum made her apologies saying that she needed to go out.

Hannah was put out. She had hoped that her mother would give her a good hard physio session. Since France, she had become more anxious about letting her lungs become even slightly congested.

Almost immediately her mother came up with a solution before she even had a chance to speak.

"Gary, I need to go over to see Belinda. Could you help out with Hannah's physio?"

Gary nodded, no hesitation, in fact he looked pleased to have been asked.

With that her mother dashed off, leaving them to clear up, and make their own way home.

"How are you coping since coming home?" Gary asked as they made their way back to the farm.

"Okay, though I'll be glad when things quieten down and the place gets back to normal"

"Not sure it ever will."

"What do you mean?"

"Well, the expansion means we should be a lot busier than before."

"I suppose so. I'm not sure I'll like it as much."

"Oh, don't worry there'll always be quiet corners to go to, I'll make certain of that."

"That's a relief."

"I wonder what Belinda wanted that made your mum rush of so quickly. Has she said anything about Adam to you?"

"No. Why would she?"

"I thought they might have had a row."

"What about?"

"Who knows, maybe he told her he still fancies her."

"What?"

"You know they were pretty close years ago. I don't think he ever got over her."

"You're kidding."

"No. After the storm they spent a lot of time together."

"True, but she spends time with lots of people, Joe included, and I can't see them getting close."

Hannah let them into the house, shed her outer clothing and hung it up. Gary flung his coat on the back of a chair in the kitchen and followed her upstairs to the physio table.

"Are you okay with having Abby as your constant shadow?" he asked.

Hannah climbed onto the table, stripped off her thick jumper and grabbed a wedge cushion so Gary could start.

"No problem, she's such a lost soul, but she seems to be settling in at school, having me there to look out for her helped. I do hope she and her Mum can sort out their differences. Her position has really made me appreciate my mum even more. How are you coping with Pete?"

"Pete? He's great, never complains about anything, he just gets on with whatever I ask him to do. I was worried it wouldn't work out, but I'm glad we gave them a break."

"Do you think they'll stay?"

"I hope so, for their sakes. Joe thinks their mum might move nearer so she can see them more. Enough talking, let's concentrate on you. Which area needs the most work?"

Hannah pointed to a spot, and closed her eyes as he started the rhythmical patting.

"Music?"

"Why not?" He stretched over and pressed the play button on her iPod and continued. His pummelling worked. Hannah soon had the desired coughing fit.

She didn't want him to stop, but was too tired to demand more.

"Fancy joining me for some hot chocolate before you go?" she asked. She'd be making one for herself to have along with her late night snack and the last of her medication for the day.

"No. But thanks for the offer. I need to head back."

Hannah was disappointed. She wanted to ask him if he knew what was bugging Edward to make him so withdrawn. It could wait. Gary had already put himself out for her, and it wasn't fair to press him to stay now.

"I promised Joe I'd drive him into town to check up on his old mate, Simon."

His explanation made her feel better because it meant he wasn't rushing off to get away from her. He was simply honouring a commitment.

Chapter 31

The week waiting for news of Rosie dragged on. Clare watched Hannah with her new shadow Abby, both of whom watched over May, who in turn kept an eye on them.

Clare was conscious of the fact that Hannah had not talked about the prospect of Rosie dying. Every attempt to broach the subject failed as Hannah always turned the conversation round.

Knowing that the three of them were there for each other left Clare no choice but to leave them to it and go off to supervise the clearing up of the storm damage.

The bulk of the fallen trees blocking the drive had either been heaved aside, or chopped and stacked. What was left would have to wait until the fields were dry enough to get heavy lifting gear on site.

Gary and Pete were systematically rechecking every pot for glass splinters, grouping them out of the way of the builders. The tender plants were crammed into the surviving greenhouse space. A new poly-tunnel was on order but would take a while before it was erected.

Clare was deeply indebted to Joe, and his ex-army friends who were more industrious than any of the crew Adam had employed to assist before he abandoned Dovedales for his London project.

The new building was progressing with the builders promising completion by the end of the month. Clare didn't dare share their confidence. Her battle with the insurance company dragged on, making her nervous about ever arriving at a fair compensation figure.

Since the storm she had done nothing about her show garden. The markers put in the ground had blown away along with her hopes, making her think about postponing for a year. Sadly the competition rules stated the prize was valid for that year only so she either had to proceed or lose the opportunity.

Much as she wanted to drop out, she knew that the decision would hurt others more than herself, the children in particular. She didn't want anyone to have cause to take the blame for her weakness. Trying to explain how hard the break up with Mike had hit her, let alone the disruption of the family unit, including moving house was impossible. The extra pressure of taking on a share of the responsibility at Dovedales and coping with the storm damage, topped by worrying about May's health, not to mention the situation with Pete and Abby had left her completely drained and terrified the show garden might stretch her beyond her limits.

Edward was also on her mind. He was barely able to hide the anger he felt towards his father for abandoning Hannah in hospital. The addition of the confusing entries on the family tree had made matters worse. If he had been able to confront his father it might have helped, but Mike had not made contact with any of them since they had flown back from France.

Clare couldn't get Edward to talk though she was sure that the discoveries he'd made would have triggered worries about the genetic issues he'd have to deal with in the future. She hadn't made a big thing of it, because she hadn't had time to check on the latest genetic findings. All she had done was suggest they make an appointment with Dr. James to ask the relevant questions.

The situation with Edward made her conscious of the fact she had focused all her energy into the fight to keep Hannah healthy, without considering the impact the disease had on Edward. This oversight was one she had to rectify. She had to become better prepared for any future problems the family were likely to face.

The phone rang.

It was Dr James.

"Rosie slipped away early yesterday morning" he said. "Her parents are still struggling to take it in. They asked me to call and let Hannah know. They wanted to be sure that someone was with her when she got the news."

Clare asked if he knew what the funeral plans were.

"Rosie asked for something simple and soon. The undertaker and the local vicar are both family friends, and they are working together to follow her wishes. It could be as early as Wednesday, I'll let you know."

She thanked him and ended the call.

The news pushed her day to day worries aside. Once again Hannah became her priority.

Clare made a quick detour via May's house. She wanted May to know in case her support was needed. Then she went to the far greenhouse to find Hannah who had gone there to work with Gary.

Hannah saw her approaching and didn't need to hear the words spoken. The fact that Clare had come to find her was enough.

"She's gone, hasn't she?" Hannah said before Clare had a chance to speak.

Clare nodded. "Dr James called. He said the end was very peaceful. Getting her home had been a good decision. He's going to call back once the funeral plans are fixed."

"Thanks. Don't worry. I'll be okay." Hannah dodged a hug by pulling a trolley, laden with plants, into the gap between them.

Clare wanted to give her a big hug and hold her while she cried, but had to accept Hannah would grieve in her own way in her own time. All she could do was keep a close watch and be there if needed. The current calm acceptance might not last.

Gary stood nearby, watching the exchange. A tiny nod was the only signal he gave to indicate he'd look out for Hannah. It was a small comfort knowing Hannah wouldn't have to deal with her grief on her own.

"Can you tell Edward?" Hannah asked. There was a break in her voice, a hint of how hard it was to hold things together.

"Don't worry, I will. Do you want to stay down here for a while?"

Hannah nodded.

Clare half wished Hannah had burst into tears and clung to her for comfort, but that was unlikely to happen. Tears would fall eventually only the timing was in doubt. It didn't feel quite so heartless to walk away, knowing Gary was there.

To please Hannah, she left the greenhouse to find Edward to break the news. She thought he'd intended to go to the library so she tried to leave a message for him. His phone didn't appear to be working. Switched off or dead, she couldn't tell. After an hour she tried again. Nothing. Eventually she went home to see if he was there. He wasn't, but the red light on the answer phone was flashing. She listened to the waiting message.

"Hi Mum. I've decided to head up to York to see Gran and Grandad. I'm fed up waiting for Dad, and need to get the project finished. Don't worry about me. I'll call tonight when I get there."

Clare knew he'd left the house very early in the morning, before she got up to do Hannah's physio. She'd assumed he was heading out for an early morning run, and had been pleased, thinking he was back into training with enthusiasm.

It never occurred to her he'd take off to confront his grandparents. How would he travel, train or bus?

Her mind went into overdrive. How long was the journey? Would he have arrived? Should she warn her in-laws that he was on the way? It was probably too late, and she didn't feel her own emotional state could cope with such a potentially difficult call.

She went online and checked the bus timetable. If he had caught the earliest bus, which was also the fastest, he would be in York by now, even if it took an hour from the bus station to his grandparents' house, he was bound to have arrived.

Could she bear to wait for him to make contact as promised? The only trouble with doing that was Hannah's reaction. She had specifically asked Clare to break the news about Rosie and wouldn't understand Clare's reluctance to contact him at his grandparents without a long detailed explanation. The only sensible solution was to enlist May's help.

"May, I need a big favour. Could you call Edward at Mike's parents' house and pass on the news about Rosie? I can't explain, but I don't feel up to dealing with Hilda at the moment."

"Don't worry. I'll do it now," May answered.

Clare hated passing the task on, but May would say the right things to Edward to soften the blow. She was also less likely to get involved with the more complicated issues Edward's visit to his grandparents might have triggered.

May phoned her back ten minutes later.

"What is going on? I know you and Hilda have always had a difficult relationship, but I didn't expect to her to give me an earful about messing with other people's business. When I said I had no idea what she meant, she muttered something about Mike being on his way to collect Edward and bring him home. She sounded so angry. Anyway she hung up on me before I got to tell him about Rosie."

"Sorry. I should have warned you. I was being cowardly."

"You expected trouble?"

"Yes, I guess I did. I should never have asked you to get involved."

"What's going on?"

"While delving into the family tree Edward discovered Mike had a brother and sister that we knew nothing about. Mike has not been very helpful, so Edward has rushed off to confront his parents. I didn't know he was going, so wasn't able to warn them and give them time to prepare for awkward questions."

"No wonder she isn't herself."

"I know. Anyway thanks for trying. I'll contact Mike and ask him to break the news about Rosie."

"Good luck."

"Thanks."

She felt helpless, and wished she could go and rescue Edward, but Hannah couldn't be left at a time like this.

She wondered how Mike would react. If he'd talked to Edward when she had asked then they would never had been put in this position.

She tapped in his phone number. The message service kicked in immediately. She rang off, preferring to leave a text message than a voice message.

She wrote. "Understand you are fetching Edward. Please get him to call. Hannah's friend Rosie died. No funeral details yet, could be very soon. I think Hannah could do with his support."

She read the message over. Did it appear hostile? She hoped not, but she didn't want it to sound as if she was ready to cosy up to Mike.

Hannah had come back to May's with Gary. May asked if she and Clare were staying for supper, but Hannah shook her head. Clare quickly put on her coat to walk home with Hannah. A quiet evening in was probably a good idea. They headed home and Clare opened a tin of soup which they ate in silence. Afterwards Clare suggested Hannah needed a physio session. It felt right to make an extra effort and Clare carried on tapping away much longer than was actually necessary. Hannah still didn't cry. Maybe the tears would come in the night when she was alone.

Clare kissed her goodnight and made her way to her own bed.

She hadn't had a reply from Mike or any communication from Edward. She read as she waited. It was long after midnight before a text arrived from Mike.

"Edward's fine. Sorry about Rosie. Stopping here tonight. Very awkward situation. Will try to get Edward back in time for the funeral."

Clare was surprised at his admission of things being awkward. Could it possibly mean he'd be more open to discussing his family issues in the future?

Chapter 32

Even though she was exhausted Clare struggled to get to sleep. It had been the same every night since the storm. Tonight, she lay in bed staring at the cupboard where she had hidden the box of unopened letters. She hadn't been able to bring herself to read them, though on several occasions she had been tempted to take them down and throw them into the study fire. Burning them would not wipe out the knowledge they had ever existed, or change the present.

She'd spent a surreal evening listening to Belinda going on and on about Adam. How he had abandoned her and gone off to London. How neglected she felt. How she was considering ending their relationship. Clare had found herself in the odd position of begging Belinda not to make any rash decisions, when she really wanted to encourage Belinda to end the relationship. More because she had never thought they were suited than the desire to step into Belinda's shoes. In fact the longer the discussion lasted the less likely it became that she wanted to take Belinda's place.

Would it have been easier if Adam had stuck around? She doubted it. She still loved him, or the idea of the idyllic relationship they had when they were teenagers, but wasn't sure she could survive any long term relationship with him or anyone else. She had told him not to break up with Belinda for that reason, never expecting Belinda to be the one threatening to end the engagement.

The thing that worried her most was that Adam might think that it would change her mind and she'd welcome him back.

In the morning she had a second call from Dr James. This time he was able to tell her the funeral arrangements. She immediately sent Mike a text giving him the details. The service was scheduled for the following day, leaving little time to prepare, but maybe that was a good thing.

She wondered if Gary would tell Adam about Rosie. Not that she expected him to attend the funeral. He had only met her once at Hannah's birthday party.

Gary and May were certain to come if only to support Hannah.

Hannah took the news well. She had already decided what to wear for the occasion. She'd chosen her favourite red jumper and her new denim jeans, the clothes she would have worn to visit Rosie. She had selected a rust coloured coat and green skirt for Clare to wear, saying she didn't think Rosie wanted anyone to wear black. Clare agreed to go along with the choice because all that mattered was Hannah's happiness.

Edward sent a reassuring text to say they were on their way home slowly. They would be back in time and would come direct to the church. There was nothing in the message to indicate whether Edward was happy with the slow journey home. All she could hope was that communication between him and Mike had improved.

On the morning of the funeral, Hannah still managed to put on a brave display of coping even though it looked as if she hadn't slept at all. Clare knew the feeling and guessed her eyes had big rings round them too.

Gary offered to drive them and May to the church. The plan was to arrive there early, ahead of the funeral party.

239

They filed into the village church, took their seats in the heavily carved pews and waited. The organist played a selection of Bach pieces adding to the atmosphere in the church. Weak winter sunlight shone through the stained glass windows casting colourful dots on the pillars that lined the aisles. Hannah shivered violently, a shiver that had nothing to do with the cold. Clare put an arm around her.

Clare remembered the last time she had been in this church. It was her and Mike's first Christmas together and his parents had insisted this was the Carol service they wanted to attend. Clare hadn't known his parents well enough to question what made this particular church so important. Mike had muttered something about their having lived nearby when he was little. To avoid upsetting his mother they had agreed to drive her there. It was memorable for the wrong reasons. They had gone early so they could look round the church. Clare could still visualize the tomb in the enclosed chapel near the alter. The exquisite carved marble figures lying together on the top were beautiful, but it was the ten children lined up along the side of the tomb, two were represented by sculls on cushions held by their older siblings that had stuck in her memory. Today didn't feel like the right occasion to check if her memory was accurate.

Mike's mother had fainted before the service even began. They'd managed to revive her and get her out before the congregation arrived. Clare didn't think any of them had ever returned to the church after their move to York.

She turned to May who was sitting next to her. The last funeral Clare had attended was Arthur's. May gave Clare a weak smile, as if she knew what Clare was thinking. She looked round and saw Edward had made it. Adam was also there half hidden behind one of the pillars on the far side of the church. He nodded to acknowledge her. She nodded back and looked away without finding out if Belinda was with him. Then she spotted Mike coming in. Clare concentrated on Edward. He waved to her and reacted to her signal that she had kept a space for him and made his way up the side aisle to take his place in the pew next to Hannah. Mike followed and squeezed in beside him.

She faced the alter in an attempt to avoid making eye contact. Mike didn't have to join them. Was he that desperate to impress the children? Did he think they'd believe he'd cared about Rosie?

Edward must have been mind reading because he gave a nudge and angled his head in Mike's direction and mouthed, "It's okay."

Further conversation was impossible. The music volume increased to signal of the start of the service. The congregation stood up. Rosie's coffin was carried in, Ellen and Bill followed. The heady scent of freesias filled the nave as the procession moved up the aisle. Clare held Hannah's hand through the prayers and hymns and while Dr James spoke about Rosie, describing her bravery and unfailing capacity for cheerfulness right to the end of her short life.

Tears were blinked back or wiped away. All too soon the service was over. The coffin bearers moved into place and carried Rosie on her final journey. Ellen and Bill, supporting each other, filed out after them. Their grief was visible and painful to witness. The congregation followed the procession as it tracked across the grass to the top northwest corner of the churchyard to a freshly dug grave. The mourners circled round for the last act. Clare kept her arm around Hannah's shoulder. Edward stood further back with May and Gary. Mike had not followed, which she was grateful for. This was hardly the place for a reunion, though it might have made him feel safe as no one would make a scene at a funeral.

The coffin was positioned over the empty grave. A short prayer was said and the pallbearers lowered the casket into place and the closing blessing was said. There seemed to be reluctance on Ellen and Bill's part to throw the offered scoopful of earth onto the coffin. Somehow they found the strength, after which, they dropped a pink rose bud on top.

241

Clare imagined it must be the most painful act of all. The last thing they could do for their daughter. They had done what was expected of them, they stepped aside to let others follow their lead. Hannah bravely moved forward and added her handful of earth. Clare did likewise. Gradually the rest of the congregation took their turn. Everyone, that is, except Mike who appeared to have retreated to the farthest corner of the grounds, avoiding looking at the coffin or the grave or at the grief stricken faces of Rosie's parents and friends and even at his own daughter.

His haunted look made Clare regret her unsympathetic thoughts about him. Mike was a mess. This might be the first time he'd come close to having a chance to grieve for his siblings. From the way his parents reacted there was every possibility this was the case, which would explain the way he handled, or more accurately didn't handle Hannah's illness. Then it occurred to her, his parents had lived in the area when he was a child. Could the graves of his siblings be here? Was that what he was searching for?

She tapped Gary on the shoulder. "Keep an eye on Hannah and May."

She hurried over to Edward to find out just how well he and Mike were getting on. He gave her a hug when she reached him.

"Did you get the answers you wanted?" she asked.

"Not to start with. The olds freaked out when I asked them for information. But Dad was great when he picked me up. I think he'd had plenty of time on his way up to figure out what to say. Anyway he told me that his parents forbade him from ever speaking about either his brother or sister. He found it really hard, but thought that was normal behaviour so accepted it."

"That all makes sense. Did anyone mention where they were buried?"

"No, but he did say his family had lived in this village when he was very young. He wondered if he would recognise

242

their house."

"Did he?"

"No, but he doesn't look very happy now."

"What are you talking about?" Hannah asked.

Clare spun round, regretting her reluctance to tell Hannah about Edward's discovery. She didn't have time to explain now. The anguish on Mike's face was too real to ignore.

Edward seemed to sense her dilemma. He quickly said, "I think he needs to talk, and I'm not sure I can help."

"Don't worry, I'll go," Clare said. "But can you explain the situation to Hannah." Edward nodded. "Then go on ahead with Gary. I'll get your father to bring me when he's ready."

May had joined them. She drew Hannah away, Edward followed. They crossed the church yard, joining the other mourners as they left to go to the village hall.

Mike had stopped pacing and staring at headstones when she tapped him on the shoulder. He seemed grateful for her presence when she stopped beside him and didn't pull away when she touched his hand.

"What are you looking for?"

"Their graves."

"They didn't tell you where they were?"

"No never. They told me I must never mention their names." Clare could almost hear his mother repeating that mantra to him. His father would have been instructed to remain silent too. What a terrible way to deal with grief. She didn't suppose for one minute they might have wondered if it would help Mike to talk about his brother and sister. Or that he might need to understand more about their deaths even if he was only three. She could sense that he'd never had any help to cope with the loss of his siblings.

She tightened her grip on his hand. "You can talk to me about Lily and Patrick anytime you want." She deliberately spoke their names. Saying them made them seem more real.

She needed to gauge his reaction.

Mike struggled to swallow. She had touched a raw nerve.

"It never occurred to me to ask where they were buried until today," he mumbled. "I hadn't realized it was important to find out until just now."

"I don't suppose you know why they died?"

He touched her hand. "I don't. No one ever told me anything, but after Hannah was diagnosed with Cystic Fibrosis, I began to wonder. I didn't want to face it. That's why I lied to the doctor when he asked if anyone in the family might have had it. I couldn't accept she might die like my sister and brother. It was easier to refuse to accept that Hannah was ill. Sorry I didn't handle it well, did I?"

"It would have helped if I'd known why you couldn't deal with it. I'd like to hear more about Lily sometime."

"Thanks, I'd appreciate that. You should go to Hannah now, I think she needs you."

"I sent her off with May and Gary and Edward. I said I'd get you to drive me to the hall where they have organized refreshments."

"I don't think I'm up to going to pay my respects."

"Try. It might help Hannah. I think she was very touched that you came today."

"I only came because I had to bring Edward."

"Yes, but you stayed. Trust me, that counts."

As Clare walked to Mike's car, she remembered Mike as he had been when they first married. Back then concern for others had always been at the forefront of everything he did. After Hannah was born he'd become less engaged with people around him. She was so involved with keeping Hannah fit that it was a while before she noticed. As Hannah grew the remoteness increased a little at a time until one day she had felt as if she was living with a stranger.

Arriving at the wake with Mike felt odd, but at the same time his presence added a comforting ring of normality about it. She wondered what everyone would make of their appearing together. The gossip would spread fast, that's for sure.

Mike quickly moved to the quietest corner of the room, leaving her to circulate. Dr James joined him there. The conversation looked rather stilted to start with, but soon they seemed to be engaged in deep discussion to the point where they were ignoring everyone else around them. Clare wondered what topic kept them so animated. She didn't for one second think Mike would ask Dr James for his advice on dealing with grief either for him or for Hannah. The only person who dared interrupt their intense debate was Hannah. She gave her father a nudge followed by a brief kiss on the cheek. He kissed her back, said something to her, which seemed to satisfy her and she walked away.

Mike carried on his intense discussion with the doctor. Clare wondered if she should rescue the doctor. Maybe Mike was being overbearing, but she didn't have the energy to become embroiled in anything deep.

Adam tapped her on the shoulder.

"Good to see you," he said. "I hoped I'd get a chance to talk to you. Gary says they're going to recover the tree tomorrow morning. He's persuaded me to give a hand before I head off back to London. The early start suits me as I need to be on my way after lunch." he said.

"How's the London project?" she asked, hoping to keep the conversation neutral.

"Fine, but intense. Working in a confined space with parking restrictions is a nightmare."

"Guess we're lucky on that score."

"I'd better head off now. Belinda and I have stuff to sort out."

She didn't dare ask what stuff. Had Belinda gone ahead with her threat to break their engagement, or was she going to persevere?

The gathering was beginning to thin out. Clare looked round to see who was left. She had to figure out a plan for getting the family home.

May was sitting quietly at a table near the door. Gary was nearby. Hannah was hugging Rosie's parents. Her hugs appeared to be appreciated. Clare was pleased. Ellen and Bill deserved every scrap of comfort on offer. Edward had joined Mike, but both were looking more at ease than they had for a long time. They looked in her direction, then at each other, nodded and headed over to her.

"My stuff is in Dad's car, he's offered to drop me home. Do you want to come with us, or will you go with Gary?" Edward said.

Clare wanted to refuse, but at the same time didn't want to make Edward feel uncomfortable with his newfound relationship with his father.

"Let me check with Gary. I think May is ready to leave now."

She went over to Gary. "May's looking tired, Mike has offered to take us home, so if you'd like to go ahead with May I think she'd be pleased."

"Sounds like a good plan," he answered. "See you all tomorrow when we attempt to lift that tree."

"Yes."

Clare went to May to thank her for all her support and gave her a kiss goodbye.

When she got back to Mike and Edward, Hannah had joined them.

"Fancy fish and chips?" Mike asked. "The kids are both keen, we can pick them up on the way back."

Clare suspected it was a cunning plan on his part to get into her house. If they went home with fish and chips, they would be duty bound to offer to let him come in and eat with them. She nodded. Fine, if that's what the kids wanted she would go with it.

"Great idea, meet you at the car."

She said good bye to Ellen and Bill and then joined the family outside.

246

When they got to the fish and chip shop, Mike gave Edward some cash and suggested he and Hannah go in to place the order.

The minute they were out of earshot he said, "Clare, sorry. I didn't mean to gate crash your evening. I won't come in if you would rather I didn't."

"Don't worry. If it's okay with the kids its fine with me," she answered. Her desires were immaterial, what the children wanted was far more important.

When they got back to the house, Mike waited for her to suggest where he should sit. He quietly surveyed the kitchen and displayed approval in his expression. He waited for the food to be served and he had their full attention.

"Now we are all together, I want to say something." He looked to Clare for permission to continue. "I owe you all an apology. I have let you all down one way or another."

He looked at them in turn. No one responded. Clare wasn't sure if he expected a response.

"I don't expect you to act as if nothing happened. But I hope one day you'll feel that you can turn to me for support."

Clare felt she must say something. "Thank you, Mike. Meanwhile, I suggest we eat."

"Good idea," he said with a smile, as he reached for the ketchup bottle.

"Hannah, on the way back from York, Edward told me about your plans for working with horses and sick children. I know I was against your leaving school, but having seen you with Rosie on your birthday and witnessed the joy that outing gave her, I'm prepared to give you whatever support you need."

Clare and Hannah looked at each other in disbelief. Getting him to approve the idea had worried them, having him volunteer to help without any pressure was a shock.

"No need to look so startled. I do mean it."

"I'm sure you do." Clare said.

247

"Thanks, Dad." Hannah chipped in.

"I've also been thinking about what Edward said regarding a gap year. In the past I may have been hasty in dismissing the value of travelling abroad. If he can show me a well thought out plan, I'll give my blessing."

Clare looked across to Edward to check his reaction. His big grin said it all. She hadn't seen him looking so happy for a long while.

When their plates were empty, Mike pushed his aside. Clare offered him a coffee. He shook his head. "I think it's probably better if I go. It's been a long day. Maybe we can meet up tomorrow."

Hannah quickly spoke up. "Tomorrow we're all busy. The tree lifting equipment is going to be on site tomorrow."

"Tree lifting?" Mike queried. Clare realised he knew nothing of the show garden, or the current progress of the nursery expansion and recovery programme, which was all tied in with events that occurred after their split.

Edward started to explain. The only problem was that he threw in an invitation for Mike to come and watch.

Clare wanted to object, but knew it would sound petty. What harm would it do if he did show up?

Once again Mike looked to her for approval before he gave his answer.

"I'd love to come, if you don't mind."

Chapter 33

It took an age for Clare to work out what noise woke her. The low loader with the digger had arrived. Voices mingled with clatters and bangs. She leapt out of bed and peered through the window. It was still dark. She grabbed some clothes, hurried to pull them on and made her way outside to see who else had turned up.

Joe had made it, but he never failed to appear when he said he would. Gary was not always on time in the mornings.

Clare hadn't been keen on the idea of having to hire equipment to rescue the tree from beside the pond. The expense being her prime concern, but she'd been out-voted by everyone including May. So the equipment had been booked and the big move was on.

Before they rescued the tree they would have to excavate a holding hole for it. The chosen spot was in the centre of the plot she'd originally marked out for her trial garden.

If they could get it in place they could judge if the tree was right for the show in six months time. The plan was to dig a large hole, then lay porous membranes down to contain the roots of the rescued tree. The tree itself would have to have its existing roots hard pruned to make it manageable and to fit its new home. Once in place, topsoil and nutrients would be packed around the relocated tree to encourage new roots to grow within the restricted space. The whole exercise was designed to make it easier to lift the tree when it was time for the show.

Joe was talking to the digger operator, explaining the first part of the plan, pointing out the location of the first hole. He had brought a can of spray paint to outline the exact dimensions and had already laid out a sheet of membrane on which to place the removed soil. She never ceased to be amazed at his efficiency.

The small digger bucket was selected and the machine inched forward putting its stabilizing legs out. Joe nipped round and placed flat stabilizer boards under each leg before they were lowered. He signalled to the driver to proceed.

Clare expected the task would take a while, so retreated to the house to put the kettle on. She needed a coffee and knew hot drinks were always welcome.

By the time she came back out with a tray filled with mugs, a very deep, neat excavation was ready. Gary and Adam were helping Joe to peg down the liner to prevent it getting tangled up in the roots when the tree went in. Next they placed strong webbing straps criss-crossed on top of the first layer of membrane, after which they tugged a much stronger fabric layer into place. This would act as a holder for the root ball for the next excavation. The webbing straps were the sort that would attach to a lifting hoist and make future moves easier. Clare loved that the three men, Joe, Gary and Adam had spent hours working out the logistics. All she prayed for now was that their efforts would succeed.

She was glad that she had added a couple of extra cups to her tray. The men downed them quickly and went back to work. With the hole prepared, they moved off to the field to start work on clearing branches round the tree, pruning the roots and fixing straps in place to help with the lifting. It was going to be a time consuming job, with lots of challenges.

The soft ground for a start, the enormous weight, let alone the awkward position the trunk was lying in.

May and the children came out to inspect the first part of the job. The chilly wind was enough to encourage May and Abby back to the kitchen. They promised to prepare a warming soup for lunch. Hannah and Edward had come out too, both keen to stay to watch the tree being raised.

Mike arrived. He apologised for being late, he stood by Clare while Hannah went to fetch some gloves. Clare took the opportunity when they were alone to ask about his parents.

"Sorry about Edward going off like that. I know you didn't want him to question them. I had tried to put him off."

"I know, he told me."

"Were they very upset?"

"Yes, but nothing they didn't deserve. Sorry that sounds harsh, but they should never have insisted on keeping silent about Lily and Patrick."

She was pleased to hear him use their names. It must have felt odd after so long having to keep quiet about them.

"Should I try to talk to them?" She didn't want to, but she couldn't help feeling sorry for them. The thought of losing her child was unimaginable, to have lost two devastating.

"Not yet, let me get my head round it first, before anyone tackles them. I know it won't be easy, but it is time they came to terms with their loss. I talked to Dr James about it, and he suggested that I get help. I wasn't sure that it would do any good so long after the event, but he says he thinks it will."

"I'm sure he's right. I'll do what I can to help too."

"Thanks, that's very generous of you. Especially after the distress I've caused you over the years."

Hannah came back with the gloves. She'd picked up an extra pair for Mike. He put them on and followed her to see if he could help with untangling the branches. He and Edward worked side by side. Adam was giving orders to them. Joe was making sure that the machine driver knew what to do. The bulk of the overlapping branches were quickly cleared, then Gary and Joe set to work cutting off the surplus roots and hauling the harness in place.

Everyone stood back and held their breath as the bucket of the digger lifted. The attached straps strained under the weight of the tree. The trunk shifted a fraction, then an inch, then another, until it was about a foot off the ground. The machine then began to swivel, easing the load away from the sodden ground.

Clare gasped. It was huge. How would they hope to keep it upright in the allocated hole?

Once clear of the other branches and tree debris, the driver lowered it onto the ground to enable a bit more pruning and sawing to proceed. The men set to work. Clare stayed back, uncomfortable at offering any advice as tree pruning on this scale was out of her league. Satisfied they had done all they had to do, the team readjusted the straps round the girth. The next stage of transporting it to its new temporary home started. Joe and Gary went to one side holding a rope attached to one of the branches. Adam and Mike walked along on the other, their rope attached to a shortened root. Their task was to stop the trunk from spinning out of control and to guide the trunk through a couple of gateways.

The slow trundle progressed without mishap. The next delicate operation was settling the tree in the hole in an upright position. The process was fascinating. Clare held her breath as the trunk dangled over the prepared place. The driver lowered the digger arm. The quartet of men pushed and shoved until they were satisfied and gave the driver the thumbs up signal. The hoist arm lowered the heavy load slowly and precisely. Extra straps lay on the ground waiting for the trunk to be placed on them. The newly pruned stubby roots were positioned over the hole.

The driver supervised the release of some straps and hitched new straps higher up the trunk. After a few more adjustments that Clare didn't quite understand, the driver used his controls to raise the arm again. The top end of the tree rose, the roots gently slid into the hole. The tree was nearly in position but at a very odd angle. He lowered the arm further and another round of repositioning straps took place. Another lift. The angle improved. Three more attempts and the tree was upright. Now a small digger started backfilling the hole while it was still supported by the harnesses.

Gary and Joe climbed into the hole to stamp and shove the earth into the gaps round the roots. Bucket load after bucket load went into the hole round the splayed roots to give the tree stability. Adam and Mike stood side by side watching. They didn't say much to each other, but what they did say seemed amicable enough.

Clare couldn't quite believe that Mike seemed so at ease. Would it last, or was this just a short lived reaction spurred by the shock of having lied to them all for so many years? She couldn't help wondering if the short tempered Mike would reappear.

With the tree in place, the whole gang headed to May's for lunch, Mike included. Clare noticed that the first thing he did on arrival was to seek May out. She got close enough to hear the conversation.

"May, I owe you my thanks for all you have done for my family. I know I behaved abominably. I'm not proud of what I did, but hope you'll be able to forgive me."

May seemed to struggle to find the right words for a response. "You don't need my forgiveness. I'm not the one you hurt. But I appreciate the apology."

"Thanks. The kids invited me; mind if I join you?"

May glanced to Clare. "Not at all, find a spot to sit down."

Edward signalled to Mike to sit next to him, a gesture Clare found touching. They certainly seemed to have bonded on the journey home. She hoped she'd have more time to talk to Edward on his own about what happened in York.

Chapter 34

Clare was very alert to the subtle difference in Mike's behaviour. He now openly discussed Cystic Fibrosis and appeared to have developed an insatiable desire to catch up with new research, leaving her struggling to keep up with his knowledge.

One thing hadn't changed though, he still hadn't attempted to do Hannah's physio even after she and Edward decided to reinstate the original arrangement of living part time at his house.

Then there was the issue of family outings. Clare was not comfortable with joining in. She didn't want Mike to think or hope she might forgive him. But Hannah had applied pressure.

"Come with us Mum."

Then to compound the dilemma, Mike had topped it with his comment.

"Don't miss out on having fun with them just because of me. I really regret not taking time off to enjoy being with them in the past."

The first few outings had been awkward, but soon Clare found herself relaxing and enjoying the easy atmosphere that came with the improved relationship the children had established with Mike.

The nursery was nearly back to the peaceful normality of the winter season. The paths for the show garden had been laid out, and were looking good. And she had even had time to do some clearing work in the walled garden so the spring plants would have a chance to shine.

Belinda had become a frequent visitor since breaking off her engagement to Adam. Belinda decided he was never going to settle in one place, and she wanted stability in her life.

"I have to admit I was a bit hurt by his reaction. I had expected him to make some attempt to persuade me to reconsider," she said when she called round to break the news to Clare.

Clare hadn't known how to respond to that so said nothing.

"So I guess I made the right decision." She laughed and went on with the comment, "You're welcome to take him back."

Clare wasn't sure if she was joking or serious, the laugh seemed rather forced.

"I don't think I'm ready for that, I'm off men for now." She hoped that would satisfy Belinda.

Clare wondered if Adam would think the same way as Belinda. She hoped not. True she had used his being with Belinda as an excuse not to explore the existing attraction between them. But it was not the only reason she had not wanted to get together with him.

When he did come back, she must ensure they never had a moment alone. She knew she was not ready to deal with any pressure on his part, so it was better never to have to face discussing his now single status.

"How's May?" Belinda asked.

Clare was so relieved to have the subject changed.

"Oh, she's really perked up. The worry about Pete and

Abby has been resolved without having to involve the authorities. Their mum has agreed to let them stay, so she is relaxed and enjoying having youngsters in the house."

"What's the mother like?"

"She's sweet, but got herself in a bad situation. Hopefully now she will get her life sorted out. The children obviously love having her back in their lives but are also very happy not to have to return to the town where she lived. She'd like to move nearer, but would have to have a job. I had wondered about employing her to work at the nursery, but think it might be a step too far and too soon."

"What's she like? I'm looking for someone to work in the shop?"

"She might suit, I'll give you her number, then you can get her to come in and decide for yourself."

While Clare wrote down the number, Belinda chatted on.

"How are the kids?"

"Busy with exam revision."

"So sad about her friend Rosie, how's she coping?"

Clare wasn't sure what to answer. It was obvious Hannah still felt the pain of losing Rosie on a daily basis, evident in the way she embraced her stable project. She had taken the comments about needing qualifications to make adults take her seriously to heart, and turned one exam project into a marketing exercise and her art portfolio was filled with a series of poster designs which were impressive. Her teachers had been so impressed with her newfound enthusiasm they had phoned Clare to comment on it.

"She seems to be okay."

"I saw Edward and Mike together the other day. They do seem to be getting on now." Belinda stopped for a second. "I'm sorry I was so interfering before. Sometimes I talk without thinking. I do it when I'm tense. And I guess the whole situation with Adam, and knowing you and he had been so close in the past, and not knowing if you both still felt the same way, made me kind of crazy."

"Come off it, you're not so bad."

"Cost me two husbands, I should know."

"Well, it seems Mike has bravely offered to give Edward driving lessons. I hope it doesn't destroy their bonding."

Then Clare had an idea.

"Maybe you can help me. Hannah is up to something. Edward's in on the conspiracy too. The pair of them are behaving the same way they did when they entered me for the show garden competition. I've asked Mike what they're up to, and from his reaction I'm guessing he's involved as well. I need you to find out what's up because I really can't handle any surprises right now."

"I'll do my best."

After Belinda left, Clare had time to enjoy some solitude. She needed to make the most of the peace because the children would be back in the morning and be there all week. Mike was heading up to York to see his parents. It was over a month since Edward had barged in asking awkward questions, and it had taken that long for them to finally accept that they needed to talk to Mike about their loss. Clare hoped they would be all right.

The children came back full of glee. Hannah had persuaded Mike to pay for Pete and Abby to have some riding lessons. Clare was very surprised at how easily he had been persuaded to accept that Pete and Abby were to be included in almost everything they did as a family.

Clare took them to their first lesson and stood by the rails with Sue to watch their progress. Pete was a natural on a horse and needed very little instruction. Abby who was much more timid, was going to need a lot more effort, but Hannah was happy about that. Abby was her first pupil and she was determined to make sure she learned to do everything perfectly.

"She's going to be a great teacher," Sue said. "I hope I haven't upset you all with my support of her ideas?"

"Not at all, we are all behind her. Admittedly at first it

took a while to get used to the idea of her doing something like that. I had rather thought she'd head to university, but see now that it really isn't what she needs."

"I haven't told Hannah yet, I'm getting married soon which means I will probably stop working here, while I can supervise her training to start with, I won't be around to back her up later on. I thought it fair to warn you."

"What will happen here, will someone else take over?"

"I really don't know. I haven't had a chance to work out what to do myself. The only thing I do know is that my going is bound to upset Hannah's plans. But I promise I'll do what I can to help."

"Thanks for the warning. I am sure we can work something out. Please don't say anything to her before her exams."

The riding session ended, the horses were led back to be unsaddled. The delight was evident in the laughter and chatter between the youngsters.

Mike returned from York, he seemed a little subdued, but told Clare his parents were beginning to come to terms with the situation. They were still planning to come down for the holidays as per usual and hoped that she would spend some time with them. Clare wasn't sure whether that was going to be easy, but didn't feel she could refuse.

She told him about her conversation with Sue at the stables.

"I am sure we can work out something, I'll go and see Sue and find out more. Hannah has really set her heart on this, and I will do everything to help her make it happen," he replied.

This was a more positive response than expected.

It was a few days before he got back to her.

"I've spoken to Sue, we need to talk. How about coming out for dinner on Saturday?"

"Aren't you taking the children bowling?"

"Yes, but they don't really need me hanging about. They

are meeting up with a big bunch of school friends. A post exam party I think. Hannah suggested I take you out to dinner to save me driving into town and back again twice."

"Okay," she agreed, half wishing Hannah would keep her bright ideas to herself. She should be concentrating on her own social life not her mother's. "That would be lovely, did you have anywhere in mind?"

"Yes. There's a new restaurant I want to try."

When Mike arrived to pick them up on Saturday, Hannah appeared looking gorgeous but somewhat overdressed for a night at the bowling alley. Clare was tempted to say something but decided it was safer not to. The last thing she wanted to do was make Hannah feel uncomfortable with what she was wearing. Maybe there was someone going to the bowling that she wanted to impress. The excited atmosphere in the car, made Clare hope that the event matched the mood.

Mike turned onto the main road, away from the bowling centre. She tapped his arm and queried where he was heading.

"Oh sorry, I forgot to tell you we are picking someone else up."

Clare relaxed and listened to Hannah teasing Edward about a girl in her class who fancied him. When they pulled up in the full carpark at Oak village hall, she assumed that whichever of Edward's friends needed the lift was at some sort of party being held there.

"I'll go and find him." Edward said as he opened the door and leapt out.

Hannah rushed off after him.

Mike reversed the car in to a parking space, ready for a quick exit. He kept the engine running as he waited for the children to return. He muttered something about the table being booked for eight.

"Shall I go and chase them up?" she asked, not wanting to sour his mood.

He shrugged. "Good idea. Time is a bit tight."

"I won't be a minute." She unstrapped her seat belt and got out.

As she walked towards the building she heard Mike cut the engine. She hoped the delay wouldn't put him in a bad mood. She pushed open the door into the hallway. No one in sight. She peered into the main hall. It was full. Full of people she knew. No wonder the children had problems getting out quickly. She worried about gate crashing the event, especially as she had no idea what it was. But she felt she had no option. She stepped through the door to be greeted by a loud cheer. She scanned the room to find the children. And realized all eyes were on her. She went to step backward out the door. Mike blocked the way.

"Three cheers for Clare" someone called out.

"Cheers Mum," Hannah said handing her a glass of champagne. It was at that moment Clare registered that this was the surprise they had been cooking up. The only thing she didn't know was what they were celebrating.

She took a deep breath, put on a big smile, and began looking to see who the guests were. May, Gary and the nursery staff were there. Joe and his gang, a cluster of the builders gang, Sue from the stables with a couple of the girls who worked with her, Mike's secretary, her mother, Mike's parents. Wow, someone had worked hard putting this crowd together. Then she spotted Uncle Norman, Rosie's parents and Dr. James. In the far corner were at least a dozen of Hannah's class mates and an equal number of Edward's friends. There were nursery customers, and a few students from her college group. There were more people sitting down, who she couldn't see, but was sure she would get to round them all in due course.

Someone shouted, "Speech."

Clare realized they expected her to say something, but what? She had no idea what they were celebrating.

"You've really caught me out here," she said. "I'm

261

delighted to see you all, but I think Hannah has some explaining to do." She swept her arm out towards Hannah. "After you."

Hannah blushed and stepped forward. "We invited everyone here to thank my mum for everything she has done for us. I know the last six months have been tough, but no matter what, you always found time to go that bit further to keep us all going." There was a round of applause.

"During this time, I began to understand some of the strains you face. In case any of you don't know, I suffer from Cystic Fibrosis, a serious condition that may shorten my life. I never wanted to tell anyone and know it must have been hard for Mum to keep it secret. I no longer want her to cover for me." She raised her glass. "Thanks for everything."

Mike stepped forward, and took over. "The other reason for this event is to congratulate Clare on winning the chance to have a show garden at the national garden show, and this is also to thank everyone who has helped with getting Dovedales back in order, so she can concentrate on creating a prize winning garden." There were cheers and claps.

Clare knew she had to say something.

"My vote of thanks goes to my children, and to May, who has inspired me, kept me motivated and most of all kept us all fed during the worst of the clear up. And on that note, did I hear someone say the hog roast is ready? Time to feast. Cheers."

The next few hours went by in a whirl as she circled round the room to chat to everyone who had come. She was surprised to find Belinda chatting to Adam, with her mother beside them. When she got near enough to speak to them her mother got in first.

"I have just apologized to Adam for my dreadful behaviour all those years ago. He's been very kind about it. I hope you'll be able to forgive me too."

Clare could only guess that May had told her about passing on the letters. But May wouldn't know Adam had found out, unless he'd told her himself.

"It was a long time ago," she answered, hoping that her mother would be satisfied with that for now.

"Adam and Belinda were telling me they have called off their engagement. I think it is such a shame, I thought they made a perfect couple. Don't you agree?"

Clare didn't believe she expected her to respond. "Excuse me a moment, I must go and talk to Mike's parents, it looks as if they are about to leave and I haven't had a chance to speak to them." She hurried away.

"What a lovely surprise," she said when she reached them.

"Oh, we were so glad to be invited. We really do want to talk to you, but I don't think this is the right place. Will you be there tomorrow?"

"Tomorrow?" Clare looked round hoping someone would fill her in.

Mike came to the rescue. "I've arranged for us to go to the churchyard to lay some flowers on the graves. I was hoping you and the children would come too."

"Of course I'll come."

They left and Mike thanked her for agreeing to go with them the next day. "It means a lot, now that they have finally accepted they must openly grieve."

After everyone had gone and the hall had been cleared, Clare had time to reflect on the massive effort it took for Hannah to announce she had Cystic Fibrosis. It was step one in the process of setting up her business. Sue's warning that she might not be there to help had been a concern, but now Clare believed Hannah had the confidence to cope with any setback calmly and efficiently. She looked across the room with pride at Hannah, who was moving chairs with Gary. They shoved the last of the stacks of chairs into the little store room and shut the door. Gary said something to Hannah that made her blush and turn slightly away from It was the first time Clare had ever seen Hannah react like that to anyone. She had wondered if the outfit was for someone special. Now she was sure Gary was the man Hannah was out to impress. If his look was anything to go by, it had worked.

That night she was alone again in the house wishing the children were there. The graveside visit would be harrowing, though she was sure Hannah and Edward would cope. The fact that Rosie had so recently been buried close by, might make it harder for Hannah, which made her really glad she had been invited to attend.

She got up early. It was a bright sunny morning, so she took a walk round the garden to see what else was coming up and to pick three posies of snowdrops to take with her. All around her were promising little shoots. It was a joy to have the responsibility for such a treasure store of plants. Her own trial garden was beginning to take shape with some of the plants they intended to use already in position showing the structure. Clare was proud of her design, and beginning to have confidence that it would look good at the show.

She dressed with care, choosing darker colours rather than full on funeral black. It was hard to imagine how difficult it must be to return to the graves after such a long time.

When she arrived at the church she was met by Norman, who had been waiting by the gate. He looked more terrified than she felt.

"Good to see you," she said.

"I'm really glad you're here. I couldn't believe it when Mike phoned and invited me along," he said opening the gate to let her though. I'm wondering how they will cope."

"I think it was about time they faced up to the past. Having it out in the open has certainly helped Mike. It has made him connect with the children in a way he never did before."

A car drew up at the gate. Hilda, Denis, Mike and the children walked together towards Clare and Norman.

264

Hilda gave Clare a hug. "Thank you for being so understanding. What we did was selfish." Clare could almost feel the tension easing out of her as she spoke. "I know it has hurt you all."

"The only thing I am sorry about was that you didn't manage to get help to deal with your grief at the time."

"I wish I had..."

"Stop wishing, the important thing is how you act now and in the future."

Denis tapped Clare on the shoulder. "Wise words. Thank you. We will try to live up to them."

Mike led his mother and father ahead to the graves he had found the week after Rosie's funeral. The headstones were clean and there were fresh flowers in place.

Clare followed with the two children and Norman. The group circled the spot. Clare gave Hannah and Edward a posy each to place on the graves. Then the vicar joined them and began to say a few prayers. When he finished, he stepped forward and took Hilda's hand in his. "I'm glad you are now able to come here at last. I hope that you will find comfort in being able to do this."

Mike then stepped towards his parents. He handed his mother something wrapped in crumpled tissue paper. Clare immediately guessed it was the battered christening mug she had found in his desk drawer. The significance of the engraving, LS for Lily Spencer, made his obsession with old silver make sense.

"I've been looking after this for a while, I wondered if you'd like to take care of it now?"

His mother's eyes filled with tears, as she stared down at his gift.

"I didn't like to clean it, in case I rubbed off her finger prints. And there are a few photos I rescued as well."

His mother flung her arms round his neck and hugged him in the first physical display of emotion Clare had ever witnessed from her in all the time she had known Mike.

Clare looked round. Hannah was moved to tears too. Edward looked a bit uncomfortable at the open grief on display.

Clare gave Hannah the third bunch of snowdrops then put an arm round her shoulder and whispered, "I think we should go and put these on Rosie's grave."

Hannah nodded, and pulled on Edward's sleeve. They eased away leaving Mike and his parents to make peace with each other and talk about their losses more privately. Norman and the vicar moved away too.

Clare positioned herself to watch the group from a distance. Hilda eventually released Mike from her hug, but he kept one arm around her shoulder as she wiped away her tears, and reached out to grip his father's hand. Clare couldn't help but be glad to witness such a tender moment.

Now she turned her attention to Hannah and Edward. Hannah placed the bunch of snowdrops on the fresh turf on Rosie's grave, then looked up and said. "We had some laughs together and that's what I want to remember."

Clare stepped forward and gave her a hug.

"She'd like that."

"Can we go and look round the church?" Edward asked. Clare nodded and followed them, relieved at the way the family had coped. It was a while before Mike and his parents came into the church.

Hilda came to Clare and gave her a hug.

"We may move back down here so we can come more often," she said, "if Mike doesn't object."

"Of course I won't object, in fact I'd love you to be closer," Mike answered with complete conviction.

Clare was pleased with his reaction, it was what his parents needed, and was a great example to set his children. This was more like the man she had chosen to marry than the one she had lived with for so many years. The burden of carrying that secret had weighed him down.

He kissed Clare on the cheek before he led his parents

and children back to the car.

Clare took her time, walking slowly with Norman as she tried to process her thoughts.

"Last time we spoke" Norman said, "you told me your marriage was over. I was surprised to see how well you and Mike were getting on today. Is there a chance of you getting back together?"

"I doubt it. But I'm happy that we're communicating as a family once more."

Authors note

When I started this book all I knew about Cystic Fibrosis was that it was a life threatening genetic disease which affected the lungs. I have during research come across some wonderfully positive people with heart rending stories who made me keen to raise awareness about the disease and to highlight the importance of the transplant donor register.

For every copy of this book sold a donation is being made to a Cystic Fibrosis Charity to help fight this disease.

Please help to increase the amount raised by spreading the word.

Leave a review on Amazon

Tell your friends

Tweet the link

If you want to know what happens next contact the author.

http://caroayre.wordpress.com/

Twitter @AyreC

Facebook- Caro Ayre Author

www.CaroAyre.co.uk

Cystic Fibrosis the reason to give

Most people don't understand what cystic fibrosis is, or what it does, until someone close to them is affected by it. They soon discover it's a life-shortening genetic condition - only half live to celebrate their fortieth birthday.

Cystic fibrosis directly affects around 10,000 people in the UK.

The faulty gene is carried by over two million people in the UK, most of whom have no idea. If two carriers have children, there's a one in four chance their child will have the condition, which slowly destroys the lungs and digestive system.

People with cystic fibrosis often look perfectly healthy. But it's a lifelong challenge involving a vast daily intake of drugs, time-consuming physiotherapy and isolation from others with the condition. It places a huge burden on those around them and the condition can critically escalate at any moment.

The Cystic Fibrosis Trust is here to beat the condition and make a daily difference to the lives of those with cystic fibrosis, and the people who care for them. Fighting it is a battle that must be won. That's why the trust is fundraising for change. Their aim is to develop better treatments and, ultimately, a cure. Cystic fibrosis *is* beatable. Find out more at: www.cysticfibrosis.org.uk or call our helpline 0300 373 1000.

For more information in US
http://www.cysticfibrosis.com

Transplants

Information about transplants can be found on the NHS Blood and Transplant website.

For people with end stage cystic fibrosis, lung transplant can be one of the only ways of improving and lengthening their quality of life. Sadly 1 in 3 will die waiting for donated lungs and many will wait three years or more to get their chance at life. To find out more about donating organs and transplantation visit the NHS's Organ Donation website.

http://www.organdonation.nhs.uk/how_to_become_a_donor/questions/

http://optn.transplant.hrsa.gov/ - USA

http://www.donatelife.gov.au/discover/about-transplantation - Australia

Caro Ayre

A childhood in Africa was followed by a move to a large Victorian house in need of love and a lot of work in a stunning rural location in Somerset.

The urge to write had always been there, but never acted on until it provided a perfect excuse to sit down between rounds of decorating, gardening and caring for bed and breakfast guests.

For more information go to:-
http://caroayre.wordpress.com/
www.CaroAyre.co.uk
Twitter @AyreC
Facebook-Caro-Ayre-Author

Feast of the Antlion

Caro Ayre

An action packed novel with a touch of romance set in Kenya.

Poachers, plane crashes, blackmail and murder are not what Sandra Harriman expected to face when she took control of a huge wildlife conservation project.

Sandra feels like an ant caught in an antlion's trap as she fights to protect her step-children's inheritance. Uncovering her dead husband's secrets leaves her wondering who can be trusted.

Kindle. http://www.amazon.co.uk/B006PZBXCI

Also in **Paperback - ISBN 978-0-9572224-0-3**
Price UK £7.99 US $10.99 Aust $14.99 Eur 9.99